AGAINST THE LIGHT

AGAINST THE LIGHT

Marjorie Eccles

This first world edition published 2016
in Great Britain and the USA by
SEVERN HOUSE PUBLISHERS LTD of
19 Cedar Road, Sutton, Surrey, England, SM2 5DA.
Trade paperback edition first published
in Great Britain and the USA 2016 by
SEVERN HOUSE PUBLISHERS LTD

British Library Cataloguing in Publication Data
A CIP catalogue record for this title is available from the British Library.

ISBN-13: 978-0-7278-8622-4 (cased)
ISBN-13: 978-1-84751-724-1 (trade paper)
ISBN-13: 978-1-78010-785-1 (e-book)

All Severn House titles are printed on acid-free paper.

Severn House Publishers support the Forest Stewardship Council™ [FSC™],
the leading international forest certification organisation.
All our titles that are printed on FSC certified paper carry the FSC logo.

Typeset by Palimpsest Book Production Ltd.,
Falkirk, Stirlingshire, Scotland.
Printed and bound in Great Britain by
TJ International, Padstow, Cornwall.

Part One

One

April, 1912

It made the headlines, of course. This time last year the newspapers had been too full of the approaching Coronation jubilations and excitements to leave much space for anything else, and since then there had been nothing half so interesting to draw in the nation's readers – only the gloomy forecast of yet more strikes to come . . . suffragettes . . . the Irish problem . . . and the German Kaiser getting too big for his boots. When it broke, the new story with its human appeal caused a mild sensation, and sent the sales of the *Daily Mail* rocketing.

Until that, too, was abruptly relegated to the back pages, eclipsed by news which stunned the world.

The *Titanic,* a luxurious ocean-going liner launched to a huge fanfare of publicity, a reputedly unsinkable vessel with over two thousand passengers on board, had been lost on its maiden voyage across the Atlantic to the United States. Unbelievably, dramatically, it had collided with an iceberg south of Newfoundland, foundered, and now lay at the bottom of the ocean.

Continents on both sides of the Atlantic mourned the fifteen hundred and more men, women and children who had lost their lives, while Alice Latimer's family were still trying to come to terms with the event that had turned their own lives upside down.

She had felt no premonitions of what was to come as she bicycled energetically homewards across London. Alice was a doctor in the time allowed – four days a week – from being the wife of a Member of Parliament. It was a busy, demanding, divided life she led, not without its problems, and as always she had several things on her mind, her main concern today being with what she'd find when she arrived home. Or rather, what she hoped not to find.

She pushed on, feeling hot, as much due to these bothersome thoughts as to the exertions of pedalling in a stuffy bicycling costume with a divided skirt and a hat that would insist on fighting its hatpins in its desire to blow away, as well as trying to avoid getting her bicycle wheel stuck in the tramlines. It had been a long day at the Dorcas Clinic and cycling from the congested back streets of insalubrious Spitalfields to the wide, tree-lined avenues and handsome houses around the Regent's Park was no mean feat, even for someone as determined as Alice. And the spring morning which had started out so beautifully, clear and sparkling, had once again given way to lowering skies which looked as though they meant business – though no one was complaining about the present capricious weather and what might be a dull summer to come. Not after the interminable months of scorching heat last year, when all London had wilted, the grass in the parks had burned off and people had collapsed of heatstroke.

He's certain to be gone, she persuaded herself, pushing aside a damp strand of hair from her overheated face. She had left the house before either of them that morning, but Edmund nearly always kept his promises (he was a politician after all) and he wouldn't have reneged on his offer to speak to Dudley and – diplomatically of course – let him know he had outstayed his welcome.

'But please, no money when he leaves – absolutely not, Edmund,' she'd warned last night. Her cousin had never asked for money, but the suggestion had always hovered. Independent-minded as she herself was, she felt it was more than time he learned to stand on his own feet. And yet, she still felt bad about sending him away. It was she who'd urged him to stay in the first place after all, another of those impulses of hers that she'd come to regret. The time had come for him to depart, however, and asking him to leave would come better from Edmund, who would never let himself be swayed by sad brown eyes and a mute appeal, like a spaniel being rejected by his master. Like any politician he could, when occasion demanded it, be quite ruthless.

'Very well, you have my word – though I must admit I'd be happy to give him almost anything to go away. I really cannot take much more of his determination to be unobtrusive.'

Alice laughed. A joke from Edmund these days was to be savoured, even such a small one. They came so rarely lately, swamped as he was by the cares and responsibilities of office that came with the occupation of a ministerial position in Prime Minister Herbert Henry Asquith's Liberal government.

Dudley Nichol was in fact Alice's only living blood relation, though he was a cousin so far removed she barely knew him. He had arrived unannounced, a slight, willowy, rather helpless young man of twenty-six, a virtual stranger from the distant past, and because Alice was glad to welcome anyone even vaguely related to her, he'd been given a cordial invitation to visit for a while. It was unfortunate that he seemed to have interpreted it as meaning an indefinite stay. Anxious not to be in the way but always *there*. He found things to do during the day but evenings were no longer their own.

Alice liked him, however. He had an odd, quirky humour Edmund couldn't share, and they laughed together, although Edmund had to admit he had intelligent and perceptive observations to make when the two of them spoke about current affairs, even though Dudley invariably withdrew when the discussions threatened to become too serious. He spent a good deal of time each day in his room, endlessly scribbling. At what? Alice had wondered, intrigued. Not a novel or anything like that – he'd confessed sadly that his education wasn't up to that sort of thing when she'd bluntly put the question. But he hadn't said what it was he wrote so assiduously. Letters to a sweetheart, maybe. That little-boy-lost look, the occasional impish smile spiced with a hint of mischief, could tug at the heartstrings, and that shy smile must have set many a woman a-flutter.

'At least we'll have the place to ourselves again,' Edmund had said.

'I don't know where he'll go, though.' Alice was still worried.

'There's always Violet,' he replied dryly, surprising her that he'd even noticed the odd rapport which had sprung up between his sister and Dudley. 'In which case we wouldn't be rid of him at all.' Since they lived at such close quarters, that was undeniable.

'Dudley wouldn't presume.'

Edmund said nothing more but his eyebrows rose.

His sister and her husband shared with the Latimers the large house which had come to Edmund on the death of his father, and it was true that Dudley did wander along in a desultory way to spend rather a lot of time during the day with Violet, in the intervals between disappearing somewhere on vague, unspecified business. In fact, his existence altogether seemed to have been pretty aimless since the death of his adored mother, when he was eighteen. Alice had listened to accounts of the various attempts he'd subsequently made to earn a precarious living – a catalogue of beginnings and failures – with more patience than she would otherwise have done, had she not known only too well what it felt like to be suddenly left alone in the world, bereft of the one person who had meant everything.

Just when her own life as a newly qualified doctor was opening out in front of her, her father had died of a massive heart attack. Francis Nichol had been a doctor himself, an untidy, improvident but kindly and well-loved man who had accumulated debts through not pressing his bills, and his affairs had been left in chaos. After the debts had been settled, his practice in a small Herefordshire town, which Alice had been planning to join, had perforce been discontinued, leaving her adrift and practically penniless. It was at that point, when she was at such a low ebb, feeling her life was in bits and her natural buoyancy having totally deserted her, she had met Edmund Latimer. Handsome, well-to-do and distinguished-looking, possessed of presence and a quiet but undeniable authority, he had stepped in and taken the guiding reins and before she knew it, she had found herself the wife of a politician. A man with a growing reputation, Edmund was always busy with one thing and another, shouldering responsibilities in the demanding Parliamentary career for which he'd abandoned his law practice. He was also nearly twenty years older than she was; but none of that had seemed to matter.

She would never cease to be grateful to him, more especially since, unlike most men, he made no objections to the idea of his wife working, as she now did voluntarily among the sick and the poor at the Dorcas Free Clinic. And yet, accompanying him to the endless social occasions and dull dinners that went with his position, and playing the hostess when required, she often needed to stifle a sense of rebellion by telling herself that was after all part of the bargain. She knew that, divested of her working garb, bathed and scented, her hair released from its simple, easily managed knot and newly arranged into fashionable rolls and puffs, and wearing the sophisticated and expensive clothes Edmund insisted she bought, she could be transformed into an exemplary Parliamentary wife who could hold her own with the best of them. It mattered to Edmund that, unlike the Prime Minister, he was thought to have approval in his choice of the right wife. She was no dazzling beauty, never that, but some of his colleagues, at least, appreciated intelligent conversation and respected the competent, professional woman behind the pretty face, which he liked to see. It was only when he thought that anything approaching flirting with his younger associates was going on that he frowned. Perhaps because it reminded him too much of the difference in their ages.

It had never occurred to her when she agreed to marry him that there would come a time when she'd question the wisdom of trying to keep up the medical work she was trained for and loved, as well as the obligations entailed in marrying him. It was never meant to be for long, only until the children they had both hoped for arrived, Edmund as much as Alice. Five years later, and still childless, however, Alice had begun to feel herself increasingly dissatisfied with the situation. But in her busy life, she found it necessary to slot matters into different compartments, and she hadn't yet found the time (or perhaps was afraid) to open that particular one and seriously think about what it might mean.

Manessa House, large, prosperous, white-stuccoed, many windowed and symmetrically built, stood at the end of its short, tidy sweep of gravel. It was at its best in summer, when the quiet garden that stretched out to the back would be filled with the scent of roses, and when its backdrop of trees, now just beginning to green over, was in full leaf. Even this cold, drizzly afternoon couldn't spoil the handsome, dignified look of the house in the tree-lined avenue. Inherited by Edmund from his father, Henry Latimer, who had outlived both his wives, each of whom had given him a child, its size and its various staircases and passageways made it a viable proposition for him to allow his much younger half-sister Violet Martens and her husband to occupy half of it, without either family getting too much in each other's way. Alice was in fact very careful not to abuse the easy accessibility the arrangement offered. Friendly relations were maintained by treading softly where Violet was concerned. On the other hand, a visit to see her adorable baby niece was the highlight of each day and something Alice did her best not to miss.

There was no sign of Edmund's recently acquired Napier on the drive, despite the fact that they were due to dine out – dine out or make up a theatre party, Alice couldn't remember which without consulting her diary. Wheeling her bicycle round the back to park it in an outhouse, she felt a stab of guilt in hoping some Parliamentary business might hold Edmund up for long enough to prevent them going out at all. At the end of a long day's work at the clinic among the poor who led such desperate lives, it was sometimes hard to summon up enough enthusiasm to prepare herself for a glittering social occasion. She was therefore not in the least displeased, when she reached the spacious hall, to find that a telephone message had been left, to say that Edmund had indeed been detained. Quite possibly a question was being raised in the House which was likely to lead to a lively debate and a late sitting. Perhaps a vote was expected, when his presence would be essential. The Government's extremely slim majority after the last election meant that Mr Asquith, the Prime Minster – H.H. as he was generally known among his colleagues – needed every bit of support he could get, and not only on the ever present Irish problem which was yet again dominating all other business. Among other matters, he was also under relentless pressure from his Chancellor of the Exchequer, Lloyd George, and from Winston Churchill, the Home Secretary, to push through controversial vote-catching domestic reforms. Edmund kept a modest set of rooms near Westminster, handy for the division bell, where he could stay the night if the occasion warranted it.

Alice read his message again. It ended by saying she must not feel there was any real necessity for her to go alone to what she now recalled was one of those tiresome soirées. She was grateful for that; without doubt it would be so overcrowded her absence was unlikely to be unduly remarked on, and right now, a free evening alone, a bath, supper on a tray and a book was certainly a far more appealing proposition. She stifled the idea that the message might subtly have suggested that although she *could* avoid the occasion if she wished, it might in fact be diplomatic for her to attend.

Pulling out her hatpins as she ran up the graceful central staircase, she paused for a moment to squint at the clock at the foot of the stairs. As usual, the house was immaculate. The waxed floors shone and smelled of beeswax. In a large vase on the hall table, stiffly arranged daffodils stood to attention. The brass stair-rods were newly polished, as was the mahogany long case clock, ticking regular seconds away into the silence. Although the lives of the two families did not overlap much, a shared staff was employed to run this large, two-household establishment, both of which were ruled by Mrs Lowther, their housekeeper. Violet also had a personal maid whom she allowed to assist Alice on odd occasions, when her hair needed to be dressed more elaborately than usual, for instance. A forty-year-old daughter of the vicarage with an expression permanently soured by resentment at her unmarried state, Newcombe was evidently not pleased at this. But she did as she was told. She was devoted to Violet.

Alice tossed her hat on to the bed in her bedroom and shrugged herself out of her jacket. She hesitated as she emerged from the room. Was it wishful thinking that the place had the feeling of air undisturbed by any human presence? It wasn't until she found Dudley's room deserted and its cupboards empty that she allowed herself to believe it. Relief surged through her. No note or letter, though. She hadn't been looking for thanks, but she was disappointed he hadn't even said goodbye. She turned to leave and her eye caught a glint of something showing underneath the bed valance, a glint which proved to be the gilded page-edges of a small book. How very odd – a Roman Catholic prayer book, red leather with flimsy, well-thumbed pages. Inside was written: *To Dudley, from Mother, on your First Communion.*

Dudley, religious? A devout Catholic? He had given no indication of any such beliefs during all the time he'd been with them – nor of any beliefs at all, for that matter. The notion cast a whole new light on him. But in that case, how careless of him to have left the missal behind. A precious possession from his adored mother, what was more. He would be mortified. Oh, Heavens, did that mean he would return for it?

The nondescript man with the pale face had been leaning against the wall in the set-back gateway to one of the large, prosperous houses further along the wide street for over half an hour before Alice appeared. He waited until she and her bicycle had disappeared down the drive of Manessa House, then stubbed out his cigarette, turned up the collar of his shabby suit jacket against the rain, now coming down with serious intent, and sloped away with his hands shoved into his trouser pockets, his head down. How he lived made him suspicious of everyone and he'd had to make sure, to see for himself, confirm what he'd been told. Now, after three days' watching, he was satisfied they could guarantee the routine of the house.

At the palace of Westminster where the two houses of Parliament sat, behind the stately and imposing chambers in which the means of governing the nation and drawing up its laws was debated, lay a maze of corridors and staircases leading to offices in which the business of implementing them was conducted.

Edmund had just been called to Downing Street, to see the Prime Minister.

'Do me a favour, will you?' he asked David Moresby, who happened to be in his office with him at a time when the secretaries had left in search of their afternoon cup of tea. 'Telephone my wife for me and make my apologies, there's a good fellow?' He hurriedly gathered papers together, tall and well built, sober and distinguished-looking in the Parliamentary uniform of pinstriped trousers and frock coat, his dark hair turning silver. He had a birthmark, a port wine stain that ran diagonally across his forehead, but he made nothing of it – and neither did anyone else after a while, except to see it as a mark of distinction. Though courteous and urbane with everyone, he was always a man to hold his own counsel, with something reticent about the eyes. Yet, like all politicians, he was something of an actor, and more than most, he was a good one. Presenting himself as quiet and self-controlled, it was repugnant to him to do anything outrageous or attention-craving. His speeches in the House of Commons were moderate and reasonable, winning him the trust and respect of his colleagues. Such histrionics as Lloyd George was capable of were anathema to him.

'We're expected at the Essendines – tell her I'll be home as soon as I can, if you would, but I believe she might wish to go ahead without me.'

'Of course, Minister,' David replied good-naturedly.

'Thank you, Moresby, I'll do the same for you some time.'

David stood looking thoughtfully after the departing figure. It was unlike Latimer, who was scrupulously polite with everyone and meticulous in consideration of his wife's feelings, not to have taken a few minutes to speak to her himself, even though David was friendly enough with both Latimer and his wife to be asked to do it for him. Still, an urgent summons to the Prime Minister at Number

Ten wasn't something anyone delayed answering. While he still had the matter in his mind he stayed in Latimer's office to make the telephone call from there. Taking a seat and adjusting the knees of his immaculately pressed trousers, he picked up the telephone. The wind blew grit against the windows and from the framed sepia print on the wall Queen Victoria looked down, unamused, as he dialled the operator and waited to be connected.

When the position of his Parliamentary Private Secretary had become vacant, Edmund Latimer had immediately offered it to David Moresby, a younger MP on whom he'd had his eye for some time. The post was acknowledged as a stepping stone to governmental office for an ambitious man and David, a backbencher with his own Derbyshire constituency, was ideally suited to it in every way, even if reaching the heights of PPS was sometimes looked on as a doubtful honour. Making oneself aware of everything that was going on, being on good terms with members of all parties in order to gauge the mood of the House, listening to gossip, liaising with the party Whips and reporting back to his Minister, as well as attending to work linked to his own constituency, was not necessarily a path to appeal to everyone. The position was, in fact, slightly suspect in some eyes. But David had given no indication so far that his integrity, or his capacity for hard work, was in any way compromised. Personable and agreeable, with a lazy smile that belied a formidable energy and staying power, saved from self-importance by the possession of an ironic sense of humour, he was respected as a sound, reliable, up and coming young MP.

Alice wasn't yet home to answer the telephone, but he spoke to her sister-in-law, who promised to pass on the message. He repeated what Latimer had said, that Alice might wish to go on without him. 'On the other hand, Mrs Martens,' he said, after a pause, adding his own view, 'I imagine there's absolutely no obligation on Mrs Latimer to attend . . . it's only one of those tiresome bashes where there'll be too many people and too much to eat and drink. Though of course, she'll be aware of that.'

'I'm sure she will be,' answered Violet, who would have given her eye teeth to attend such a brilliant gathering. 'I'm sure she'll understand that perfectly well.'

David had no sooner put the earpiece back on its hook than the office door flew open. Unlike those who were familiar with its eccentricities, the young woman who stood there wasn't in time to grab it before it crashed against the wall and ricocheted back towards her. She managed to dodge it but lost hold of her briefcase in the process, and its contents scattered over the floor.

A decidedly unladylike exclamation was uttered, hardly according with the neatly dressed figure and pretty face presented to him. The fiery blush as she bent to retrieve the papers and stuff them back into the case showed her mortification at having let it slip.

'Here, let me help.'

'Thank you, I'm so sorry! I mean, I didn't . . . I – I seem to have lost my way. I was looking for the tea room.'

'Then you've certainly strayed a long way.'

'I never did have the sense of direction,' she said ruefully as the last of the papers was stowed away. 'And I'm not familiar with the layout here yet. I'm so sorry to have intruded.'

'Not at all. Westminster's a rabbit warren. It's almost mandatory to lose your way until you get the hang of it.'

'Would you put me in the way of the tea room, then?'

'As it happens I'm going in that direction,' he said, aware of a sudden thirst. 'Allow me.'

Over tea and toasted teacake, when she learned David's name and what his position was she flushed again with embarrassment but she was naturally talkative and soon recovered. She told him her name was Mona Reagan and that she had just started work in the office of Joe Devlin, the fiery Irish Nationalist MP for Belfast West, popularly known as Wee Joe.

He had noted at once the lilt of her Irish accent, and he liked the smile in her deep blue eyes and the way tendrils of silky blue-black hair escaped its knot and clung to her white neck. He smiled, feeling the first stirrings of interest, imagining her as the country girl she told him she was. Wearing a red petticoat maybe, bare-footed, her hair hanging loose and blowing free in the wind across the Irish peat bogs. She was from County Down, where her family still lived on the shores of Lough Neagh, she told him.

'So what made you leave them and come over here?' he asked.

'I'd already left home. I was in Belfast to train as a teacher but I wasn't cut out for it. It was the job with Devlin that came up and brought me to vile, wicked London.' She laughed. 'But if the number of my mother's Hail Marys and the candles the nuns have lit for me count for anything, I won't come to any harm.' She noticed the clock on the wall. 'I'd better go. I only slipped out for a cup of tea and I've been gone for twenty-five minutes. I've enjoyed the talk with you – though we're supposed to be enemies, aren't we?'

'I wouldn't put it quite like that.' But there was no denying that the man she was working for, Wee Joe Devlin, was a thorn in the flesh of the Government, one of those Irish Catholic Nationalist MPs, led by John Redmond, who were demanding Home Rule, a Parliament in Dublin devolved from the United Kingdom. It was not an issue for which Asquith, or the rest of the Cabinet, had much enthusiasm, and to which the Conservatives and the House of Lords were implacably opposed. Indeed, the country as a whole, with its deep distrust of Roman Catholicism, was generally thought to be against Ireland being governed by Papists, as they saw it. But after his slim majority at the last election, Asquith needed the support of these Nationalists for his own domestic reforms – and they were not averse to blackmail: Home Rule in return for their votes.

'You're on our side – for the moment,' David reminded her. 'But it can't be easy, working for Devlin.' A firebrand, an accomplished, rousing speechmaker, champion of the working class, Joe Devlin was full of Irish charm and humour, but also hot-tempered, and a fiend for hard work.

'You'd have a job keeping up with him,' she agreed. 'But he's a charmer, right enough, so nobody minds. Anyway, I don't have to keep up – my job's only filing and typing and menial work of that class.'

The nonchalance of that intrigued him. Redmond's Nationalists, his whole team, top to bottom, most of them a good deal less moderate than their leader, were not precisely known for their tepid opinions. But of course those who were employed in lowly positions behind the scenes didn't necessarily have to hold the same views, or any views at all, come to that.

'I promise not to burst in on your privacy again,' she said as they parted. 'I don't suppose we'll meet again.'

'Westminster's a small place.' He picked up her briefcase and handed it over. 'You'd better get the clasp on this seen to.' It was an odd thing, to be carrying a briefcase weighing a ton around when you were merely in search of a cup of tea . . . nearly as odd as mistaking a room with the Right Honourable Edmund

Latimer's name on the door for a tea room. Again his interest stirred, and he knew he'd be keeping a lookout for Mona Reagan. He was a man who liked women, and she would not be the first he'd encouraged. He was a single, moderately wealthy man with excellent prospects who was marked down as a good catch for young women on the lookout for a husband, though he had so far adroitly avoided the net.

That she was in the enemy camp, as she had seen it, need not matter, nor need anything else. Neither of them was in any danger. He smiled at her. Why not? he thought with a certain resignation. It was no use wishing for what you couldn't have. The woman he loved was irrevocably married to someone else. She didn't know it, but she held his heart in her hands and always would. Forever.

Two

In case Violet had made the effort to be in her daughter's nursery for her teatime – and to be fair, she usually did – and in order to avoid raised eyebrows, before going to the nursery Alice had changed her bicycling skirt for a conventional one and tucked her shirtwaist into a wide belt, washed her hands and face and smoothed her hair. She was glad she had when she found Violet was indeed there with Lucy and her nanny, who was supervising her tea. Violet, with her unerring fashion sense, noticed every detail of other people's dress. Today she was immaculately dressed as ever, her tiny figure enhanced by a fashionably narrow-skirted dress of self-striped lavender moiré trimmed with satin ribbon the same colour as her name, a colour that gave her large blue eyes something of the same hue.

She was observing her baby daughter's teatime with a slight smile, her little pug cradled on her lap. She was not a demonstrative mother. One did one's duty and had children. They were little darlings, of course, but it was as well one only needed to see them after breakfast and before bedtime and could leave the messier aspects of their upbringing to a capable and sensible nursemaid such as this new one, a replacement for the previous nanny, who had departed in high dudgeon a month ago after a sharp exchange of words with Violet. Emma was promising, even though she was from one of the poorer parts of London. The baby had taken to her and she had a cheerful disposition.

Lucy was sitting in her high chair, clutching a piece of sticky malt loaf, delighting as it squelched between her fingers on its way to make approximate contact with her mouth. She beamed as Alice came in, dropped the cake and held out her arms.

'Just a minute!' Emma deftly intervened with a damp flannel before allowing Alice to pick the baby up. 'Don't let the little mischief make a muck-up of your blouse, Doctor!'

Violet opened her mouth to protest at such uncouth language, then changed her mind, in case she should be left nanny-less once more, but Alice just laughed. Emma was a high-spirited girl with a quick repartee. Where she came from, in the East End, such language came naturally and it didn't mean she was any less caring of the child.

Taking safe hold of Lucy needed careful manoeuvring, so encumbered was she with her numerous embroidered petticoats, but once in her arms, Alice hugged tight the warm, wriggling little body inside them and was given a sloppy kiss in return. She was accustomed to keeping a tight rein on her emotions – if she had not, the hopeless situations she came across daily at the Dorcas would have overwhelmed her long since. But where Lucy was concerned . . . The fierceness of her love for this child sometimes frightened her. Edmund, too, showed a tenderness towards her one would not have believed him capable of. He might, she thought, with a fleeting pang, have made a surprisingly good father.

Seven months old Lucy had three teeth, eyes like forget-me-nots and silky hair the colour of a new-minted sovereign. 'Marigold, we'll call her,' the besotted father had declared, delighted when she was born.

'We had a marmalade kitchen cat once called that,' returned Violet coolly, killing the idea stone dead, adjusting his tie and smiling at him in the way that brooked no opposition. 'I thought we had long ago decided on Lucinda. It's a pretty name, and far more appropriate.'

'Oh, righto.' Ferdie had hidden his disappointment. He usually found it expedient to agree with Violet, since he never won an argument with her. He was a bit of an ass, Alice thought, but such a thoroughly nice fellow his inadequacies in the mental department could be overlooked. And at least he'd asserted himself by demanding that the name of his own dead mother, Amalia, be added to the baby's, and he himself shortened Lucinda to Lucy, and sometimes used Marigold as a pet name when Violet wasn't there to object. Rather to Violet's annoyance, she'd become Lucy to everyone else, too.

Ferdie, for all he was an ass, could charm the birds off the trees with his good nature and his laughing dark eyes. The son of a Portuguese mother and a Belgian father, he allegedly worked with his father, Emil, at the family-owned Martens bank, but was still able to find time to visit his clubs, play sports and generally live an easy, amusing life. Money slipped through his fingers like wind through a sieve and it was his misfortune to have married someone equally extravagant. He and Violet made an attractively handsome couple but they were perennially short of money – Martens Senior not being inclined to shell out as much as Violet thought he should – but socially much in demand, if not in the set she really aspired to. She gathered herself now, preparing to leave Lucy to the nanny's ministrations in order to dress for whatever the evening held for her and Ferdie.

'You've seen the message from Edmund, I suppose, Alice?'

'Thank you, I have.'

'I took the call. It was David Moresby I spoke to.'

'Edmund didn't telephone himself?' Alice asked, surprised.

'Apparently he was closeted with Mr Asquith on urgent business.' A glint of malice appeared in the blue eyes (*you are not as important as the PM*) which Alice pretended not to see.

'Ah. Then I can't expect him home until late.' Or possibly not at all. Her eyes darkened at the thought of how frequent this had lately become, and how often, when he did come home, his case was stuffed with papers, which he worked on until late into the night. What with Lloyd George, the House of Lords and the Home Rulers, Asquith wasn't the only one who wasn't having it easy at the moment.

Violet presently stood up. 'I must leave you to Nanny, now, Lucinda, darling,' she said. 'I'm sure it's nearly your bedtime.'

Alice scrambled from the fluffy hearthrug where she'd been playing in an undignified way with the baby, much to Lucy's crowing delight, then bent to pick the child up to hand her to her mother. Although she herself was no more than medium height, she felt at a clumsy disadvantage compared to Violet, who was tiny, although she compensated by holding herself very straight and keeping her head high. She was like one of the exquisite pieces of china Edmund's mother had collected – a Dresden shepherdess, perhaps – which Violet had scornfully banished when she and Ferdie took over their part of the house, though Edmund had kept the collection and indeed added to it with discrimination. She had a firm chin and a polite, social, closed-lips smile that tucked itself in at the corners, and she allowed this to appear as Alice held Lucy out and Lucy lunged towards her. She graciously accepted a damp kiss on the cheek but attempted nothing further than smoothing her daughter's hair, since the pug was still clasped in her arms. Lucy reached out and grabbed a handful of its fur. The dog snapped and bared its teeth and Lucy's face crumpled.

'Naughty Lulu!' Violet admonished the dog, kissing the top of its head. Then suddenly and rather fiercely, she put the pug down and took hold of the little one, hugging her tightly and laying her cheek on the bright curls. 'Good night, darling Lucinda. Be a good baby for Nanny.' It was an unaccustomed sign of affection, but she was already extracting a wisp of lace handkerchief from her sleeve and dabbing the cheek her daughter had wetly kissed as she left the room.

Alice herself felt no inclination to leave. The nursery rooms were upstairs, facing out over the garden, plainly furnished but spacious and airy, pleasant, as were all the others in the Martens part of the house. It had been generous of Edmund, when his sister had married Ferdinand Martens, to allow them to share the house, saving them the expense of setting up an establishment of their own. Violet had made a clean sweep, banishing the solid, fine-quality mahogany and plush which had been her parents' choice in favour of clean, modern lines and the soft colours of mid blue, eau-de-nil and neutral beiges that were currently in vogue. The same taste she showed when choosing her own wardrobe ensured she had made a good job of the redecoration: even here in the old nursery, which now had sunny primrose yellow walls, although it still held a specially made child-sized desk, used first by Edmund and later by Violet, an old basket chair and a dilapidated rocking horse she and Edmund had almost ridden to death. Alice sometimes felt she ought to follow Violet's example and revamp their part of the house, too, but Edmund was against it and so it was left as it was. The stately solidity was in its own way timeless and reassuring, she had to admit, but in any case, if Violet had time to waste poring over pattern books and upholstery samples, Alice certainly had not.

She sighed. She had tried, with Violet. They were more or less the same age and she had once hoped that she would become the sister Alice had never had. But for Violet there was no room for more than one woman in the lives of either her husband or her brother.

It was time for her to go, and Lucy eventually allowed herself to be surrendered to her nursemaid. She was not a difficult child and had already formed an attachment to this new nanny, and since Alice had been instrumental in securing Emma's services, she was happy to see the arrangement working well. Emma, strong, practical and down-to-earth, was proving herself far superior to the last woman, who had been none of these things.

'All's set,' the nondescript man who'd been watching the house told the others, though a close look at his face would have revealed that he wasn't nondescript at all. It was his talent to keep his expression neutral, whatever he was feeling, not to meet anyone's gaze directly lest they should encounter his eyes and what they might read in them. 'There'll be no problem, that I can see.'

Edmund did, after all, choose to come home rather than spend the night in his rooms. Alice was reading in her bedroom, and feeling her eyelids beginning to droop when she heard him come in. The fire had died to a few embers and the room had grown chilly. The coffee-coloured crêpe-de-Chine and ecru lace of her new wrap, while undoubtedly elegant, wasn't designed for warmth. She shivered a little and had just closed her book when he tapped quietly on her door, then gently pushed it open.

'Ah, I'm glad I haven't disturbed you, my dear,' he said, coming in when he saw she was not yet in bed and asleep, bending to kiss her cheek. He kept on his long, dark overcoat and his gloves, which meant he wasn't going to stay. He glanced at the book she'd been reading, on the table next to the chair which had been drawn up to the fire. '*Alice in Wonderland* again?'

'Oh, I like rereading it, it's such nonsense it makes me smile.' It never failed, while at the same time the adventures of that other, imaginary Alice seemed to draw parallels with her own, especially with the White Rabbit, forever watching the time . . . and sometimes, aware of her more managing moments, making Alice wonder if she might not be a reincarnation of the Queen of Hearts.

'Well, I'm sure it's been more profitable for you than the crush at the Essendines.'

'I took your message to mean there was no necessity for me to go.'

He raised a brow. 'Was that what Moresby said? Well, he was right, as usual. Stout fellow, always has a sense for these things. It was too crowded – not to mention that the best of the supper was gone when I got there. But I salvaged these for you, I know how you like them.'

The thought of Edmund filching chocolate truffles and hiding them in his pocket delighted her, and she turned a laughing face up to him as he bent to put the small linen-wrapped parcel on the table by her side. He was the sort of man who always had a clean handkerchief handy for emergencies. 'I hope no one saw you risking your dignity!' He smiled faintly. 'Perhaps I should have gone, all the same,' she added guiltily. 'You managed it.'

'No, no, you did the sensible thing, you wouldn't have enjoyed it. I simply put in an appearance . . . it was in my mind to bring you home and save you from Lowther.'

It was typical of Edmund to remember that getting to the Essendines would have meant being driven in the now rather elderly motor car by Lowther, the housekeeper's husband, gardener and odd-job man who had learned to drive and now also acted as chauffeur when needed. He had been with the Latimer family since he was a young man and was not really up to either job now, but he would have been insulted if asked to retire, even with a pension. He'd grown into a grumbling old man of rigid opinions, especially on other road users, which he did not hesitate to voice, and his sarcastic commentaries, not to say his own idiosyncratic driving, were hardly conducive to a comfortable ride. Alice (whom he stubbornly insisted on addressing as 'Mrs Latimer, madam') preferred not to be driven by him at all except when really necessary, mostly when the weather was too inclement to allow for bicycling, and Edmund refused to let him near the new Napier, which he enjoyed driving himself. One of these days, she told herself, Edmund would relent and consent to her learning to drive. Or perhaps she would face his disapproval of such an unfeminine activity, and learn anyway.

'You're terribly late.' The Essendines' social had been an early evening affair.

'Yes, I went with Palfreyman for something to eat afterwards.'

She raised her eyebrows. Hugh Palfreyman was not someone for whom Edmund had much patience.

'Yes, I know he's a bore, but there was something we needed to talk over,' he said. 'And now I must leave you. Don't stay up reading too long.' Alice stretched a hand up to smooth the tired lines on his face but he intercepted it, placed a kiss in the palm and returned it to her.

'Sit down for a while, Edmund, and tell me about your day.'

He shook his head. 'I have this speech tomorrow that I must get off my hands.'

'You work too hard.' He had seemed tired recently, or at least not quite himself, and she had worried over it a little because she couldn't think of any reason why he should be. It couldn't be money, surely? He was by no means rich, but he had a settled income. That had crossed her mind, though really, it amounted to nothing more than a slight hesitation over a dressmaker's bill when previously he had actually encouraged lavish spending on clothes, a frown over the amount of money needed for wine. Tonight, he looked even more tired than usual.

'We're all of us overworked at the moment. And we all feel it, except Lloyd George and Winston, who seem to thrive on it.'

Alice grimaced. Who couldn't admire the charismatic Chancellor of the Exchequer, Lloyd George, his 'People's Budget' and his passionate, relentless pushing forward of proposals to alleviate the poverty of the working classes, by imposing hitherto unheard of taxes on the wealthy? Admire, yes – but she was uneasy with the fiery Welsh orator, who was a womaniser and gave her the uncomfortable impression he was undressing her with his eyes when he looked at her. Churchill was a different matter, always amusing with his salty humour, but the two of them were in cahoots, equally determined on the need to generate more social reforms.

'I'll come to Westminster and listen to you tomorrow.' Edmund himself was a good speaker and Alice enjoyed listening to him, even if her opinions didn't always coincide with his.

'I wouldn't want to subject you to that,' he smiled, referring to the Ladies' Gallery where she must sit, which was notoriously uncomfortable, having a metal grille across its width, through which it was difficult to hear and almost impossible to see. 'And you have little enough free time. Don't worry your head over it, my dear.' He turned to go.

'I do wish you wouldn't patronize me, Edmund,' she said, with a touch of asperity. 'You know that anything that concerns you as my husband concerns me.'

'Do I do that? I wasn't aware of it.' He smiled again but this time it was distinctly cooler, and his reply was very slightly distant. It had been the wrong thing for her to say. Too personal. She had embarrassed him. 'Goodnight, my dear.'

'Goodnight, Edmund.' She watched him walk to the door. 'By the way, thank you for speaking to Dudley.'

He paused. 'Dudley? No, I'm afraid I didn't have the chance. He was still in bed when I left this morning.'

'Well, he's gone now.'

'Has he, by Jove? Permanently?'

'I don't know, but he's taken his clothes and everything, so I assume he won't be back.' Unless he comes for his prayer book, she thought, but she didn't mention this. 'He didn't leave a note.'

'How very ungrateful of him.' Perhaps he didn't mean that to sound as if this lack of manners somehow reflected on her family, however distant the relationship between her and Dudley was, and perhaps he saw this belatedly. 'You were quite fond of him, weren't you?'

Absurdly, she felt herself blush, 'In a way.'

He smiled. 'Well, at least we'll have the house to ourselves again. I find him rather a tiresome young man, dare I say it. Don't stay up reading too long. Sleep well, my dear.'

The door closed between them and she leaned back, turning her head against the back of the chair. The crocheted antimacassar scratched against her face as if it were scratching against her heart. Although he was always scrupulously polite, kind and considerate, there was more than a streak of ruthlessness in Edmund as far as his work was concerned, which she could understand, but it could extend, perhaps more than he was aware of, into his private life as well. Had he any idea how much his exclusion of her, his reserve, hurt? And not only in respect of his profession. She was aware that there were other aspects of his private life he did not share with her, but it was so evidently deeply distasteful to him to discuss that she had given up the attempt. It was how he was, she told herself.

Resolutely, she put her book away, got ready for bed and slid between the cool, clean linen sheets. She listened to Edmund moving about in his own room, taking his time over exchanging his formal clothes for his velvet smoking jacket and slippers, and then heard him go down to his study, where he would undoubtedly work until after midnight. While she waited for oblivion, she willed herself not to worry. If she allowed the niggling doubts that wormed themselves insidiously and all too often into her mind lately to take hold, might she not have to face the fact that her overimpulsive nature had caused her to consent to a too hasty marriage?

As he changed, Edmund's mind turned over the day's events.

One way and another it had been an exhausting day. Dominated by Home Rule, yet again. That seemingly unsolvable problem, the great argument that had rumbled on for decades – forever, it seemed. On the one hand, the Catholic majority in Ireland who felt they had the right to have their own Parliament in Dublin, to make Irish laws for Irish people, and not to be governed by those emanating from a Westminster Parliament in London. On the other were the Protestants and landlords in the six counties of Ulster, descendants of English colonists granted plantations of confiscated lands there (from whence stemmed all the present troubles) who preferred anything to being ruled by a wild bunch of Catholics and knew they would fare better if the English Parliament retained some jurisdiction over their affairs. What did Redmond's hotheads know of governing a country? Down the years, blood had been spilled over it, men had died fighting for their cause and many others were still prepared to follow them. Because of it, Irish Fenians had even attempted, within living memory, to blow up the Houses of Parliament. If matters continued this way, Irishmen fighting among themselves, things could only get worse.

He sighed, uncapped his fountain pen but didn't immediately begin work on his speech. Instead, the events of the evening began to turn themselves over and over in his mind. He had almost resolved to absent himself from that evening's events and go straight on with what he had to do, but at the last moment, despite a slight headache, decided otherwise. It would be circumspect to put in an appearance at the large and imposing town house where Lady Essendine saw no reason why persons of note and MPs of all persuasion should not mingle amicably. He would indulge in a few minutes' no doubt frivolous chit-chat, do the conventional, expected thing, shake a few hands and then leave. It took longer than he anticipated, however, to make his escape, owing to the number of friends and acquaintances who greeted him and drew him into conversation. It had been a mistake to come at all, he thought, as his headache worsened. The brilliantly lit room, filled with the buzz of talk and laughter, stylishly dressed ladies, the smell of cigars and the perfume of massed lilies, was overpoweringly hot and he drank rather more champagne than he had intended.

His eyes strayed across the room while ostensibly listening to H.H.'s beguiling and fashionable wife, Margot, whose famously wicked and outspoken observations, mostly on other people, at last succeeded in bringing out a reluctant smile. They talked a little longer then, accustomed to more rapt attention than he was giving her, she tapped his arm with a long white hand and passed on to fascinate the infinitely more susceptible Lloyd George. Edmund crossed the room to speak with a lady who until then had been at the centre of an admiring group but was momentarily alone except for one weak-chinned individual he did not recognize, and with whom she was chatting in a desultory manner. 'Mrs Fiore, good evening.'

'Mr Latimer, how nice to see you.' She gave the young man a nod and a charming smile, whereupon he melted away. 'I'm afraid you've missed supper.'

'I came only to show myself, and to escort my wife home, but I see she is not here.'

'No.' Their eyes met, and held for several moments. Constance (Connie) Fiore was an American, a woman of perhaps forty-five, tall and with a rich crown of brown hair, worldly, expensively dressed, who lived her life on the fringes of the political world. She was a clever woman, a widow. Her husband's wealth, so it was said, had come from his Italian immigrant family who had made a fortune by opening a chain of restaurants across the United States. It was rumoured she was the centre of many a political intrigue and it was certain she had the ear of more than one cabinet minister.

They talked of this and that for some time. 'By the way, I'd like you to meet my friend, Molly Childers,' she said presently. 'Let me take you across. You know she's American, like me, and very rich?'

He followed her glance across the room and saw an attractive dark-haired woman, seemingly the centre of a group of those intellectuals whose society, Edmund knew, she and her husband favoured.

He had no objection to meeting Mrs Childers, but he had his own reasons for not wanting to speak to her husband tonight. A slight and unassuming man, Erskine Childers was Cambridge-educated, an aspiring Liberal candidate who was also a published author, one of his books being a highly successful thriller, *The Riddle of the Sands.* At present he held a respected position in the House of Commons whereby he was responsible for the recording of all Parliamentary business. He was of Anglo-Irish extraction and was in fact at that moment one of a group including several Irish Nationalists. The others were bending their attention to what Childers was expounding with some intensity, almost certainly on what had come to be his favourite subject: Irish Nationalism. Childers' mild manner concealed a sometimes burning intensity. Together he and these particular Nationalists, to whom moderation on the subject of Home Rule was unknown, were too much for Edmund tonight. He had had more than enough of Ireland for one day.

'Some other time, Connie. Regretfully, I must leave now.'

'So soon? Well, come and see me when you can, Edmund.' Their eyes met once again as he pressed her hand; then he went to find his hostess to make his excuses, and left.

answer him. Passed out, or fallen asleep most like. As I said, I thought they'd been out on the razzle. I carried on till I got here then I says, "Here we are, sir," but he doesn't stir, does he, so I goes and opens the door to give him a prod. Wondering what to do with him, see, hoping he hadn't been bleedin' sick. I've had drunks like that before, but usually it's taking them home and leaving 'em to somebody else. Gawd! I've seen some sights in my time but that . . . 'Orrible, it were. Didn't take me long to see he wasn't with us no more, I can tell you.' He took a red-spotted handkerchief from his pocket, blew his nose loudly and gave a rattling cough.

'Nasty shock,' Inskip agreed.

'You can say that again. Not nice at all, and blood all over me cab!'

'We'll see about getting it cleaned up for you when we've finished with it.'

'Finished with it? And what am I supposed to do without it meantime? I've already been diddled out of one fare tonight. It ain't my fault he got hisself topped.' He coughed again, his eyes streamed and he put his head in his hands. The moustache drooped mousily.

Inskip had every sympathy with him. The fellow was not only aggrieved, he was understandably worried, since his livelihood depended on this motor. He walked over to Gaines, who was with the doctor, and spoke to him for a while. He came back with the news that the inspector would see he was provided with a substitute vehicle until his own could be returned to him. 'You may as well go now, Mr Sheldyke, get yourself to bed. Come in and see us tomorrow morning and we'll see about arranging it. We'll need you to sign what you've just told us, as well. Don't forget to leave your address.'

The cabbie didn't know it, but he wasn't yet ruled out as a suspect. There was only his word for it that there had been two passengers. If the victim had been alone and flashed money about, who was to say the cabbie hadn't killed him and relieved him of it? There was no blood on his clothing but if he lived so near he could have stepped home to change it and got rid of the money before calling the police. Inskip didn't really think it likely – there was no doubt he felt as rotten with his cold as he looked, and he seemed genuinely shaken, but who wouldn't be if they'd just killed someone?

Sheldyke didn't seem altogether reassured by what he'd been told,

Part Two

Three

It was three in the morning and the taxicab driver, a scrawny middle-aged fellow with a wilting, grey-brown moustache, gruesomely reminiscent of a dead mouse, was trying to calm his nerves with a cigarette while the police doctor examined the body in his cab, drawn up a little further away. He had a nasty cold, a broad Cockney accent and his name was Ron Sheldyke.

'I'm not easy shocked, and that's the truth,' he told Joseph Inskip, the Detective Sergeant from Scotland Yard, thickly, 'not after driving one and all around for thirty years – some of the things what goes on in the back seats you wouldn't believe, make a sailor blush, it would. But this beats the lot.'

He sat hunched on the running board of the police vehicle, drew deep on the cigarette, coughed and then let it dangle from his fingers while he began again on what he had already told Inskip and Detective Inspector Gaines when they arrived, as if by repeating it he could lessen the impact. 'I was finished for the night, see, fair knackered and on me way home for a hot drink and me bed, when these two blokes hailed me in Bishopsgate. It was raining like the clappers and they wanted to go to somewhere Finchley way, but I wasn't for going that far, not for double the fare I wasn't, and in the end they agreed to me taking them as far as here, Edgware Road. It wasn't out me way, see, I live just off Praed Street, five minutes from here. They'd pick up another cab when I dropped them, they said. Good luck, this time of night, I thought, but didn't argue. A fare's a fare. "Off we go, then, cabbie!" says the younger one – that's the poor sod in there.'

He indicated his cab and Inskip opened his mouth to frame a question, but there was no stopping him.

'Spoke like a toff, he did, polite and all that, and they was laughing a lot . . . I reckoned they'd been making a night of it. But before we got here the big fella leans forward and tells me to stop. out goodnight, still having a laugh, and then he was out and into the rain with only a "Goodnight, then." The other one but he thankfully staggered off, shivering, in search of a hot drink and his bed, and Inskip rejoined Gaines and the doctor, having now finished his examination, while they waited for the ambulance to come so the body could be removed from the cab. The dead man was propped upright, his head to one side, slumped against the side of the cab, almost as if he might have fallen heavily asleep. But the wide bloody gash just under his jaw instantly removed any suppositions of that sort. One side of his clothing was soaked with the blood that had flowed from the wound and pooled on to the leather seats. 'Somebody knew what he was doing,' remarked the doctor, 'severed the jugular and the carotid vein, clean as a whistle. Poor devil,' he added. He was elderly, on the point of retiring, a man who had seen it all before and whom nothing could surprise, but he hadn't yet lost his compassion.

'The driver says he heard nothing, but wouldn't he have cried out when he was attacked, Doctor Fenton?' Gaines asked.

'He'd hardly have known what was happening. Death would have been instantaneous, or very nearly. And he may have been in a drunken sleep when it happened . . . smelling like that, I don't need to examine him to know he'd had fair amount.'

The victim was a young man of under medium height, slightly built. His now blood-soaked tweeds were well worn, his shirt cuffs slightly frayed. His shoes were down at heel and badly in need of resoling, but as far as anyone could tell, everything he wore appeared to have once been of good quality. Hopefully, there might be a tailor's label inside when it was possible to divest him of his suit.

'He wore glasses,' Gaines remarked, 'look at the mark across the bridge of his nose.' But if they had fallen off, there was no sign of them. 'Ask the cabbie tomorrow if he remembers him wearing them, Joseph.' After addressing him formally as 'Sergeant', ever since they'd first begun to work together, the inspector had lately gone so far as to call him 'Joseph' on occasion. Inskip took that as a step forward in their hitherto fairly cool, though not actively unfriendly, relationship. 'Or a hat,' he added. 'No sign of that, either.'

It was slightly bizarre to think of the spectacles being removed after he was dead, either because they'd been knocked off accidentally in the attack and the killer had simply taken them with him, which seemed unnecessary, or even if they had been the expensive, gold-rimmed sort which could have been sold, since robbery as the motive for the murder wasn't immediately apparent: although the victim's pockets were empty of everything but a handkerchief tucked into his top pocket, and a few coins of low denomination in those of his trousers, he still wore an old-fashioned but expensive gold 'Albert' watch chain stretched across his waistcoat, to which was attached a gold half-hunter of some considerable value. From the chain also depended a gold wedding ring. Had this young man tragically lost his wife? It seemed reasonable to assume that if he'd been the sort of person who had been moved to keep her ring, he might also have had her photograph, or even a lock of her hair, tucked into his wallet. Except that any wallet he might have had was missing. Maybe it had held paper money and had been taken for that – though that still begged the question of why the gold watch and chain had been left.

It was in the nature of their work – their fate, George Gaines sometimes thought – to face the sordid details of life, and all too often death, but nothing saddened him more than the futile waste of a young life. And this man was young, still in his twenties, he guessed, with most of his life before him, now abruptly cut off, for whatever reason. Not apparently through any sudden quarrel, according to the cabbie. Both his fares had been in high spirits when they entered his cab, and he would certainly have heard if it had degenerated into something else, and indeed, the murderer – chilling thought – had still been laughing when he left the cab. No, this killing indicated malicious forethought: the possession of a knife ready to be used for the murder, the quick, no doubt planned, exit.

'Let's have a look at that handkerchief. There might be a laundry mark.'

Inskip gingerly inserted two fingers and eased out the folded handkerchief that was tucked into the top pocket with two jaunty points showing, but its fine, hemstitched cotton was scarcely soiled, the thickness of the tweed having protected it somewhat. He shook it out, showing the ironed creases it still retained, but there was no laundry mark. Home laundered, then. His shirt, what part of it that wasn't blood-soaked, revealed itself as snowy white and his collar was stiffly starched. A man who had pretty obviously come down in the world was unlikely to have servants to wash his linen, so if the wedding ring *had* belonged to his dead wife, perhaps he'd returned to the parental home to live. Gaines did not welcome the thought of having to inform a mother of the bloody murder of her son.

Inskip bent to retrieve a folded scrap of paper which had come out with the handkerchief and fluttered to the ground. It too had escaped the worst of the bloodstains. It was folded into four and when he opened it, the address pencilled on it was clearly readable. He stared, and went on staring.

'Well?' Gaines' voice roused him. 'What is it?'

'I'm not sure I believe this, sir. It says Nine Catesby Street.'

'And?'

'That's my Auntie Orla's address!'

Four

Unrefreshed after a restless night, her body stiff from unconsciously lying tensed while she slept, Alice woke late, to another cold but sparkling spring morning, the sort of day that had made her father say he wished he could bottle it and give it to his patients as medicine. One of those days when it felt good to be alive. And indeed, it was impossible to give way to the sort of thoughts that had drifted through her mind while she slept; they were even now slipping away as the bright sunshine filled her room and came to rest on the chocolate truffles, still wrapped in the white linen handkerchief. She moved them to one side, out of the sun, still amused at the thought of Edmund – *Edmund* – snaffling them! He hadn't forgotten her, even as he socialized, though it didn't appear as though he'd enjoyed the event. It had been thoughtful of David Moresby, always with his finger on the pulse, to give the tactful reminder that she herself hadn't been under any obligation to attend.

It was some time since she'd seen David. Disconcertingly blue eyes that tended to laugh at odd moments. The dark unruly hair disciplined with a judicious amount of brilliantine but still sometimes looking as though he shoved his fingers through it. Popular, ambitious, easy with people, bespoke suits that showed off a lithe figure, he was all set to become the rising young politician he aspired to be, though David Moresby occupying a similar position to Edmund would be an entirely different proposition, she thought. Perhaps if she'd gone to the Essendines' last night it wouldn't have been as boring as she had imagined it would be. They could have shared a joke or two at the expense of the more pompous of those present. David was undoubtedly a young man in a hurry, but one who didn't let his ambition overrule his sense of humour.

A glance out of the window revealed no sign of the Napier below. Edmund must have left earlier and let her sleep on without disturbing her, knowing it wasn't her scheduled day at the Dorcas. The reminder caused her to hesitate. For a wonder, she had nothing else planned to fill her time that day. So why not profitably spend it at the clinic?

Edmund would no doubt say she was 'wasting' her free day. She refused to allow the sneaking suspicion that he thought of it as something to keep her from mischief to linger, and decided she would cycle there, hoping the day wouldn't cloud over and bring the rain to catch her on her way home, as it had yesterday. If it did, so much the worse. She wasn't in the mood to suffer one of Lowther's sour monologues, and the exercise would ease the stiffness from muscles that had been tensed and unrelaxed all night.

Coincidences like this just didn't happen, Inskip told himself. His Jewish friend, the tailor who made the natty suits Inskip indulged himself with, said that the Hebrew word for coincidence could be rearranged to mean 'only from God' which meant there had to be a reason for it. Be that as it may, he knocked on his aunt's door in the East End and waited with a tingling sense of anticipation.

Unlovely as it was, busy, workaday Catesby Street was no different to any other in the confusion of streets and alleys round here, where mean houses, shops, sheds and tenements, crammed together in various stages of neglect and disrepair, rose to the sky, obscuring any light that might venture to penetrate its murk. Even this bright, breezy day couldn't banish the vile, acrid stink from the tannery close by. From behind the street came children's voices in the play-ground of the nearby elementary school, shrill above the hoarse calls of a rag-and-bone man perched on a cart being dragged along by a dispirited horse. More raised voices came from two women who were loudly berating the owner of a makeshift market stall over the bulged apples he was trying to pass off as sound. And it looked as though a fight might be starting in a crowd collected outside the public house on the corner. Luckily, before Inskip could be expected to intervene, the door was opened.

'Why, if this isn't a miracle – just when I've been asking myself if I was ever going to see you again, Joseph. You're as welcome as the day!' His diminutive Aunt Orla beamed, opened her arms and reached up to fold him in a pillowy embrace. 'I suppose you'll be telling me you've been too busy again to come and see your old auntie!'

'Never too busy for that – and hey, I was here only last week, remember?'

'Last week, last month, it seems longer,' she returned equably. 'And what are we doing, standing on the doorstep? Will you come in then, and let me be having a proper look of you. Sure you're a real bobby-dazzler!'

Inskip was pleased she'd noticed his new suit. But had she really forgotten he'd called to see her only last week? Or was it just a way of making him feel guilty? Orla was sharp, and on reflection, he had to admit it might just have been two weeks . . . perhaps three? . . . since his last visit. He'd always been close to her, his favourite aunt, and he tried to make it in his way to pop in and see her regularly. But it was true, the boss hadn't left him time for much else just lately; Gaines could be a bit of a slavedriver on occasion. It gave him a pang of remorse to think it had only now occurred to him that she might be lonely, living alone, despite her cronies from St Bede's Church, and that was maybe why she took in lodgers. He vowed to *make* more time for her in future.

Following her into the steamy kitchen, the familiar laundry sights and smells greeted him: a copper simmering in the corner, a scent of warm, ironed linen and yellow Sunlight soap. It was crowded with two dolly tubs and a mangle, as well as the kitchen table and chairs. Two flat irons heated on the open coal range. He ducked under the laden wooden ceiling rack worked by a pulley, used for laundry on wet days – and on days like this, too, when the odds were not great on it coming in from the line outside without smuts. The moist heat bathed around him – the Turkish baths down the road were less steamy – but he wouldn't have dreamed of suggesting it would be more comfortable in the parlour, which he knew would be no less cluttered.

Orla Maclusky was his mother's sister. Despite a sprinkling of grey in her dark curly hair and the extra pounds she'd accumulated over the years, she'd lost none of her Irish beauty. Her skin bloomed like a young woman's, except where the laughter lines showed, and her eyes were as bright and blue as they had been when she'd first left the shores of Erin with his parents for England. She'd come to London in her twenties but she still had a lot of the Irish in her speech, richly embellishing the acquired accent of East London, particularly in moments of excitement, or stress.

She'd never married, but she'd done well for herself with the little business she ran, the profits from it enabling her to buy a modest house in this poor district, where she had set up as a dealer in second-hand clothes. Nothing ratty, she insisted, priding herself on the quality of the garments she sold to those who could afford them, earning a good reputation by never offering anything for sale unless it was clean, and in reasonable repair. Her trade kept her ceaselessly busy, washing, ironing, mending and setting out the clothes for display in her front room, yet she still found the time and energy to take in the occasional lodger to augment her income.

He let her rattle on until he had the opportunity to steer the conversation the way he wanted it to go. 'Well, then, how is the new resident?' he asked when they were sitting down with their tea steaming in front of them.

'My lodger, is it? Now, that's funny you should ask. He came back only yesterday. I'd scarcely seen neither the hide nor the hair of him for more than a month until then.'

'He'd left you?'

'Not for good. His things were still here and I knew he'd come back. And so he did.'

'You weren't bothered at him disappearing like that, Auntie Orla? Anyone else would have thrown him out. Sounds as though he was up to something fishy.'

'The police are giving you a nasty suspicious mind, Joseph. Lennie's not one of your bad lads. I like him, and besides, he'd paid his rent well in advance, although he doesn't have much money to spare. But things are going to get better for him soon, he says, and I believe him. He's quiet and considerate – and he never misses going to mass,' she added, taking the opportunity of throwing out a broad hint to Inskip, which he pretended not to hear. 'He never goes out much, or not until lately. Keeps his room tidy and has his meals with me.' She thought about what he'd said for a moment. 'But I *have* been a bit worried, to tell the truth. I think he hasn't been well, he looks delicate to me. He didn't come home last night. I don't suppose he'd have gone out at all if Danny hadn't persuaded him.'

'Danny?'

'Danny O'Rourke,' she said carefully, watching him. 'He came to see me last night.'

'And you let him in?' said Inskip, when he could. '*O'Rourke?*'

'Would I have left him on the doorstep, and he with messages from the cousins still in the old country? The old folk there still remember me, I'll have you know.' She sighed a little, a faraway look in her eyes. Did she still hanker after going back to Ireland? he'd sometimes wondered. She always welcomed anyone who brought her news of her old home with open arms. But O'Rourke being back in London was not welcome news for anyone, especially Inskip. There were unresolved issues between them, going back a long way. Once there'd been a girl, Cathleen, who could have amounted to a great deal for Inskip, had she not been dazzled by smiling eyes, and been taken in by the blarney. He might have learned to live with that if O'Rourke hadn't taken off and disappeared when she became pregnant. A good Irish Catholic girl, having a baby out of wedlock, an absent father . . . it had been too much for Cathleen and she had let the river claim her life.

How dared the bastard show his face back here? Inskip wasn't the only one who had matters to settle with him. Cathleen's parents, and her three brothers, had never forgiven him for the sadness and shame he had brought on them.

Orla, watching him, divined his thoughts. 'Sure, it's tempting to believe that one's the divil on three legs,' she said, crossing herself even as she spoke. 'He's back here for something, that's for sure, but as Father Finucane tells us, forgiveness is . . .' Catching Inskip's eye, she stopped and hastily changed direction. 'Only yesterday he was wondering why he never sees you at mass lately? Father Finucane, I mean.'

Inskip bit his tongue. This was familiar ground but he wasn't about to get into a religious discussion with Orla. He never won when he did, because in matters of faith she was entirely illogical, and he knew no counter-arguments anyway. Instead, feeling the rising of his temper at what he'd just heard, but sternly ordering himself to stay calm, he asked, 'What does he look like, your lodger?'

'What?' She stared. 'Oh the poor wee man's nothing special, but he has lovely eyes when he takes his specs off. And lovely manners on him. He's been well brought up, that's for sure, though he needs somebody to look after him, some nice girl, I'm thinking. He tells me he's been living in lodgings ever since his poor mother was taken.'

'Nothing special, you say – but you'd recognize him again if you saw him?'

'Well, wasn't it only yesterday he sat where you are, eating his bacon and cabbage and saying how good it was? Of course I'd know him!'

'What was his name again?'

'Leonard. Lennie, he said to call him. Lennie Croxton.' A growing uneasiness widened her eyes. 'There's something wrong, isn't there?'

'Yes, Auntie. I'm sorry to have to tell you, but I'm afraid it's possible your Lennie might have come to a sad end.'

A good deed in a naughty world, the Dorcas in more ways than one shone amid the crumbling poverty that surrounded it, the tall tenements that excluded light and air, the foetid alleys and noisome courts. It occupied the ground floor of one of the many hand- some old Spitalfields houses built originally by Huguenot silk merchants, most of them now fallen into sad disrepair. When Doctor Sam Weston had wished to set up his practice, he and his newly married wife, Hannah, with the aid of a small but timely legacy from her godmother, had bought the property and renovated and repaired as much of it as they could afford, although water still occasionally leaked through the roof into the attics above the upstairs rooms where they lived with their growing young family. And not the least of it was that the paintwork outside was flaking and badly in need of repainting, apart from a board which announced itself as Dorcas House, a free clinic for mothers and babies, and was kept clean and shining by Nurse Peg, as was the doctor's brass nameplate. Inside, it was as welcoming and reassuring as fresh paint, clean, scrubbed floors throughout, light colours on the walls and a few cheerful pictures could make it.

Alice, Sam, and his wife, Hannah, had all met when they were medical students. Hannah had been born into a well-to-do lifestyle, but she accepted with good grace the conditions and surroundings in which she now had to bring up her small twin boys, with another baby almost ready to be born, making it impossible for her to continue to work as a doctor. She took life philosophically and shared her husband's dedication to the work being done at the clinic, though she sighed a little when he fell asleep over his supper after yet another day when he'd scarcely been off his feet. Unlike Hannah, he came from working-class stock, with no income except what he earned. It was only Hannah's modest personal income which enabled him to maintain his family and his small practice, as well as the clinic. It certainly wasn't a flow of rich patients able to pay the bills. As often as not in this desperately poverty-stricken district, they stayed unpaid. In that respect, Sam was just such another man as Alice's father had been, almost a saint in his unstinting care for his patients. But sainthood didn't pay the bills and their finances could only be stretched so far. Money was a constant worry.

Today, when Alice arrived at the Dorcas, the waiting room was already full of wan-faced women and a great many children, some of them barefoot, even on a cold day like this, and at least one of whom, she noticed with resigned pity, had a bad case of rickets. Most of them showed signs of malnutrition. She hoped the suspicious flush on the face of one child wouldn't turn out to be the first indication of measles or something worse, otherwise the clinic would very quickly have an epidemic on their hands and Heaven alone knew how they'd cope with that.

Sam was surprised at her unexpected appearance, but pleased to see her. It meant he could be out on his rounds while she took care of those in the waiting room. The air around Sam Weston always seemed to crackle with energy and within ten minutes, he had shrugged on his coat and his stocky frame disappeared out of the door, seeming to leave a vacuum behind when he departed.

Alice's first patient was that same flushed little boy she had noticed, brought in by his mother. Her quick, professional glance told her that the mother was not far away from having another little life to worry about, too. She wasn't yet thirty, but looked fifty. The effort it must have cost to keep herself, the boy and her other children clean and decent was incalculable. Heavy-eyed and listless, the boy should have been in bed, but as Alice examined him she was thankful to find he appeared to be suffering nothing more than a heavy cold and a cough, one worrying enough to have caused his mother to bring him here. The clinic was usually a last resort. Many of the women so disliked seeking help from what they saw as a charity, they often left it too late.

'Nothing seriously worrying, Mrs Cribbins, nothing more than the cough.'

Nothing more than a cough, indeed! she thought as she wrote out a prescription for linctus. In the conditions in which this family lived, six of them in a two-roomed apartment in a house they shared with three other families, a cough like that could signal disaster – bronchitis, even tuberculosis. 'Take him home and keep him warm and in bed. Hand this to Nurse Peg and she'll get Mr Lubetkin to make up a bottle to ease his chest.' Mrs Lambert, known to all as Nurse Peg, was a motherly, late-middle aged woman who had trained as a hospital nurse, brought up a family of four and now that they had flown the nest wanted to use her skills as a nurse again – though not in a hospital. She was bossy and would stand no nonsense, but she was also kind, and the patients respected her. Mr Lubetkin was an elderly Polish Jew who had been a pharmacist in his own country before being forced to flee from religious persecution there, and now worked in the little room at the back they used as a dispensary, rolling pills and making up countless bottles of medicine.

Alice gave the little boy a striped humbug from the jar on her desk, smiling to see how his eyes brightened a little but noticing how sparrow-thin his arms were as he took it. 'Promise to take the medicine, Ollie? It's not nasty, in fact it tastes – really nice.' She'd almost said it tasted of raspberries, but she doubted if he'd ever seen a raspberry, never mind tasted one. He needed milk, eggs and butter, and his mother would be able to give him none of these. She would have liked to have pressed money into her hand but Mrs Cribbins was proud, and even a few coins might have been seen as an insult. Instead, she stood up and fetched a small parcel of Lucy's outgrown baby clothes she had brought in the previous day. 'Maybe you or someone else will find these useful, Mrs Cribbins. My niece is seven months old now and these are too small for her. Amazing how quickly they grow, isn't it?'

This was something Mrs Cribbins understood. Baby clothes and other outgrown children's garments were acceptable – everyone passed them on, once, twice, half-a-dozen times. As she fingered the quality of the long gowns, the lacy woollen matinee coats, tiny bootees, soft flannel vests, and little bonnets, and exclaimed at the hand embroidery, done by Violet, who was an exquisite needlewoman and had sewn a whole layette to relieve the boredom before Lucy's birth, her sudden smile for a moment made her the young woman she once was. Such beautiful clothes might have to be sold rather than used for the new baby, but that didn't matter.

Patient after patient came in as the day wore on. At midday, Hannah came downstairs and invited her to share lunch. 'I've made soup. Sam's likely to forget he hasn't eaten and won't be home,' she said with a wry smile, 'but the terrible twins have had their lunch and I've put them down for a nap. I'd welcome a spot of adult conversation.'

Alice could understand that. The two boys were engaging little imps of three who demanded all their mother's attention. Friends since their medical student days, half an hour with gentle Hannah was always welcome and she happily accepted the offer of soup and a chat.

Late in the afternoon, the stream of patients gradually dwindled and at last, the waiting room was empty, allowing Alice to write up her records. She was tired, but nowhere near as tired as after one or other of the social events in her divided life. This, after all, was what she'd once dedicated her life to, nevertheless it shocked her to find herself suddenly aware that she felt more at home here than in her own home, at Manessa House.

The telephone ringing somewhere outside the room made her jump. Incoming telephone calls to the clinic were rare. Sam had felt it necessary to have it installed, but it was used only infrequently, when it was necessary to gain an urgent admission to one of the hospitals or for some other emergency. It was rarely, if ever, used as a method of summoning him. Few around here could afford to summon the doctor at all unless the need was desperate, and in any case almost none of them had access to a telephone or were familiar with its use. In an emergency, a boy would be sent running to the surgery, knocking the doctor up if it was night time.

The ringing eventually ceased as Nurse Peg answered the call. Alice heard her speaking loudly – even she mistrusted the capabilities of the new-fangled gadget, quite rightly in most cases, since the inevitable crackling and hissing on the line often made carrying on a conversation a feat of endurance. A moment later she came in, her broad face pale and concerned. 'That telephone call – it's for you, Doctor. I'm afraid you're needed at home.'

Comforted by the tea, Orla had told Inskip everything she knew about her lodger, which in effect amounted to not much at all, and in the end, though she didn't want to do it, she made no objections when he asked her, and went with him to identify the body of the dead man found in the taxicab.

'Yes, that's Lennie,' she told them sadly. She bowed her head and said a prayer and when she opened her eyes she had tears in them.

Inskip put his arms round her, then took her home again and made another pot of strong tea.

'We'll have to search his room,' he said, wondering why he felt apologetic.

'Go ahead, if you think it'll be of any use. He was a gentleman, but he didn't have much.'

She was right. Lennie Croxton's sole possession, apart from a few spare clothes, was a framed, rather faded snapshot of a pleasant-faced woman standing in a garden with two young children, a boy and a girl, an arm around each of them. His mother, his sister and himself? It would seem so. There was a resemblance. But his mother, according to Orla, was dead. The wedding ring on his watch chain had almost certainly belonged to her – and if that was his sister in the photograph, she could be married and living anywhere. Lennie had left nothing behind to indicate how it might be possible to get in touch with her. There were two other people in the snapshot but they wouldn't be much use either, just a man and a woman, almost off the picture, evidently not meant to be in the photo at all but caught by the camera.

Downstairs once more, he questioned Orla again about her lodger, but there was little more she could tell. She believed his guess about the photo was right – yes, his mother was dead and in fact she was almost certain the sister, too, had died at a young age. As to any other aspects of his life, his aunt was ignorant. Her lodger had spent most of his time in his room, except when he came down to share his dinner with her. What had they talked about, then, sitting there together in the kitchen?

'Oh, this and that. He liked to hear about everything that was going on in the parish. And it fascinated him to hear about the old country, what we got up to as children, going potato picking in the field with the Da . . . and all that . . . before the Famine that forced us over here . . .' Her voice trailed off. 'Well, you know how all that was. The hardness of the times.'

'There's some that think they still are.'

'That *know* they are,' she corrected him. 'And with good reason.' For several minutes they spoke of the troubled land across the sea, then Orla sighed, stirred the piled fire, picked up the half-empty coal scuttle and shunted what was left in it into the grate. More flames roared up the chimney.

Inskip wiped the sweat off his brow.

Indeed he did know what Orla meant, he thought as he took the scuttle down to the coal-cellar and refilled it for her. He himself was only one remove from first generation Irish immigrants, refugees from the potato famine in which a million people had died. Like Orla, his parents had fled Ireland and settled with their four sons in London's East End. After their mother, then their father died, all the boys, adults by then, had emigrated to the United States. Three of them were still there, leading successful lives in Boston. Only Inskip had returned – escaped, he liked to think – homesick for the warm life of the streets where he had grown up. He stayed, despite the letters from his older brothers which came extolling America, if you took the opportunities available and worked hard. They tried to seduce him back with stories of the money they were making, their spacious houses, central heating, motor cars and all the food you could eat. Inskip ignored the seductions. It was nothing to the vibrant, if squalid, life he was familiar with, its polyglot population from all over the place, its crumbling tenements, its teeming, noisy, and often hazardous street life, where people often lived on the edge of the law but mostly looked out for each other. And not the least reason he stayed here was because he felt alive by being kept on his toes with his work in the police, especially since he had become a detective at Scotland Yard.

He took the scuttle back, washed his hands at the stone sink and tried to prise out more information about Lennie Croxton from Orla, but it was evident that in their conversations over their meals together it was she who'd done the talking and Croxton the listening, giving nothing of himself away.

'Did he have a job, a profession?'

'I don't know, but he never failed to pay his rent. I had the impression he was a clerk somewhere but you can't force a person if they don't want to talk about themselves,' she said sadly. 'I suppose he might have had some private means . . . this wasn't the life he'd been born to, that's for sure. I told you, he was a gentleman, he didn't give himself airs but he was educated and used to better things.'

He thought she must have had a hard time repressing her curiosity, not having anything to satisfy her or to pass on to her church cronies, who enjoyed nothing better than gossip – what they called the craik. 'What were his interests, his friends?'

'I don't know of any friends.' She was beginning to look distressed. 'Listen, he was just a quiet young man that never harmed a living soul.'

She was trying to convince herself that her nice young lodger couldn't have been implicated in anything sleazy, that neither his reticence, nor his apparent lack of friends or acquaintances, his unexplained absence and his having no visible means of support, had anything to do with his grisly end. As for the uncharacteristic rapport he'd struck up with O'Rourke . . . Inskip just didn't believe that.

'Where was O'Rourke staying?' he asked his aunt.

She gave him a steady look. Despite what she wanted to believe, the implications of what had passed hadn't really escaped her. 'He didn't say. It was a surprise to me to see him back at all. I expect he still has friends here, though.'

'I'm sure he has,' said Inskip, thinking of the sort of friends they would be, and that he knew where to find them, though he wouldn't bet much on the chances of O'Rourke being with any of them now. With his capacity for dodging trouble and disappearing like smoke, he was very likely out of the country already, maybe back in Ireland, or even further away, in any case holing up somewhere where he couldn't be found. Everything pointed to him as the killer who had got into the cab with Lennie Croxton and cut his throat, and hopefully the cabbie would have no difficulty in identifying him as the 'big fella' who'd been his second passenger . . . if he could be found. But why had the mild-mannered Lennie Croxton his aunt knew been associating at all with a rogue like O'Rourke? And what the hell was O'Rourke up to?

'So they knew one another, O'Rourke and your Lennie?' he said, in spite of not believing at all in such an unlikely friendship.

She shook her head, 'They'd never met, until Danny came to see me. I think they just took a liking to each other, you know, the way it happens sometimes.' But she didn't look too certain.

Neither was Inskip putting much store by that, though he knew what she meant. People did initially take to the man. O'Rourke, when he wanted to, could charm birds off trees, use his silver tongue to convince anyone of anything . . . look at Cathleen. Even perhaps to persuading a young chap of mild disposition and irreproachable habits whom he'd only just met to go out carousing with him? Inskip's natural cynicism, plus his police training, took over and told him no. Things had been going on beneath the surface that indicated at least one of those things he'd just heard about Croxton might not be true . . . His mysterious absence over the last month, for instance, indicated he'd been leading a secret life. At the very least his behaviour had been such as to excite suspicion, but he didn't disillusion Orla further.

'If you hear anything about where that O'Rourke is, you just let me know, Auntie,' he said as he got up to leave.

'I will. It's not right that such a decent young fellow should have been killed like that. I'll ask around,' she promised. 'Someone will know.' He nodded his thanks. The Catholic community round here was tightly integrated, and not much would escape the old gossips at St Bede's – not forgetting Father Finucane himself. A visit to him might in fact be profitable. Daniel O'Rourke hadn't left a lot behind him in the way of sympathy when he'd scarpered like the lily-livered coward he was, leaving behind the wreckage he'd caused to a young woman's life.

At that point, Inskip gave himself a mental shake. This was getting personal. Despite his background, he never thought of himself as particularly Irish. He didn't go out of his way to associate with the many Irish expatriates in London, nor did he go to mass – and anyway, he was only Irish on his mother's side. The Inskips had been imports from England to the godforsaken island across the Irish Sea through a seventeenth-century ancestor who'd been a servant to one of those English colonists. But despite himself, Inskip felt drawn further and further into the coils of the present tangled situation by the mysterious ties of race and blood. And the mere fact that it was O'Rourke they were looking for gave a particular fillip to his determination that he must be found, somehow. And not only for murdering Lennie Croxton. Memory turned like a knife in his gut – however belatedly revenge came, it would be sweet. He made an instant decision not to make public the extent of his previous connection to the man – at least not just yet – only to tell Gaines that he knew who O'Rourke was. Which would, unfortunately, entail the superintendent, Renshaw, being informed.

Renshaw wouldn't have got where he was if he hadn't been a good man in his younger days, but desk-bound responsibilities and caution had come with promotion. He hung on to his job nowadays through going strictly by the book. Inskip couldn't be sure, but he suspected that if he revealed too much about his connection with O'Rourke the super might find a convenient reason to have him taken off the case, pronto. He was wary of Inskip in any case, saw him as something of a loose cannon, that much Inskip knew. He preferred working with the more predictable Gaines, a more experienced, steadier, if slower-thinking man who nevertheless was one of his best detectives. On the other hand, Inskip and Gaines had grown into working well together and Renshaw knew it.

He couldn't – and wouldn't – keep his connection to O'Rourke quiet for too long. But before Renshaw got to hear of it, he had enquiries of his own to make, unhampered by anything the superintendent might decide was the more cautious line to follow. In fact, it was Leonard Croxton who looked like being more of a problem than finding O'Rourke might be. Who was he, and what had he been up to, that it was necessary for someone to murder him? Where had he disappeared to during the last few weeks? Tracing him would be difficult, if not impossible. The starting point had to be O'Rourke, and where he had stayed.

Five

It had been Mrs Lowther who had made the telephone call to
Alice at the Dorcas, which said everything for the urgency of the
situation. For nothing less would she have brought herself to use
the mysterious Instrument, as she referred to it. She had come to
acknowledge, grudgingly, that it was useful in emergencies, but she
still approached it gingerly when forced to use it. She didn't rightly
see how it could work, except by some sort of black magic.

Kidnapped.

A fantasy word, one so unfamiliar in ordinary life you could
scarcely take in what it meant. Something that happened in books,
or to other people. Not to the Martens family. Not to *Lucy*! This
had to be some awful, horrible mistake. But the telephone message,
though garbled, had left little room for doubt.

Alice found them waiting for the police in Violet's morning room,
a small room overlooking the side of the house, Violet herself, in
floods of tears, and Lucy's nanny, white-faced and obviously upset.
The cup rattled on the saucer as Emma, a normally unflappable
person, handed tea to Violet, who waved it aside, too incoherent
for speech. Alice gulped hers and waited for further enlightenment,
but over Violet's drooping head Emma would not meet her eyes
and looked away. Guilty? Lucy was her charge, after all. Or just
unwilling to be drawn? Whichever was true, perhaps it was better
that Violet shouldn't have to listen while the distressing details were
repeated. When the police arrived, the events would all need to be
gone over again, anyway.

So Alice, still numb with shock, curbed her impatience and remained
pretty much in the dark. Lowther, who'd been sent to fetch her home,
had also stubbornly refused to go into details, though she'd had to
share the front seat of the motor with him, due to her bicycle having
to be wedged, not without difficulty, into the back beside the seats.
She knew nothing except that Lucy had been taken for her afternoon
outing to the Regent's Park and there she had disappeared. 'Baby
carriage and all,' said Lowther, not without a certain relish.

'Disappeared? How on earth—?'

'You'll know soon enough, Mrs Latimer, madam,' he'd grunted, but with a sort of gruff sympathy. After which he became clam-like, infuriatingly refusing to say more, if indeed he knew anything, which Alice suspected he did not.

'Where are the police, why are they not here yet? Violet was demanding fretfully. Her handkerchief was screwed into a ball, her pretty face was blotched and her feathery eyelashes were dark and spiky with tears. 'And oh, why did Ferdie have to choose today, of all days, to go racing?' she moaned. Alice, on the other hand, was rather glad Ferdie wasn't here and hoped, not yet knowing any details, that all this was a temporary misunderstanding that would all be resolved before he arrived home. If Violet, oh-so-controlled Violet, was in a state of collapse, it was hard to imagine what the effect of this would be on Ferdie. He had set off the previous day as a passenger in his friend Fitzwilliam's open tourer to drive to the races in Worcester, where Fitz had a horse running. They had planned to stay the night there, and should by now be on their way home. Hopefully, straight home, if the horse hadn't won, with no stops for celebration.

'And why isn't Edmund here yet?' Violet sobbed.

'Edmund?'

It appeared that he, the one to whom everyone, especially Violet, automatically turned for support in this family when authority was needed, had been sitting in committee when he'd been called out to receive her message, and though shocked and appalled, it had been impossible for him to come home at that precise moment. Leave it with him, he'd said, and he'd be there as soon as ever possible. And of course he would, Alice said reassuringly, pressing Violet's heaving shoulder. Where Lucy was concerned, Edmund would have moved the earth.

A measure of how much she needed comfort, Violet allowed Alice's hand to stay there for a moment before shrugging it off. She sat twisting her rings round on her slim fingers. Her normal poise had completely deserted her, although not to the point where she looked in the least dishevelled: the form-fitting coat-and-skirt outfit she was still wearing was uncreased and elegant as her clothes always were, although its sombre bottle-green only exaggerated her pallor.

The table was laid for tea with a stiffly starched white cloth, cups and saucers and a plate of scones which no one wanted. The light,

modern room today felt oddly cold. It struck Alice for the first
time that although the last word in modernity, there was nothing
precisely comfortable about Violet's choice of furnishings. She
walked to the window. The sun, which had lived up to its early
promise and been out all day, now, in the late afternoon, had disappeared. It was windless and the garden was still. A blackbird's evening
song sounded, piercingly clear. This contradictory year had started
out mild and brought the blossom out early and now it had fluttered down from the one cherry tree always the first to flower, to
make a snowy carpet on the grass, a mute reminder that this was
where Lucy's pram usually stood when she was put outside to sleep
in the fresh air. The garden, too, looked exceedingly chilly. There
might even be a late frost tonight by the look of the cold sky,
turning from duck-egg blue to pale green as the light faded. And
out there, somewhere, was little Lucy.

Stoical enough as a rule, DI Gaines had been more than a trifle
miffed at having this additional investigation thrust upon him, being
ordered to drop everything and jump through hoops like a circus
performer, all for something which he felt could have been resolved
without the intervention of Scotland Yard. But when the direction
had come from on high, as this one had, querying the whys and
wherefores was not an option. Especially since it had come via
Edmund Latimer, MP, no less, pulling rank and quick to invoke the
services of the Yard, the natural inclinations of prominent politicians
like him being to demand nothing less than the best.

'It's probably nothing much – you know how these mothers can
panic over some mistake or other,' the childless Renshaw had told
Gaines, rather sharply in the face of his obvious reluctance when
the case was given to him. 'Soon over and no harm done. But you'd
better go and make a good impression.'

Gaines was momentarily rendered speechless, that the idea of a
mistake over a baby's disappearance could be entertained, even for
one single moment. A *baby*, not even a toddler who had wandered
off and got itself lost.

The pause had given Renshaw the opportunity to administer the
final clinch. 'Besides, this other business isn't properly under way
yet, is it?'

This other business, the small matter of a murder. Not to mention that, in the way these things happen, just at the point when some breathing space was needed, every criminal in London, or so it seemed, had decided to step up their activity. But Gaines sighed and resigned himself to the inevitable. The whole department was stretched to capacity, but that didn't mean to say there was any question that the disappearance of a baby didn't have the highest priority. It was normal to have several cases on the go at once, nor would it be the first time he was required to juggle two important ones at the same time. He didn't want anyone else to take over his investigation on the taxicab murder, but since it was true that it wasn't going anywhere much at the moment . . .

Although Inskip's interview with his Aunt Orla had established the identity of the victim and turned up a promising lead on the Irishman, O'Rourke, the search for him, not to mention ferreting out details of the victim himself, gave every indication of being a slow business. It was a bonus that Inskip knew the Irish folk O'Rourke had been known to associate with and who were likely to know where he was, but they were not talking. Frustrating, to say the least, when they were almost certain of the identity of the murderer, that the business of finding him might stretch out for months. But gathering information at this stage was the most they could do, and Renshaw knew it. In any case, whether the child's disappearance was being regarded lightly by other people or not, it wasn't in Gaines' nature to dismiss the distress of any mother in such circumstances, however it should turn out. So he had set off with as much grace as he could muster, summoning Inskip to accompany him.

'What's up with you, then?' he asked on the way there, sensing Inskip wasn't quite with him. The sergeant didn't always listen as closely as he should, his mind on its own trajectory.

'Oh, nothing, sir.'

Gaines didn't press him, though something was evidently bothering him.

At Manessa House, while the three women waited, ten minutes stretched out into what felt like an hour. But at last, there was the sound of voices, footsteps outside. The door opened and two burly men were shown in. They still looked like policemen despite the fact that they were wearing plain clothes, though the younger man's attire was anything but.

'Well, if it isn't the Lord Mayor of London!' The exclamation came from Emma, the baby's nanny. Too late, she pressed her lips together. Remarks like that were scarcely in order today, however involuntary, but no one else had seemed to notice.

Not even the dandified younger man to whom the remark was addressed. 'Nice to see you again, too, Miss Pavel.'

'You know each other, then . . .?' Alice stopped, hearing herself stating the obvious.

'We've met before,' Emma said.

'Indeed we have, Miss Pavel.' The senior man, who had a drooping moustache that made him look older than he probably was, and wore a slightly rumpled suit in sharp contrast to the other's smart brown check, gave Emma a smile and took charge, introducing himself as Detective Chief Inspector George Gaines and the Lord Mayor as Detective Sergeant Joseph Inskip, both from Scotland Yard.

'Scotland Yard?' repeated Violet sharply. Instinctively, she had sat up straighter when they entered, her hand going to her hair. She need not have worried. Its loops and swirls were smooth and immaculate, undisturbed despite the last frantic hour or two.

'That's right, Mrs Martens.' Gaines spoke reassuringly, giving no indication of his feelings, but as he went on there was something in his manner that said it wasn't his idea to be investigating this, a domestic matter normally not within his remit.

It wasn't surprising to Alice, however. Once her husband had been told, strings would have been pulled. The name of Edmund Latimer, MP was sufficient to open doors closed to lesser mortals, a facility which he didn't hesitate to use when necessary. It caused Alice uneasiness from time to time but in this case she wasn't about to cavil at unfairness and privilege, even when it meant invoking the services of Scotland Yard for what to this officer was no doubt something which would turn out to be a storm in a teacup, however catastrophic and earth-shattering it might be to a baby's parents.

Whatever he felt, he was giving the matter his full attention, and wasted no time in getting down to the facts of the disappearance; a mystery in itself, that it could have happened at all, the apparent abduction of a baby in charge of her nursemaid, in broad daylight, in a well-populated public park. 'Take me through what happened,' he said encouragingly to Emma.

Emma hesitated. 'I—'

'Nanny wasn't there,' interposed Violet, swallowing another sob. 'I had given her the afternoon off to go and visit her mother.'

'Then who was in charge of the baby?'

'I was. I took her there myself. Oh, if only I had not!'

'*You* did, Violet?' The idea of her sister-in-law performing the duties of nursemaid and looking after her own child struck Alice as so extraordinary her tact deserted her.

'Yes, me, her mother! Why not?' replied Violet sharply, stung into forgetting her tears for a brief moment. 'There was no one else to do it in any case. Mrs Lowther – our housekeeper, Inspector Gaines – is usually only too delighted to have the chance to look after Baby, but she'd gone to buy new sheets at Swan and Edgar's.' She paused then added pointedly, 'Now they're functioning properly again after those dreadful suffragettes smashed their windows last month!' Gaines coughed. 'Well, anyway, she wasn't here, and all the other servants were too busy to attend to Lucinda. But she was restless for some reason, she would keep on crying and her little face was awfully red.'

'She's teething, Mrs Martens,' put in Emma.

'Yes, of course, I know that, Nanny. But I couldn't settle her, Inspector. I know Nanny takes her to the park every afternoon and I thought wheeling her there might lull her to sleep. Which eventually it did. I was afraid she might wake again if I stopped, but I was tired of walking around like that, so I risked it and found a seat.'

'Whereabouts in the park was this?' asked Inskip.

'What? Oh, I don't remember exactly where . . . somewhere,' she said vaguely. 'There were nursemaids with prams and a lot of little children running around and making a great deal of noise further along, so I chose a seat well away from them, where it was quiet.'

The noisy children, Alice suspected, were an excuse and she guessed this hadn't escaped either policeman. The park was frequented on a daily basis by nursemaids and their charges and, in common with most of the women in Violet's circle, she wouldn't have known what to do if she'd found herself in the midst of a gaggle of them. Facing their disapproval, moreover. A lady like that, wheeling her own child out! Unheard of!

'What happened next?' asked Gaines.

'Why, nothing. Except that a woman came and sat on the seat beside me.' The sergeant, who was doing the note-taking, looked alert. 'But she began cooing over Lucinda, who was still asleep,

and when I showed my annoyance that she might wake her, she
moved away. It was warm and pleasant in the sun and – well, I'm
afraid I became a little drowsy myself.'

The sergeant's mouth turned down but both men studiously
avoided comment. Alice knew that Violet invariably stayed in bed
until noon after a late night, and often took a nap before dressing
to go out for the evening. She and Ferdie rarely arrived home before
the small hours. It was hardly surprising she had dropped off.

'I swear I closed my eyes for no more than a few minutes,' she
protested, 'but when I woke up, my baby had gone!' A fresh bout
of tears threatened.

'Can you describe this woman, the one who sat beside you?'
Gaines asked.

'What? Well, no. She was just . . . She was only there for a minute
or so and I don't recall at all what she looked like.'

No further explanation was needed to tell them that she had
not been a 'lady', then. Women like Mrs Martens were able to
recognize, sum up and remember every detail of a woman from
their own social strata from twenty yards away.

'What does it matter, anyway? She walked away and disappeared
towards the lake.' Suddenly, her hand went to her mouth. 'Oh. Oh,
you don't – you can't mean *she* might have been the one – oh, dear
God, no! The lake!'

'No, I don't mean that, not at all, not the lake,' Gaines said
hastily, 'though she might, just possibly, have been the one who
took her away. But,' he was quick to add, 'we don't want to jump to
conclusions of any sort, just yet.'

Alice could guess what he held back from saying. Such things
did happen: women pushed to madness in a frantic desire for a
child they couldn't have, or after the death of one which, with all
the newly vaunted medical advancements nowadays, still happened
only too frequently, as well she knew. Mother love, the longing for
a child, was after all one of the most powerful instincts on earth.
If some such poor, crazed creature had taken Lucy the odds were
that she could be lost forever in the teeming, anonymous population of London, or even be many miles from here by now. Or had
Violet in her fright been nearer the mark, and had it been some
woman mad in another, more terrifying way? Driven to kill, perhaps.
There had in the past been a horrific spate of child murders by a

woman horribly named by the press as 'The Angel Maker', and the memory still haunted parents' nightmares. No wonder Violet had reacted like that at the thought of the lake.

She stopped such thoughts abruptly. Violet was saying, with a sort of hopeless resignation, 'If that's so, if some woman has her, then we shall never get her back.' She fell wretchedly silent and yet, Alice thought, mixed up with the distress and shock, some other emotion was there, something watchful and wary. Defiance? Yes, of course, that was it, against the blame and criticism she felt were directed against her, neither of which Violet ever took easily.

'I'm sorry, Mrs Martens,' Gaines began again, breaking the silence. 'Difficult as it is, you must not let yourself think like that. It's only been an hour or two. Lucy may have been taken away in a moment of madness, by someone who'll think better of it. We can still hope for her return. Meanwhile—' He cleared his throat and looked faintly embarrassed as he added, 'I'm a family man myself and I know how painful this must be, but I'm afraid I shall have to take you in some detail through everything if we're to get anywhere. Are you sure you can't remember the location of the seat where you chose to sit? It might be important.'

'No – well, not exactly. I suppose it might have been some-where near the Gloucester Gate but I can't be sure. When I found she was gone I began rushing around like a madwoman, stopping people and asking if they'd seen anything. I was at my wits' end and quite lost my bearings.'

Alice could understand this: the insane urge to feel that *someone* must surely have noticed a person wheeling a perambulator with a beautiful golden-haired baby inside. But Lucy's bright hair wouldn't have been visible, would it? Not even if the hinged hood was let down – and certainly not under one of the ridiculously fancy white bonnets Violet decreed for her child, with its crocheted ruffle surrounding her round, baby's face like an elaborate pie-frill.

'If anyone noticed someone unusual wheeling the pram, it would be one of those nannies,' Emma put in suddenly.

'Would they know it?' Gaines asked. 'From any other pram?'

'It's hard to miss.' She described it: an old wicker baby carriage resurrected from the attics where it had reposed for many a year, ever since the last baby, Violet herself, in fact, had ceased to need it. She had thought it 'amusing' to use it for her own baby. In fact, it was light and easily manoeuvrable, though it was much deplored by the departed Nanny Struthers, so old-fashioned looking it was, and possibly unhygienic into the bargain. Moreover, the other nannies she met in the park on their daily excursions looked down on it because it didn't conform to the modern, streamlined ones other fashionable mothers decreed for their own charges. 'Everybody knows it, all the other nannies, anyway,' she said.

'We'll talk to them,' Gaines promised.

Inskip commendably held his tongue as he took down their names, or rather the ones they were known to the others by, which was the name of their employer: Nannies Cavendish or Lyttleton, Ponsonby, or de Grey, as if they were family-owned. But they didn't mind that, Emma said, meeting Inskip's expression, rather did they see it as a source of pride. The more illustrious the name, the higher the nanny's ranking among her contemporaries.

'Did no one offer to help you in your search?' Gaines asked, turning again to Violet. 'These nursemaids, perhaps?'

'No. In the end I did go to look for them and ask, of course, but they had all gone home. It was after four by then, you see.' Which was self-explanatory, the immutable nursery tea time, when the park emptied of children and their keepers. The two policemen exchanged looks, eloquent of the opportunity lost by Mrs Martens in not requesting their help immediately. Violet herself, seeming only now to realize how remiss she'd been, began a hurried explanation. 'I didn't think of asking them until it occurred to me that one of those naughty children might have wheeled Lucinda away while my eyes were closed. To play a trick. For a . . . for a joke, you know,' she finished lamely.

'*A joke?*' The sergeant looked incredulous, as well he might.

But the notion of something like that wasn't perhaps altogether so very far-fetched, thought Alice. A trick it might have been, though certainly not one played by any of those children under the eagle eyes of their nannies. Those were women not only paid by parents to look after their offspring but also to present quiet, well-behaved children to the world, and it was their mission in life and a source of pride to see this was carried out. Little imps of mischief the children might be, in the way of any normal child, at times, but they would have been kept firmly under control in public and scolded if they misbehaved. It was inconceivable that any wayward child could have escaped their constant vigilance. It *was* just possible though, however unlikely, that taking Lucy was indeed some malicious trick played by someone . . . to teach Violet not to go to sleep while looking after her baby? Or perhaps someone with a deeper grudge against her – or Ferdie – to cause them anxiety and distress before the child was returned unharmed.

'It's easy to be wise after the event, Mrs Martens,' Gaines was saying, 'but with hindsight, the incident should have been reported straight away. Police are always patrolling the park.' There was no need to remind any of them what an extent that was: four hundred acres of recreation areas, paths and woodland glades, avenues of trees, and not least the boating lake. And where were they likely to find anyone who might have noticed a woman trundling an old-fashioned wicker pram through the park gates and out to those thronged pavements beyond? She might have been given a cursory glance but the sight wasn't so remarkable as to excite curiosity.

'How was I to know about the police? I never saw any,' Violet returned petulantly. 'After a while, I realized it was useless to look further and came home. My husband is away at the races and I don't expect him home until later, so I telephoned my brother . . . Edmund Latimer.'

She didn't seem to feel that needed any further elucidation. Which of course it did not, thought Gaines sourly. The name having caused such a stir among the upper echelons, that was the reason he was here. Meanwhile time was sliding by, the child remained missing and with every hour that passed there was less chance of finding her. Faced with the anxiety and distress of her mother, Gaines was suddenly ashamed of his own feelings and put them determinedly to one side. Besides, he was beginning to get that intuitive sense, the indescribable tingle which told him that maybe this enquiry might well be heading in a direction far from that anticipated, adding to the mounting sense of urgency.

But at that point Alice Latimer, who had said little so far, stepped forward to bring the questioning of Mrs Martens to a halt. She had been through enough, she said firmly. Since Gaines was inclined to agree, and in any case Violet Martens was too emotionally agitated to get much more from her, he allowed her personal maid, Newcombe, to be sent for.

When she arrived he took the opportunity to put a few brief

questions to her. After noting she'd been in her bedroom all afternoon with a severe migraine and had known nothing until Mrs Lowther came to tell her what had happened, he didn't press her further. She was a rather sulky-looking woman with a pale face, heavy dark brows and a small mouth, and the tight little frown creasing her forehead made it evident the headache might be real, and she might still be suffering. She spoke very gently, however, to Mrs Martens, who finally, if reluctantly, gave in to his assurances that everything possible would be done to find her child and allowed herself to be persuaded away, murmuring fretfully about tonight's dinner party engagement that must be cancelled.

Gaines sent Inskip off with Emma Pavel to talk to the servants, or anyone else who might conceivably throw even a glimpse of retrospective light on the situation, while he talked to Alice Latimer, the one he thought likely to be a stabilizing influence in what seemed to him to be a rather oddly assorted household. She had a slender grace that gave an initial impression of delicacy, but her brisk tone as she spoke soon dispelled the notion. He suspected she was pretty tough underneath. She was, after all, trained to be calm and capable in emergencies, and she was showing admirable good sense, a welcome relief from the overwrought Mrs Martens. At the same time, there was something else that made Gaines think twice about her. She was the child's aunt, of course, it was natural that she should be distressed, but she was trying very hard not to show how much. He guessed she was holding herself in very tightly.

'What happens next?' she asked, giving him a direct glance through clear grey eyes. 'Where do you start in these cases?'

The question was not easily answered. The truth was there were no set procedures already laid down for a crime which thankfully happened rarely in this country. Children did, unhappily, disappear, and more died in suspicious circumstances – unwanted babies were a case in point, although there were enough of those, God only knew, to supply the needs of the desperately childless women who were prepared to pay to adopt them. There was no necessity to steal a child . . . unless, of course, you didn't have the means to buy one.

'We've already alerted the park police about what's happened,' he told her. 'They're familiar with everything that goes on there and they're searching, even now. They'll be making enquiries from all the regulars to find if anyone noticed anything. It's quite likely the incident could have been a spontaneous action, unplanned, the work of a moment, happening too quickly for anyone to have been aware of what was going on. But rest assured, we won't let the grass grow under our feet. Your little Lucy – any child – matters too much for that.'

His tone, what she saw in his face, seemed to give her reassurance. 'Thank you, I'm sure that is so.'

'But patience is required, Mrs Latimer . . . I beg your pardon, *Doctor* Latimer.'

She shook her head. 'Mrs, if you please. My husband prefers that, and so do I, when I'm not working, that is.' He wondered at the order in which she'd stated the preferences. 'But as far as patience goes,' she added wryly, 'that's something I've yet to acquire, I'm afraid.'

'There's always a chance, you know, that someone may come forward with information about the unexpected appearance of a seven-month-old baby in some neighbour's household.'

How slim this chance was he didn't say, nevertheless there was one. He knew from his own experience as a father how difficult it would be to conceal the presence of a baby for long. They cried, for one thing, which this little Lucy might well be doing at some length, given the circumstances, and neighbours might hear. Or, presuming reasonable care was being taken of her, there might be washing hanging out on the line to dry, baby clothes where there had been none hung out before . . . drying nappies and so on before a fire was a miserable business. But it would be a very brave – or disturbed – woman who would dare to keep a baby under such circumstances and he felt increasingly certain that was not what had happened to Lucy.

He still felt bound to caution that there was little that could be done at that precise moment. 'If nothing turns up within the next few hours, we will, of course, have to make a public appeal for information, or for the baby's return, but that isn't what we need to do just now.'

There was a lengthy pause. 'Make no mistake, Inspector, I'm not ignorant of how dreadfully the longing for a child, or the inability to have one, can affect a woman, to the point where reason departs and she snatches a baby and keeps her hidden. But there are other possibilities why Lucy's been taken – are there not?'

There was no point in prevaricating with her. She had guessed what was really going through his mind. Despite what he'd said, it seemed to him more than possible this was an organized kidnap for money, and a demand in exchange for the return of the child would come sooner or later. 'Yes,' he admitted. 'Yes, I think it's quite possible a ransom note might soon be sent.'

'I thought as much. That's unfortunate, because I can assure you, whoever believes Lucy's parents have that kind of money is very much mistaken.' She made a poor attempt at a wry smile, though he thought she might be quite used to smiling properly, in normal circumstances, and that it would have been worth waiting for when it came.

Wealth was of course relative, depending on your circumstances. To a large part of the general public, and especially to those at the lower end of the social scale, those who strove to earn a miserable pittance in order to exist at all – to them, it must seem that anyone able to afford living in Manessa House must lead a life of unimaginable luxury, with money to squander. Especially when the baby's father was, after all, the son of the well-known Martens banking family, and therefore must be rich beyond the dreams of avarice. The other side of the coin, tradesmen's bills left unpaid by the rich while they themselves ate caviare, would hardly enter into it. Luxury to one man could be penury to another.

Mrs Latimer had an uncanny knack of picking up his thoughts. 'Nor is the Martens Bank a philanthropic organization, Inspector,' she said dryly.

He took that to mean she was referring specifically to Emil Martens, the Belgian-born owner of the bank, and that he would not be an easy mark. Martens was indeed well known as the head of such a prestigious concern, but although he made a show of public benevolence in the way of charity donations she seemed to be saying that he was, despite appearances to the contrary, not one who would allow himself easily to be subjected to emotional blackmail, or to meet monetary demands which his son and his wife could not. Gaines wondered about that. Perhaps the banker was against a lifestyle he considered extravagant? Certainly everything about Violet Martens spoke of expensive tastes, even her surroundings: this room was decorated in the new style, and a deceptively simple décor like this didn't come cheap. She was fashionably dressed and coiffured, she had servants, a personal maid, her nanny and a social life that was evidently very important to her to keep up. As for her husband . . . taking time off work to go racing with a crowd of other men didn't give the impression of a responsible banker. Perhaps he was a gambler, and money went on the gee-gees. Very likely a raffish sort of fellow, anyway.

He said to Mrs Latimer, 'You should hold on to the fact that if it does turn out to be a case of ransom, Lucy will almost certainly be safe. She'll be taken care of as long as there's hope of money for her return.'

'But what if —' Her voice shook a little. 'What if the ransom is refused? Because Ferdie can't pay?' She hesitated and then went on in a rush, 'Believe me, Emil Martens is quite capable of refusing. To be brutally frank, Inspector, he's never shown any interest whatsoever in his granddaughter. I doubt he barely remembers her name.'

The kidnappers would not return the child if there was nothing in it for them, but the idea of Lucy's body turning up – or not turning up at all – was too nightmarish a scenario to put into words. He would have liked to say there was a chance that if the parents showed themselves willing to cooperate with the police and indicated willingness to agree to paying a ransom, there could always be the possibility of those responsible being traced and intercepted, but that was a subject better left for the moment.

'Is there *nothing* we can do, Inspector?'

'You can make sure everyone in the household is warned to keep silent.' Advice to concentrate on practicalities was something which often helped more than you'd think. 'Tell them not to speak to anyone, anyone at all, about this. You understand why? It may be resolved quickly and without the press getting hold of it, but if they do and the police are known to be involved it could put Lucy in real danger.'

Yes, of course she understood the importance of that, but all the staff, she said with certainty, were absolutely loyal people who, apart from the two youngest maids, had been with them for years and would keep the business to themselves if they were asked not to talk.

Even so, Gaines knew it was unlikely such a happening could be kept secret for long. The gentlemen of the press would get wind of the story, probably sooner rather than later. A careless word from someone, however unintentional, to some other servant, or some acquaintance, and the cat would be out of the bag. He pitied the inhabitants of Manessa House when the news broke. And yet there was simply nothing to be done to hurry the kidnappers along.

Inskip returned at that point and after further reassurances that they would keep in close touch, Mrs Latimer accompanied them to the front door. Before they could take their leave a motor drew up outside the house. From it leaped an elegant fellow whom Inskip, for one, recognized as wearing the last word in sporting fashions. He was a well set up young chap with a healthy complexion. In no time at all, he had unstrapped a valise from the luggage rack, given the car door a friendly double slap on the side and with a toot-toot from its wild-haired driver, a roar and a showy spitting of gravel the car had disappeared out of the gates. Ferdinand Martens strode cheerfully towards the house. When he saw his sister-in-law and the two policemen, and took in their grave faces, he stopped dead.

'I say, is something up?'

'Come into the morning room, Ferdie,' Alice said.

They all trooped back inside, Ferdie following uncertainly. Once in the morning room, his eyes went from Alice to the police, his senses suddenly alerted. 'Where's Violet?' he asked. His voice sharpened. 'It's Lucy, isn't it? Something's happened to Lucy.'

Alice's look appealed to Gaines, who nodded and told Ferdie as briefly as possible what had transpired that day while he'd been away.

All colour drained from his face. His knees buckled, he would surely have fallen if his hands hadn't grasped the back of a chair. 'Sit down Ferdie,' Alice said, fearing an emergency on her hands. Lucy was the light of his life but still, she hadn't expected quite such an extreme reaction. 'I'll ring for some tea. Or perhaps some brandy?' She might as well not have spoken. 'Ferdie?'

He shook his head as if to clear it and waved away the suggestion. 'Carry on, please, Inspector. I'm listening.'

Alice said, 'Wait.' She went out and returned with brandy in a glass. 'Drink this,' she said firmly, and watched while he did.

His colour began to return as he sat silently listening to what little more Gaines had to say. 'And that's it?' he asked, when it was told. 'That's all?'

Gaines had to wonder how much he'd taken in. He did not seem to be quick on the uptake, an easy-going charmer with not much under the surface, and it was hard to imagine what was going on behind that slightly vacuous expression. But the disappearance of his child had without question hit him like a physical blow, and he must be struggling not to think the unthinkable. 'You know as much as we do at this moment, sir.'

Martens shook his head, turned to Alice and said, 'I did hear correctly, didn't I? Do I understand that it was *Violet* who had taken Lucy to the park?' Alice said yes, it was. 'Where is she?'

'In her bedroom, resting. She's awfully distressed, Ferdie.'

'I must see her.'

As if on cue, the door was pushed open and Violet, wrapped in a silk peignoir, and her hair let down, rushed back into the room and flung herself towards him with uncharacteristic lack of control. 'I heard the motor car. Oh, Ferdie what have I done? I blame myself! How can I ever—'

'Don't be such a silly goose, Violet, nobody's blaming you,' he interrupted, almost absently, releasing himself from her arms, and though he did it quite gently, she was forced to flop into a chair. This was evidently not the response she had expected. She looked affronted, but then gave him a nervous, almost frightened glance. To give her nervous hands something to do she snatched up some nearby fancywork she was currently engaged on, stabbing a needle at the fine rows of smocking destined for a baby's dress as if her life depended on it.

Gaines stood, preparing to go. Having just repeated everything that had previously been said, there was nothing to be done by staying and he was already balking at the thought that it would have to be gone over yet once more, in his report to his superiors at the Yard. But how much worse it was for this bereft family, who would without doubt worry at it endlessly, like a dog at a bone, until there was nothing left. It was what happened when people tried to make sense of something that appeared to have no rational explanation, something that descended like a bolt out of the blue. 'We'll be in touch, sir.' He added awkwardly, 'I'm so sorry, Mrs Martens, Mr Martens. Every effort will be made, I promise you. This sort of thing affects all of us.'

'Thank you, Inspector. I appreciate what you're doing.' Martens' blank expression did not change but he automatically held out his hand, cold as ice.

Six

The chill of approaching evening could be felt as Gaines and his sergeant left Manessa House and the young mother and father to their anxiety, though Gaines had begun to see that the latter, as soon as his high spirits had so suddenly drained away with the shocking news that awaited him, was not so young as he had at first seemed – nearer forty than thirty, he guessed. Vastly different, in any case, from the fellow who had sprung so blithely from his friend's motor car.

In view of the urgency when the summons had come, the expense of taking a taxi-cab from the Yard had been justified, but Gaines couldn't see the super looking kindly on one for the return journey. Official motor cars were a luxury not readily allotted for use by the hoi polloi. The two of them hopped on to a packed omnibus. There was no room downstairs and they managed to find the last two, separate, seats upstairs on the open deck. The journey was slow. London was going about its daily, noisy business, home-going office workers in pinstripe and bowler hat thronging the pavements, street vendors shouting, motor cabs hooting and jostling for position with horse-drawn traffic, making for frequent stops and rowdy altercations between drivers. The racket from the omnibus's engine was considerable and the din rising to the upper deck was enough to preclude conversation, even had they been sitting together. It wasn't until they'd dismounted at Trafalgar Square to walk the rest of the way and set their steps in the direction of Scotland Yard that there was any opportunity to talk.

'Tell me what you got from the servants,' Gaines said.

'Nothing much. Nothing we hadn't already heard at any rate.' Sensing some reservation, Gaines raised an eyebrow but Inskip merely went on to enumerate the staff employed at Manessa House.

The combined household was a relaxed one, it seemed, employing just a few servants. No butler or footmen, just the cook-housekeeper, Mrs Lowther, who was in charge of them all; the prim, middle-aged parlour maid, Ivy Hewson, who had admitted them when they arrived and a couple of younger maids lower down the hierarchy. Mrs Lowther's husband acted as chauffeur, handyman and gardener, and a woman came in every Monday to do the laundry. Extra help was brought in when either family entertained at home, but their social obligations were more often fulfilled by booking a table at a restaurant, making up a theatre party and so on. Even including Newcombe, Mrs Martens' personal maid, and Emma, the baby's nanny, it was a fairly modest staff compared with most households of the same social standing. All of them were apparently trustworthy, confirming what Mrs Latimer had stated.

'Let's not forget the previous nanny, though. Struthers, wasn't it? The one there was some unpleasantness with when she left. Maybe she still has a grudge to settle. And she'd be in a position to know how the household functioned, where they were all likely to be at any given time. Get hold of her.'

Inskip made a doubtful face, but he nodded agreement and after that Gaines didn't seem inclined to speak further. Nothing more was said until they were in the office, having divested themselves of their coats and were drinking tea which young DC Watts, ever on the alert for promotion prospects, brought in without being asked. Gaines, still silent, thoughtfully stirred sugar into his cup, and Inskip didn't have a mind to interrupt his cogitations, guessing uneasily where it might lead. But eventually the inspector gave him a sideways look and asked, 'So what else have you to tell me? About that young woman,' he added, as Inskip tried, without success, to look mystified. 'Emma Pavel . . . is there something going on between you?'

'Not that I'm aware of.' Inskip could feel himself reddening.

'More's the pity, then. She's a decent lass – well set up, and sharp-witted—'

'Not to say sharp-tongued.'

'You could do worse. I had a feeling when we were on the Challoner case that you'd taken a fancy to her. I was wrong, then?'

Inskip couldn't think what to say. He had discovered aspects of Gaines' character quite alien to his own: the inspector was in fact a church-going Methodist and a deacon at his local place of worship. It was something he'd found hard to swallow, that a tough London policeman like Gaines could also be a Bible-thumper. It probably explained why he swore only rarely, and was to all intents and purposes almost teetotal. He was a bit strait-laced, in Inskip's opinion, unwilling to admit it was often he who was the more easily shocked at some of the things they encountered. All the same, Inskip had come to respect him as astute but fair-minded and not open to easy condemnation of anyone, even the criminal classes they had to deal with.

'So what did Emma have to tell you?' he asked at last, evidently having given up his attempts at matchmaking, for which Inskip thanked the Lord.

'Nothing much, but – well, there was something, sir.'

After he had questioned the other servants, Inskip had sought out Emma and found her wandering in the garden, aimless at having been deprived of her duties. 'Oh, it's you,' she said when she saw him. 'What do you want, then?'

It wasn't like the young woman he remembered to be ungracious. Quick with a comeback, yes, but that was par for the course where they both came from. He decided it was unintentional.

'Just a bit of a chat. The inspector won't be ready to go just yet.' He watched her scooping up a handful of fallen cherry blossom petals, rubbing them through her fingers and letting them drop, one by one. 'We don't half meet in some funny circumstances, Emma. Pity it takes something like this.'

They had first met the previous year, when Russian anarchists had been causing mayhem in London's East End, and she had been working as a maid in the family of a woman who had been shot dead, a murder that he and Gaines had been called in to investigate. He'd been hoping to come across her again although, committed bachelor that he was, he had to admit he hadn't made overly strenuous efforts to find her. At the back of his mind, maybe, he didn't want to admit that Emma probably saw very little in him to admire, much less to want a renewal of their acquaintance.

'You're looking well. Being a nanny suits you,' he pressed on. Although somehow, he didn't see the independent-minded young woman he'd come to know willingly going back into service after that time, even though she wasn't educated for much else. The truth was, of course, it wasn't often a matter of choice for such as Emma, with her background, as well he knew. It was pretty much the same as his, and he didn't need to be told what a struggle it was to get away from it.

'It's better than what I was doing before. I'd no mind to be a parlour maid all my life.' She seemed to feel that becoming a nursemaid to a privileged baby was a big step up in the servant hierarchy, and maybe it was. She'd always been one intent on bettering herself, not content to accept the role assigned to her by reason of being born poor, and a woman into the bargain.

'Still friendly with those pesky women's rights folks, are you then? Breaking windows and causing bother?'

'I never did any of that,' she returned sharply, 'and well you know it, Joseph Inskip. Mind you, that doesn't mean I don't still think they're in the right. But I've given up the meetings, working for them. I couldn't stomach it . . . not after what happened.'

The murder of her mistress had been unutterably shocking, disrupting a well-to-do, pleasant and harmonious household where the servants had been fairly treated and Emma herself had developed a particular friendship with a young cousin of the family, now studying at Cambridge, who had been involved with the suffragette movement. Those same suffragettes who, for a while, as well as some Latvian revolutionaries who had settled in the East End, had been suspected of being involved in the murder.

'So how come you ended up here?'

'Well,' she said, 'the house in Egremont Gardens was given up, you know, what with Miss Kitty being married, and the master off across the world. They gave me good references but with my ma not being so perky lately, I went back to stay with her till I found another position that would suit me – not so easy, though.' She made a face. 'Anyway, you know the Dorcas Clinic – Doctor Weston?' she asked. Inskip nodded. Who didn't, around where he lived? 'Well, his wife needed a bit of help with their little 'uns when she fell pregnant again, and I went there for just a bit, to help till she got herself sorted. Then little Lucy's nanny took it into her head to pack her bags without notice and Doctor Alice recommended me. She seemed to think I was good with babies.'

She would be, of course. She had helped her widowed mother bring up a family of younger siblings until they were all off her hands.

'They treat you all right here, then, do they?'

'Mrs Martens can be a bit— But yes, it's all right.'

A silence fell. He cleared his throat. 'I was thinking, Emma, you and me. Maybe we could . . . well, you know, we could go out somewhere . . . you must have days off . . .' His voice trailed away. 'I was just wondering.'

'Oh, were you? Think a lot of yourself, Sergeant Inskip, don't you?'

He coloured, allowing his fingers to smooth down the fine broadcloth of the suit his Aunt Orla had so admired. It fitted him superbly, showing off his well-muscled figure. He had a handsome face and a lithe body. The ladies didn't usually take the mickey.

'Well, all right,' she relented, a smile tugging at the corners of her mouth. 'I'll think about it – when we get little Lucy back. I can't, not just now.'

For a few minutes he'd succeeded in making her forget what was happening, but now he watched her fingers pleating her apron, her face thoroughly miserable again as her mind went back over the day's events. 'She'll be missing her dolly, poor lamb.' It was a rag doll, she explained, home-made by Mrs Martens' old nanny, who now lived in retirement and had nothing better to do. It was a funny little thing, made shabby by much love, and wouldn't have been allowed in the pram with Lucy when Violet had wheeled her out, but Lucy wouldn't go to sleep without it.

'It's not your fault, Em. You know that.'

She laughed shortly. 'Well, I never thought it was! Only, I just wish I hadn't asked for this particular afternoon off, and I wouldn't have, only I'd had a message that my ma had been taken real bad . . . I wish it had been me with the baby. Catch anybody trying to make off with her then!'

They wouldn't have dared. She wouldn't have fallen asleep in the sun anyway, that was for sure. Inskip's acquaintance with mothers of babies was small, but the idea of this one taking forty winks while her baby was snatched from beside her stuck in his craw.

She said suddenly, 'What your boss said, about some woman taking her because she hasn't a baby of her own. He might have something there, I suppose, but if it was, it was somebody who knew they'd only have Mrs Martens to bother with.'

He stared. 'Supposing they did know that, they couldn't have known she would take the baby to the park. Or that she was going to fall asleep.'

'She didn't need to be asleep. Even if she'd been wide awake, they could have just grabbed the baby and made off. A lady like her wouldn't have the first idea of how to put up a fight. Not even with a woman – and I can't see a man wheeling the pram away.'

'She's right about that,' Gaines said some time later, when they were exchanging the impressions they'd gained, and Inskip had finished recounting this last bit of his conversation with Emma.

'Yes. Had to be a woman, didn't it, sir?'

Of course it did. The unparalleled sight of a man pushing a baby carriage would have excited comment. Love and care for his children as dearly as Gaines had when they were babies, even he wouldn't have brought himself to be seen doing that. No self-respecting man would. It was woman's work, just as it was the husband's job to go out to work and provide for his family. No, a man intent on taking Lucy would almost certainly have simply lifted the child out of the pram and left it, rapidly making off with her through the nearby gate – where no doubt a motor car would have been waiting.

'Something queer going on there, I reckon, all the same, sir,' Inskip went on after a moment's hesitation. Thinking of little else for the last hour he'd come to some conclusions of his own. 'It doesn't seem like a random snatch. Too convenient . . . the very day Emma had begged time off, the housekeeper off to buy bed-linen, the father out of the way for the day. The lady's maid indisposed, and the mother left to look after her own baby. Somebody was in the know, as Emma said.'

He had straddled a chair and rested both arms along its back, supporting his chin. His face was pugnacious. It hadn't taken long for Gaines to work out that he was feeling resentful at what Gaines had told him. He reproved himself for mentioning to the sergeant that it was unlikely they'd be allowed to run two big cases at once and if this turned out to be a big one, having regard to the positions of the people involved, the taxicab murder would very likely be taken out of their hands, however unpalatable the reason was. Since then Inskip had been pretty quiet. It was clear that in his opinion, the other should have priority and Gaines wondered, not for the first time, what Inskip wasn't telling him about the suspect, Daniel O'Rourke. He wasn't yet prepared to push him. From what he knew of his sergeant, he would tell him in his own good time.

'So what are you suggesting?'

'It's been done before. And you must admit it looks odd.'

'No,' said Gaines firmly. 'I mean yes, it is odd – but Martens? His grief was too genuine for that. Think again.'

Inskip thought, and saw Gaines was following where it led. 'Violet Martens—' he began.

'Faking the kidnap to extract money from Martens senior? Except that in this case money looks unlikely to be easily forthcoming, if at all. I told you what Alice Latimer said about the grandfather and how he won't part with money. Which would make the whole affair pointless, if the parents are involved.'

'Unless they imagined Martens Senior would come to the rescue when it came to the crunch?'

'Forget it, Joseph. From what I heard, there's absolutely no certainty of that. Emil Martens would apparently call the kidnappers' bluff rather than pay up.'

'Whatever they ask for, it would be a drop in the bucket to him. He's Martens' Bank, for God's sake! What sort of grandfather is he?'

'The sort whose money means more to him than the anxiety of his son or even the safety of his granddaughter? According to Mrs Latimer, he never shows the slightest interest in the child.'

Could anyone be that heartless and unfeeling? Unfortunately, where money was concerned, they both knew only too well that some people could be – and more. If ransom was the ultimate purpose of the snatch, then it looked as though the kidnappers didn't know, or had underestimated, the character or wealth of Emil Martens. There was always an outside chance, of course, that if it came to the crunch he *would* pay up, but it would be foolhardy in the extreme to rely on that.

Money obviously meant a great deal to that family, especially to Violet Martens. Her clothes and her surroundings had indicated as much. But it was also very obvious to Gaines that she was perhaps even more acutely conscious of her social position and the need to keep up appearances, and he felt sure that if nothing else, then to risk the notoriety the kidnapping of her own child would inevitably bring, if it came out, would have prevented it. He also thought that the very notion of bringing herself to act like a common criminal would be too infra dig for her to stomach. He shook his head. 'They'd have to be pretty desperate. Put the idea out of your mind.'

After a while, Inskip spread his hands, ready to admit Gaines was right. 'So what if it isn't money the kidnappers are after? What if it's some other form of blackmail?'

Gaines threw him a quick look. This was Inskip: mostly bull-headed but sometimes disconcertingly intuitive. He had a natural-born savvy and a restless energy that Gaines acknowledged complemented his own more stolid character. Inskip had come up through the ranks through his own competence, but because of his rough background, his face didn't always fit with those who mattered. Gaines didn't see it like that, but he acknowledged his sergeant needed the brake put on him sometimes – a kick up the backside when he was being stroppy, as more than one person had remarked. That said, Gaines was happy enough with their partnership. It worked well.

He turned over what they'd just discussed, while the uneasy intuition he'd had about this case almost from the first grew. The possibilities for blackmail, in the sort of well-respected family they were dealing with, seemed few on the surface, but one could never tell. Some scandal from the past being revived? The threat to expose an affair either Martens or his wife was having? Would either be enough to exert a hold over them, big enough to demand money they didn't have? In that case why take the baby as well? An added persuasion?

Suddenly he sat up straighter. The Martens were not the only ones in the family open to blackmail. If Inskip had put his finger on it and money wasn't the objective, perhaps it wasn't the parents who were being targeted. Alice Latimer and seemingly her husband were extremely fond of the child. And Latimer, in his position, was certainly vulnerable to coercion in many ways. Unless the child was found quickly enough to be able to hush the affair up, it was going to make news, a high-profile case, involving him whether he wanted it or not, even though it wasn't his own child who was missing. Perhaps the kidnappers thought he would be prepared to pay to keep his own name out of the papers, though Gaines thought cynically that as a politician he would be more likely to turn the situation to his advantage. From what little he had heard of the man, there appeared to be nothing that said he wasn't fair and honest, but Gaines had a jaundiced view of the breed in general, who in his opinion would stop at little to excite sympathy and gain votes. And these were uneasy times in politics. Anyone reading the newspapers as carefully as Gaines, who considered it a necessary part of his job to keep abreast of current affairs, knew that. If it wasn't the coal miners, the Irish Sinn Fein or the Kaiser, it was the suffragettes causing more disruptions to gain what they wanted.

He sat staring down at his paper-strewn desk. They seemed to dog his cases, these suffragettes, perhaps because they took great care to make sure they were kept in the forefront of the public eye and therefore tended never to be far from his mind. Wasn't this the sort of crime more likely to occur to a woman than to a man? Maybe, but would even the least maternal of those militant women (and there were enough of them!) go so far as to do that – to another woman? Inskip's oft-stated view of these viragos, clever and well-to-do as they often were, was that they would stop at nothing. But in this case, Gaines thought it was probably unnecessary for the suffragettes to have to resort to blackmail in order to get Latimer's backing for whatever it was they wanted. He seemingly did not object to women's independence, or to his wife following her own career as a doctor, and he probably was not at all hostile, in theory, to the cause of women's emancipation – as indeed many Liberals were not. The reason they didn't give the cause their wholehearted support was the fear that, given the franchise, most of the women would vote Conservative.

He sighed. The involvement of Edmund Latimer seemed another unlikely scenario, and they hadn't yet reached the point of grasping at straws. It was nothing more than speculation, yet it was all they had at this point. In a short while the search being conducted even now over the Regent's Park's four hundred acres of parkland and gardens, with the further grassy acres of Primrose Hill adjacent to it, would have to be abandoned as darkness fell. It would be resumed in the morning. Every nook and cranny – and they were countless – where a baby might be hidden, would be searched . . . but a baby in a pram? The most Gaines expected to be found, if anything, was the pram itself abandoned in some deserted corner. Frustrating as it was, there was little to be done at this precise moment, apart from ensuring that an alert had been put out to all police stations. Nothing more constructive than to wait upon events, see what the following day brought, until those responsible made their demands known. A ransom note. Or even, if fortune favoured them (or miracles happened) a sighting of the child.

And all the time there was something about all this that was scratching away at the surface of his mind, irritating as a sharp piece of grit in the shoe.

He sighed. 'All right,' he said to Inskip. 'If someone at the house is likely to be involved, we'll talk to the servants again – Mrs Martens' maid, and the housekeeper, come to that. And don't forget that ex-nanny.' He drummed his fingers on the desk and for a while debated whether an interview with Emil Martens might not be necessary at some point. Not just yet, he thought. Meanwhile, there was the murder of Lennie Croxton which was evidently more uppermost in Inskip's mind. 'Make yourself scarce, then, and don't forget your report, either. You might try and make it legible while you're at it.'

Paper and ink were not Inskip's forte.

Seven

The stated belief of Doctor Francis Nichol, Alice's father, had always been that the capacity of human beings to surprise was limitless, and for a while, when Ferdie had been told of his beloved child's abduction, Alice had believed it true of him.

He was normally a person soon cast down, even by a critical word – though spurred on just as easily by kindness. He drifted through life, good-looking, amiable, feckless. Well-meaning, even though things rarely seemed to work out for him. Brought up by an indulgent mother to consider the lifestyle he followed as the only suitable one for a gentleman, he had then not been allowed the means to carry it on by his money-making father. Violet continually complained about Martens Senior being tight-fisted and he certainly was that, but Alice was inclined to think his attitude stemmed more from having the measure of his son. They said the apple never fell far from the tree; in Ferdie's case it must have been blown down by the wind to land so very far away.

And yet this Ferdie, after the first stunned moments, had reacted to what had confronted him on coming home more calmly than she would have thought possible. The worst thing possible for Ferdie Martens had happened, the abduction of his adored little Lucy, but instead of breaking down in tears or even rushing out blindly in a futile search for his child, as might have been expected of him, he had stood as if turned to stone, silent and with all colour leached from his handsome face, as if the news had consumed every emotion he was capable of feeling.

Left alone after the police had gone, there seemed nothing to be said that hadn't already been said and yet what else could they talk about? Silence was not an alternative: it left room for too much that couldn't be contemplated. But at last, when the subject of the ransom was brought up yet again, Ferdie jumped up. 'I've had enough, Violet,' he said. 'I don't want to talk about it any more.' He went to the drinks cabinet and poured brandy for all three of them. Perhaps he shouldn't have another, but he looked as though he needed it. Alice had been about to leave them, feeling she had no place here and it was more than time they were left to deal with the frightening situation on their own, but Ferdie was handing her the drink, so she stayed.

'I wish Edmund would come home,' Violet said, her hands tight together. Ferdie looked at her and said nothing.

By now she had managed to regain more control of herself and was once more the Violet who was always so careful to present a calm face to the world, having remembered that whatever the provocation, tears, frowns or showing temper were luxuries one could not afford when one was approaching thirty. But her hands were still clutching the embroidery she'd automatically picked up when she first took her seat, and a fine mess she was making of the soft tussore silk. She threw it down again and sat up straighter. 'I don't believe Lucinda has been taken by some —' her voice faltered despite herself — 'by some madwoman who feels entitled to steal someone else's child. However disagreeable it is to talk about it, I'm sure there will be a ransom . . . and before that comes we must talk about it and find a way of getting it, if we want to see Lucy again.'

'And where,' Ferdie asked flatly, his face still white, 'do you suppose I am to find the sort of money they'll want, for God's sake?'

'Your father?' she came back sharply.

'I can try,' he replied. 'I *will* try, if there's no alternative. But don't expect miracles.' He couldn't disguise the bitterness in his voice.

'Why should he not pay?' Violet asked coldly. 'You have a perfect right to it. You'll succeed your father in the bank when he retires, after all.'

He laughed shortly. 'That doesn't mean its funds are mine to make free with right now. And as for retiring . . . he's by no means ready to let go of the reins just yet. Nor for the foreseeable future.'

'He'll relent if it comes to the point. Any grandfather with any feeling would.'

'I wouldn't bet on it. I can't think about it now, but put it right out of your mind, he's a non-starter.' He took a good pull of his brandy and stared down into his glass for some time until, almost as though he had deliberately turned his thoughts to another channel, he said, 'And to think, talking of betting, that I actually won a pony at Worcester.'

'Five hundred pounds?' Violet's face was a study.

'Then lost it all on Fitz's Amadeus. It turned out to be a donkey – as usual, with my rotten luck. If I'd been at home and not gallivanting off after the gee-gees this wouldn't have happened.'

'The police will find Lucy, never fear, Ferdie,' Alice said.

There was a heavy pause.

Ferdie looked up from contemplating what was left of his brandy. It had brought a little colour to his face. 'Never mind the police. I'm going to find out whoever has done this, and if I get my hands on him, I will kill him,' he said simply.

And amazingly, despite the desperate odds, and should poor Ferdie ever be able to summon up the necessary intellect to trace the kidnappers, Alice believed he would.

Part Three

Eight

Sunday, and four days now since Lucy had disappeared. Despite an increasing sense of helplessness, Gaines was keeping in frequent touch with the parents, but there was nothing to report to them. He was, however, pragmatic enough to realize there was nothing to be gained by panic, frustrated as they were by having absolutely nothing to go on, extensive though the enquiries had been. No strangers had been noticed hanging about the house. Anyone who might have been remotely concerned had been seen, and written off, from the milkman, the butcher's boy, the lad from the grocer's, even to the man who delivered the fish direct from Billingsgate. The only one who hadn't been spoken to was the young relation of Mrs Latimer's who had been staying with them. No one seemed to know where he was, but in any case, he'd already left before Lucy disappeared. Every police station had been alerted, flyers posted all over the city, although she might have been taken – almost certainly had, Gaines believed gloomily – many miles far from London by now. He could think of nothing more they could do, except concentrate on the other case, the taxi-cab murder, which wasn't getting much further either. Despite this lack of activity, he felt himself exhausted, emotionally and physically.

Now that the press had got hold of the Lucy story, it was hot news on every front page, but by this time Gaines, increasingly desperate, was willing to concede the usefulness of publicity. Amid the more lurid speculation about what might have happened, which couldn't be avoided, it was at least keeping an agog public on their toes with advice to look out for the child, and something might come of that. The press were making sure the interest was maintained, which wasn't difficult, not only because of the human interest: this baby wasn't any abducted child, after all, she was from the well-known Martens banking family – and also the niece of the politician Edmund Latimer, who was on his way to the top of the party and might one day even become prime minister.

Meanwhile, the *Daily Mail* was offering a reward for anyone who came forward with information that might lead to Lucy's whereabouts, with the result that dozens of sightings of the baby had come in, all of which must be followed up, though most of them were improbable, if not impossible: she'd been spotted at Fort William in the Scottish Highlands only a few hours after she was kidnapped . . . seen in the Grand Hotel at Scarborough with a suspicious-looking couple the same night . . . being carried on to the Irish ferry at Fishguard. A clairvoyant had come forward, claiming that if she held one of the baby's garments she could sense where she was.

'Have we chased up the nanny yet?' Gaines had asked Inskip. 'Not Emma, the previous one who left under a cloud.'

'She was going back home to Scotland, they said. Seems Ferdie Martens had paid for her ticket, very generous in the circumstances, but they were probably glad to get rid of her.'

Gaines was instantly alert. 'Scotland? Whereabouts in Scotland?'

'Dumfries. About two hundred miles from Fort William, I'd guess,' replied Inskip, following his train of thought. 'And more than five hundred from London,' he added pointedly.

'But did she actually go back to Dumfries?'

'Yes, she did.' It had been worth following up. A wire sent to the local police in Dumfries, rather than submitting to the vagaries of a long-distance telephone call, had established that Miss Struthers had returned home, and had, in fact, been there ever since.

Unless prevented from doing so by the urgency of what he was working on, Sundays for Gaines were sacrosanct to home and family. On this Sunday morning, after attendance at his church, he had found himself drawn willy-nilly to the office, while knowing there was nothing he could do. There he found most of the Sunday newspapers stacked on his desk. He flicked through them desultorily but there was nothing of moment, except for the leading article in the *News of the World* which claimed the police were not coming up to expectations on the matter of finding 'Baby Lucy', as she was now known to everyone – the first time any of the papers had expressed this opinion, but probably not the last. He shoved it aside in disgust and went home to his Sunday dinner. He owed it to his wife and family to spend the day of rest in a normal way, and he was determined to get a good night's sleep, where nothing less than the return of the missing baby – or another murder – would get him from his bed.

Inskip, determined not to waste the Sunday, had prevailed on Emma to come out with him for an hour, on the pretext that she needed to get away from the silent, unhappy house. Emma, who could scarcely tolerate a life in which there was nothing to do but sit around waiting, had not in the end needed much persuasion.

They walked along to the Regent's Park. It was crowded. A pleasant Sunday afternoon with no hint of rain and with the trees bursting into leaf was a popular time to stroll along the avenues there, find a bench to sit on and admire the colourful flower beds, or simply to enjoy mixing with the crowds. Canvas seats were set out in rows by the bandstand if a band was playing. Today, it was the band of the Coldstream Guards, at the moment playing selections from Gilbert and Sullivan. Inskip cursed himself, suddenly aware that this place, where Lucy had been taken, was probably not the best choice of venue, though Emma hadn't objected.

She was looking very smart, in her best coat and skirt, but despite the perky feather in her hat she was downcast, unable to banish the awful sense of apprehension that no one living in Manessa House could now escape. Although Inskip never felt himself off duty and had few inhibitions, it was to his own surprise that he found himself today deliberately avoiding mention of Lucy. He hadn't consciously asked Emma out in order to give her a bit of respite from the situation, but it seemed perhaps his subconscious had dictated it. The subject was, however, clearly uppermost in Emma's mind, unable to be dismissed so easily, and when she showed signs of wanting to talk of it he took the opportunity to listen.

'She must have been snatched by somebody who knew what they were doing, but I've been over it all so often and I still can't make head nor tail of it.'

'Emma, we've asked everyone this, I know, but you still can't recall anyone taking a particular interest in Lucy? No visitors who'd taken to coming more regularly than usual, for instance?'

'I don't see visitors to the house. The nursery's where I spend most of the day, with Lucy, except when Mrs Martens would ring to show Lucy off to one of her friends who was paying a call.'

'Regular visitors?'

'Some of them were, yes. And that cousin of Doctor Latimer's was always hanging about, though he wasn't exactly a *visitor* to the house, seeing he was living there.'

'You mean Dudley Nichol?' She nodded. 'He came to see the baby?'

'What, him?' She laughed. 'Lord, no, he'd no interest in Lucy. He was like most young fellows of his age, scared to death of babies, like as they're something from another planet. It was Mrs Martens he came to see.'

Inskip said carefully, 'Was there something going on, do you think?'

'He'd taken a bit of a shine to her, I reckon. Shouldn't be surprised if he'd fancied he was a bit in love with her.'

'And Mrs Martens?'

Emma pursed her lips. Inskip understood the unspoken thought as clearly as if she'd said it aloud. *Mrs Martens is in love with nobody but herself.* But she only said, 'I'd be surprised, but I couldn't really say. You should ask Miss Newcombe, if you want to know that. She had a bit of a soft spot for him because he was nice to her, which not everyone is, because she isn't ever nice to anybody. If you see what I mean.'

'A bit of jealousy there, maybe?'

'Jealousy? Lord, no! She wouldn't be jealous of Mrs Martens. She'd try to get the top brick off the chimney for her if the mistress asked for it.' She paused. 'Leastways, I don't think she was jealous of a bit of flirting, but you'd never know. She's deep, that one.'

Could she have been resentful enough to have taken the baby? Not unless she'd arranged for someone else to do it for her. She herself had undoubtedly been prostrate with a headache that afternoon. Mrs Lowther had sympathetically taken her a cup of tea and one of her own headache powders at the time Lucy had been abducted.

The band had changed its selection to *The Merry Widow*. The mellow trombone notes of 'Vilia's Song' floated across the golden afternoon to where they were sitting. When he reached out and took hold of Emma's hand she didn't pull away, or not for a few minutes. 'Vilia, oh Vilia, the witch of the wood . . .' Inskip, who couldn't even hum in tune, tapped the rhythm of the music out on his knee and even Emma attempted a small smile.

*   *   *

That night, Gaines did in fact get an undisturbed night's sleep but the terrible news that erupted on that Monday morning was nothing to do with 'Baby Lucy', nor of another murder. The story that was destined to banish the kidnapped child from the front page was a catastrophe no one would ever have predicted in a million years. Newsboys on the street corners were already shouting out the sensational news as he made his way to Scotland Yard.

Throughout that night, the telegraph lines between the United States and Great Britain had become red hot, with newsrooms and printing presses going mad in the headlong rush to be first with this tremendous scoop, and the world had awakened to learn of the sinking of that modern marvel, the passenger liner *Titanic*. The enormity of the tragedy was more than enough to dominate every newspaper in the land, to which even the high-profile kidnapping of a child in London took second place.

Nine

Prosser Street, Inskip saw as he viewed the terrace of tall houses, had once in its life been several steps up from the place where his Auntie Orla lived although, in the way of London, where working-class respectability could live just around the corner from abject poverty, it was only a few streets away, almost cheek by jowl, with Catesby Street. Once handsome, the houses had obviously started to go downhill several decades ago, even before the hideous municipal baths building taking up the length of one side, its yellow London brick now streaked and smoke-grimed, had completed the process. However, although every house showed signs of multiple occupancy, the street hadn't yet entirely degenerated into a slum. It was quiet, compared with those surrounding it, and its very silence, the absence of any noisy street life going on outside its closed doors, made it slightly forbidding. The prospect wasn't improved much today by the rain which had begun to come down hard and was failing to escape down the rubbish-clogged gutters and leaving puddles on the broken-flagged pavement.

The wind was blowing rain into his face but as he drew near the house he was heading for, he saw that two young women, one with dark curls escaping from under her hat, the other a flamboyant redhead of the type he didn't care for, had paused on the muddy pavement. They were laughing and trying to dodge the rain as they struggled to put up a recalcitrant half-open umbrella, and they shared the joke of it with him as he reached the foot of the steps.

'Allow me,' he said, reaching out for the umbrella, but at that moment the spring that controlled it decided to work and up it went. 'And all without my assistance.' He smiled, sketched a half salute, then took the steps to the front door in a couple of strides and pressed the bell.

'No use ringing, it doesn't work, and anyway, there's no one at home,' called a voice behind him. He turned round and saw it was the dark-haired girl who had spoken. She was pretty, with a white skin, blue eyes and a lovely smile.

'Unless you're looking for one of us,' said the redhead pertly.

Inskip glanced at her but he had no time for that sort of fooling around. He addressed her friend. 'The man I'm looking for is Paddy Tooley.'

'Oh, you won't find him in, he went out about half an hour ago. You've had a wasted journey.' About to turn away, she hesitated. 'If it's important, you might try the Nag – if you should happen to know it.'

He did know it, and where it was. The once glorious but now disreputable hostelry just around the corner had been built after the battle of Waterloo and named the Copenhagen in honour of the Duke of Wellington's favourite horse. It had inevitably become known as the Nag, words of more than one syllable being more than most of its regular patrons could cope with. Inskip considered. If these young women knew the people at this house, as they seemed to, or possibly if they lived here, he could probably find out straight away if this was where O'Rourke had been staying, but he was reluctant to question them. It was Paddy Tooley he wanted to see and from what he knew of him, the young woman had certainly been right: if the Nag had been his destination half an hour ago, he'd still be there, you could bet on that.

He thanked them and they parted company. The redhead was holding the umbrella, and it was the dark girl who looked back over her shoulder before they turned the corner. She dipped her head in a nod and he went the opposite way.

There were no more than a dozen men in the pub and they were immersed in the racing pages of the *Sporting Life,* possibly the only people in London that day who weren't discussing the *Titanic* disaster. In the normal manner of occupants of the Nag, most of them looked as though they were up to no good, and Paddy Tooley wasn't the exception that proved the rule. He was a huge man who combined the general appearance of an Irish navvy with the coarse, battered features of a semi-professional boxer, both of which he was. He had reddish fair hair, a red face and his small, hot brown eyes were set too close together. He stood leaning on the bar with his big fist around a pint of Guinness.

'Paddy.'

'If it isn't Joseph Inskip, by all that's wonderful. What brings you here? It's not often,' he said with patent exaggeration, 'the peelers honour us with a visit.'

'Not unless they have some purpose.'

'Oh, a purpose, is it? And what could that be?' The man might have lived half his life in England but his accent was as thick as an Irish bog. That wasn't unusual. A rich brogue was always useful if you wanted to be thought a stupid Mick – though Tooley didn't need to assume an accent for that.

'O'Rourke's what brings me here, Tooley. I'm looking for him. And never mind why.'

'Which O'Rourke would that be? Seamus, Michael— Oh, Danny? Then you're looking in the wrong place. You should be setting your sights across the sea. Nobody's heard from him since he left for the old country.'

'And when was that?'

'A week, two weeks since, I couldn't rightly remember.'

'You're lying, Tooley.'

He didn't take offence, but he looked pained. 'Ask anyone you like, eh, Maureen?' He waved expansively around and the overblown barmaid behind the counter leaned on her elbows and said don't ask her. It was only two minutes since Inskip had entered but the bar was a lot less crowded now. The Nag's clientele smelled policemen as mice smelled cats. In fact only two or three remained.

'He's been seen around. So where's he holed up?'

'I don't have the least idea in my head.'

Inskip smiled. 'That's not to be wondered at. You've been in too many fights, Paddy. Your brain's turned to mush.'

Tooley stood, feet apart, his manner not so easy now. He sized Inskip up, but evidently thought better of what he had thought to do. He deliberately drank up, then left.

'They seek him here, they seek him there, the peelers seek him everywhere.'

The sudden quip came from the landlord, who'd kept out of things so far. He was a man called Corrigan, who'd run this bar for years. A man of small stature, a smiling man who liked to think of himself as a quick wit, a bit of a rogue sometimes but well-meaning on the whole, Inskip thought. He didn't put him down. He thought he might be useful. 'Well then, have *you* seen O'Rourke lately, Corrigan?'

Corrigan picked up a pewter pot and began polishing it assiduously. 'That O'Rourke,' he said, 'he'd get himself and everyone who knows him into trouble at the drop of a hat. He can't help himself, that bloody one.'

'Does that mean you know where he is?'

'If he's around, wouldn't Tooley have told you?' Inskip thought that was a warning. O'Rourke's whereabouts were known but no one was going to talk.

'Paddy Tooley wouldn't tell me the time of day – if ever his mother had taught him how to read a clock. But you would, Corrigan, you'd let me know if you heard where O'Rourke was, wouldn't you?' He allowed his gaze to stray to the whiskey bottles behind the bar, a barrel of the stronger stuff alongside. He'd had a taste or two of it himself, without letting on that he knew it had reached here without the benefit of customs duty.

'Jayz, you're a hard man,' the landlord said. 'But it's serious, isn't it?'

'When isn't it, with O'Rourke?' He was convinced the landlord, and everyone else in the bar besides, knew all about the murder, and why he was here. His gaze drifted to the whiskey bottles once more.

'Oh God,' said Corrigan, 'the things I must do for you.'

Alice was just leaving the Dorcas, wheeling her bicycle out of the front door from the back premises where she kept it, out of temptation to any resourceful urchin who might fancy a free ride (and that was most of them) when she saw one of the policemen who had come to Manessa House after Lucy's disappearance coming towards her. 'Why, Sergeant Inskip!'

'Mrs Latimer.'

The first thing that flew into her mind was that there was some news, but she knew she would have heard from Violet or Ferdie if there had been, that it was pointless to ask. He obviously guessed what she was thinking and shook his head.

'Nothing yet, Doctor, I'm sorry.'

He said it quite gently, she thought, considering the previous impression he'd made on her, which had been that of a forceful, rather tactless man.

They stood awkwardly, not knowing what else to say. Her glance sharpened. 'Goodness, you look a bit worse for wear.' His mouth was swollen. There was a cut beneath his eye and on his cheekbone a huge swelling.

'It's nothing. All in a day's work.' He grinned, wincing as he did so and cursing the proximity of the Nag to this clinic and the bad luck that had brought her out just as he was passing, when he'd never before encountered her in the neighbourhood.

'You'd better come inside and let me have a look at it.'

'I won't bother you, Doctor.' She seemed exhausted, and there were dark circles under her eyes. 'It looks worse than it feels, I dare say.'

'No, come on, I insist. You look as though you could do with a cup of tea as well.'

A stiff whiskey was more what he'd had in mind. He was on his way home to his lodgings to get one but he gave in and followed her inside.

'Nothing broken,' she said when she had examined the swelling and cleaned the cut. 'But I'm afraid you are going to have one heck of a shiner. You're lucky it wasn't worse. Who was it? And don't tell me you walked into a door.' She had seen too many women in the same state here at the clinic, beaten up by a drunken husband, to make that mistake.

He shrugged. 'Line of duty.' She didn't need to know the details, or why. 'It happens.' He didn't want to talk about it because it had been his own fault. After leaving Corrigan polishing pots in his now nearly empty bar, he'd visited the gents in the backyard of the Nag. They were waiting for him, as he might have antici-pated had his mind not been full of what he'd just heard, or more truthfully *hadn't* heard, from Tooley. Two of them, though nothing like the build of Tooley, and he could have given a better account of himself had he not been taken by surprise. Still, he regarded what had happened to him philosophically. He ought to have known better than to come out into the street via the back alley instead of going out through the front entrance. But he reckoned he'd knocked a few teeth out and blacked an eye or two before passing out. And that one of his assailants was going to have trouble walking for a while after his foot had connected with the place that mattered. He was lucky, as Doctor Latimer had said, but he knew it hadn't been a serious attempt, it had only been meant to scare him off. Which, if he hadn't known it before, meant there was definitely something they didn't want him poking his nose into.

The tea, brought in by a woman Doctor Latimer addressed as Nurse Peg, was hot, strong and sweet, and though it wasn't the whiskey he felt he needed, it tasted good and the first few sips began to revive him. 'My!' she said when she saw his face.

'You should see the other fella.' He was recovering fast but not up to sparkling repartee yet.

She poured another cup of tea, gave it to Doctor Latimer and was about to leave when she was suddenly struck by something. 'I know you, don't I?' she said to Inskip. 'Aren't you Mrs Maclusky's nephew, the policeman?' She wore a crucifix on a silver chain around her neck. St Bede's was in the vicinity so there was no mystery about how the acquaintance had arisen. 'The one that brought her the news? Poor Orla, to have a thing like that happen! She was very fond of her lodger, such a nice young chap he was. Quiet but always pleasant. Have you caught him yet, the one that killed him?' He sighed. She wasn't the only one who thought it was that easy. She studied the plasters on his face. 'It's Danny O'Rourke you've been looking for, isn't it? You want to be careful, young man. He associates with some funny characters, that one.'

'So I've been hearing.' There was nothing secret from these church women, but this was not where he wanted to go. He went back to something else she'd said. 'It sounds as though you knew Lennie Croxton?'

'I met him once or twice when he came to mass. He'd have been a good-looking chap if it hadn't been for wearing those awful glasses. Fastened up with sticky tape, they were, but I suppose he couldn't afford new ones.'

'Yes, we found them, in pretty bad shape.' Moving Croxton's body from the cab had unearthed the spectacles, smashed to smithereens, from where they had fallen to one side, where the weight of his body had put the finishing touches to a flimsy, wire-rimmed pair already past its best.

Doctor Latimer was having difficulty in fitting the cork into the neck of the bottle of iodine she had been using for his cuts. Her normally steady hand had slipped and some of the contents had splashed on to her hand. 'Someone should find a different stopper for these bottles,' she remarked, finally managing to rub the yellow stain from her fingers with something sharp-smelling from another, unlabelled bottle. He should ask her what it was – his face was going to look bad enough for the next few days without canary yellow iodine stains adding to the decorations, but she saw him looking and saved him the trouble of asking. 'Surgical spirit, Sergeant – but soap and water will do the trick if you have patience.' She put the container down with a decisive click.

He thanked her and stood up.

She smiled. 'Well, I think you'll do now. You're going to live.'

He saw his face reflected in the glass of a picture as he left. The yellow iodine stains he'd have to put up with. A more immediate problem was how he was going to explain it all to Gaines.

Ten

After their first meeting, David Moresby had fully expected to come across Mona Reagan again, quite soon. It should not have surprised him when he didn't: she was, as she had said, employed merely as one of the office workers behind the scenes, not to flit about the corridors of Westminster. But he *was* mildly surprised, by no means convinced that their first encounter hadn't been contrived by her, and intrigued to know why she hadn't made another one in her way. He admitted that his interest had been piqued in her as an attractive young woman he would like to know better. He had in fact wondered whether he might ask her out to dinner, though he knew he should be cautious about that – about consorting with her at all, in fact, he decided on second thoughts. The village pump had nothing on Westminster when it came to gossip and he had no wish to compromise himself by being seen consorting with – well, with the enemy, as Mona herself had it.

But all of that had been pushed to the back of his mind by the kidnap of Edmund Latimer's baby niece, though Latimer himself had shown neither emotion over the child's disappearance nor concern for her safe return. It was all over Westminster, everyone had heard the story and perhaps he was sick of sympathy, weary of the press who, sensing a big story, with all their persistent chasing after him, had significantly failed to get any comment from him. In that reserved man, it was possible there lurked a deep affection for the baby and distress for his sister, but he was adept at concealing his inner feelings, putting on a poker face, and certainly not one to let a domestic crisis, however traumatic, interfere with his work. David had suspected Alice would be even more affected by what had happened. Himself, he scarcely knew the baby's parents; he had met them once or twice when the Latimers had given dinner parties to which they'd all been invited. He had sent a note to them when the baby had first gone missing, and also one to Alice, expressing his sympathy and the hope that if there was anything he could do to help in the way of easing pressure on her husband, she must let

him know. It was a platitude and he would have liked to have said
more, but natural caution held him back, fearing he might reveal
more of himself than was wise, for both of them.

He was actually thinking about her when Mona Reagan
appeared. There was no pretence this time of mistaking his office
for the tea room, as she had mistaken Latimer's. A brisk knock
and then she was there in answer to his 'Come in.' She looked
around and breathed what was evidently a sigh of relief at finding
him momentarily alone, without a secretary or a colleague working
alongside. 'Miss Reagan. How nice to see you. Please take a seat.
What can I do for you?'

She looked at the papers on his desk. 'I hope I'm not disturbing
you, but what I have to say won't take long. I'm going away and I
just wanted to say goodbye.'

'Oh, I'm sorry to hear that. You're finding the work too
difficult?'

'Not at all. Uncongenial, perhaps.' She hesitated. 'I want no more
of it, in fact. I guess I've had enough.'

'A little of Wee Joe goes a long way, I imagine,' he ventured, with
a wry smile.

The blue eyes that had held a laugh in them were serious now.
For a moment, they rested on his face, blue eyes meeting blue, then
she looked away and shrugged. 'Oh no, it's not him, perhaps it's just
London that's got too much,' she said. 'I'm going home.'

'You're going to be a teacher after all, then?' She shook her head.
'No, I suppose you're going to be married.' He realized that was a
more obvious reason, an attractive young woman like her.

'No, I'm going home to my mammy,' she said, with a hint of
self-mockery. 'At least, I suppose the truth of it is that I'm homesick.
I need some fresh air.'

'That's something you don't get much of in London.' He
wondered what she was really saying. 'I wish you well in the future.
I'm sorry our acquaintance has been so brief.' So brief, in fact, no
more than one chance meeting, that he wondered why she had
found it necessary to seek him out to make her farewells.

As if she read his thoughts she hesitated, then added, 'I came to
say goodbye because I shall be gone soon and you were so nice
to me when I burst in on your office.'

'Not mine,' he pointed out. 'The Minister's. Mr Latimer's.'

'Yes. Mr Latimer.' There was a pause. 'You want to tell him to be careful,' she said quickly then drew in her breath, looking frightened, as if she ought not to have said it.

'Careful? In what way?' He thought it a strange thing to have said. The idea of Edmund Latimer being less than careful about anything at all almost made him laugh – and anyway, how could she, in her lowly position, know enough about his doings to necessitate a warning? Unless she was simply passing on something she had overheard. But the thought of the day they had met, when she had accidentally burst into Latimer's office, flashed through his mind once more, along with several other possibilities, one of which was that Mona Reagan was attractive and Edmund Latimer not wholly . . . unsusceptible. More unusual liaisons had been known to go on behind the scenes at Westminster, but the thought had been too bizarre to entertain for more than a second. And besides . . .

She shrugged. 'He'll know what I mean.' And then, hastily, 'Don't worry, it's not important. I'd have told him myself if I ever thought there was a chance I'd get to speak to him.'

She was right. In the loftiness of Latimer's position, and her lowly one, that was unlikely. He could think of no way of detaining her and finding out more, other than to ask, 'Won't you stay and have coffee with me? There's some on its way.'

But that was no persuasion either. They shook hands and on the way out she said, 'I hope the baby will be found soon, God love her. His sister's, isn't it, Mr Latimer's, I mean?'

And then she was gone, leaving him to his mixed thoughts.

Inskip decided to stop by his Auntie Orla's the next morning on his way to pay a call on the Catholic priest. She had a parcel ready for him to pass on.

'I would have sent the poor man some of my barmbrack if it weren't for that Julia O'Keefe's jealousy,' she said. 'She can't even bake soda bread and no wonder, with a face on her that would sour the buttermilk before it reaches the mixing bowl.' She handed him a floppy brown paper parcel tied with string. 'Don't let him open this while you're there, it might embarrass you both.' Orla couldn't afford whiskey, but he guessed it was something she'd salvaged for Father Finucane that was warm to wear – nothing she couldn't give a priest, a couple of pairs of socks maybe, or a flannel shirt he could wear under his cassock.

He didn't give his police credentials when he knocked on the presbytery door and asked to see Father Finucane, but the housekeeper, after a suspicious look at his face, didn't ask him in. She probably knew him by sight and reputation. She didn't actually shut the door, but she left him standing on the steps while she went to deliver his request, and looked disappointed when she came back at having to reply that the Father would see him. He could see what Orla had meant about the woman. She had a long nose and her hair drawn tightly back from her forehead and looked as if she didn't know how to smile. Her back was straight as a ramrod as she led him to the priest's study.

'Joseph Inskip! How nice to see you, boy!' Father Finucane waved him to a seat, smiled and thanked him for the parcel, which he thankfully didn't attempt to open, then looked enquiringly at Inskip with a pair of bright, intelligent and kindly eyes – a short, dumpy man who looked nothing special but was regarded by his parishioners as someone only a little below the God he represented. 'How's the world been treating you? Not well by the look of that face,' he said jocularly. 'I don't think you've been in this room since I was preparing you for your first communion, but I'm not going to pretend surprise. I don't think you're here for spiritual consolation.'

'I am not, Father,' Inskip admitted. The priest couldn't have forgotten the events which had led up to Cathleen's death and O'Rourke's flight to escape punishment, but it was unlikely he would think Inskip had now come to confess his disillusion with a religion and a God who could allow these things to happen.

At that moment Miss O'Keefe brought in some tea, which must have been already brewed, so prompt was she. She poured it in silence, gave a nod, and went out. Father Finucane looked hopefully at the tray but there was no accompanying plate of biscuits. The housekeeper made a good pot of tea, however; it was hot and very strong. You could have stood the teaspoon in it.

Inskip thought about how to broach the subject but he was forestalled. 'You are here about Daniel O'Rourke,' the priest said directly. 'I have heard what's being rumoured . . . but of course stories like that lose nothing in the telling.' He sighed and looked infinitely sad. 'If you're looking to me to tell you where he is you'll be disappointed. He has not been here. Daniel never liked what I had to say to him, and he knows what I would say now if he has the sin of taking another man's life on his conscience.'

'We don't know that he has, not yet, Father. But I am not here about O'Rourke.' He hadn't expected the priest to know where he was, and if he did, he wouldn't say.

'Then it's about the murdered man himself, God rest his soul.' He crossed himself, and waited. Inskip said it was. 'Well, I can't help you there, either. He came to mass but he wasn't inclined to linger afterwards and I only ever spoke to him very briefly. He never came to Confession. Seemed a nice enough young fellow, that's all I can say. I was surprised to say the least to hear he'd been associating with the likes of O'Rourke.'

'Was he Irish, too?'

'That I don't know. Maybe he was, or had some leanings. We Irish stick together, in ways that are not always as commendable as they might be.' He rose from his chair and went to stand, teacup in hand, with his back to the small, smouldering fire. 'I'm sadly afraid there's too much talk of violence going around these parts, as you must know better than I do – and not only talk. What goes on in Ireland is mirrored here in a small way, and I've lost count of the times it's already resulted in bad trouble for the families of all concerned. I can't blame them for their views. As I see it, this thing they're after that they call Home Rule, it's inevitable sooner or later. But we are not renowned for patience. You cannot right centuries of wrong in a moment and I know people are sick of talk and still raw from past injustices. The older ones, those that are still proud to call themselves Fenians, can't bring themselves to believe the struggle can ever be settled by peaceful means. Nothing will be achieved with armed violence, but Nationalist, Republican, or whatever they like to call themselves, it still amounts to the same thing. They see themselves as martyrs for the cause.'

'Who are they, these people you know, specifically?' Father Finucane knew everyone, every detail about his parishioners, and would certainly be aware if anyone of them were up to no good. Inskip had put the question, fully expecting the answer no. And of course, the priest shrugged and shook his head.

'What about Tooley, Paddy Tooley?' Inskip asked carefully.

He laughed. 'I wouldn't fancy Tooley as a martyr for anything.'

He came back to the tea-tray on the desk, picked up the teapot and poured another cup of the now evil-looking brew. Inskip waved away a refill. 'I've said too much,' he said suddenly. 'Don't concern yourself with those who want to stir things up is my advice.'

'If that's what O'Rourke has come back to do, it does concern me, it's my job, and we'll get him, Father, you may be sure of that.' Nothing less could have brought him back here, surely, to stir things up or to get money. There were influential people, even priests – though not Father Finucane – who were not averse to helping, with money or anything else.

'Yes, I am afraid he must be brought to justice, but such an extremity has brought many a man to reflection and repentance.'

Did he really believe this? 'Father, I must go. Thank you for the tea.'

'It's been good to talk to you, Joseph. You've not thought about going back across the sea, then, to join your brothers? They keep in touch, you know, send contributions. It's a good life they have.'

'I have a good life here, Father.'

'Well, well, I'm glad to hear that.' The priest said nothing more as he accompanied Inskip to the door, blessing him before he left. 'Maybe you'll find it in your way to letting us see more of you at Our Lady. And think on this, Joseph. Revenge is the Lord's and it's He who will repay.'

He had remembered Cathleen, after all.

At Manessa House, Violet and Ferdie were breakfasting. Ferdie had the newspaper, still almost entirely dominated by stories of the *Titanic* disaster, propped against the coffee pot, pretending to read. But the speculations as to how the worst shipping disaster in the history of the world could possibly have happened, the rising death toll, the unexpected stories of heroism among those rescued made little impact on him. The news had shocked the world and was drawing people together, as adversity was supposed to do, though that wasn't something that applied to himself and his wife. For some reason their own personal calamity was making it difficult to communicate. Some barrier seemed to have risen between them that prevented them sharing their grief and he couldn't read what was going on behind the façade Violet was putting up. But then she had always kept her emotions severely in check. It wasn't done to wear one's heart on one's sleeve. He had always known she was tougher than he was, but he still marvelled at the stoicism she was able to adopt now, at what cost God only knew to herself. He couldn't attempt to emulate it and her constantly repeated belief that everything was bound to come right irked him. He didn't know how she got through the days, vaguely supposing she might be seeing her friends, shopping, doing all the things that normally occupied her days, but she didn't say, and he didn't ask.

Everyone else in the house was carrying on with their life, or trying to, as they had been advised. Alice was going to her clinic, every day now, and Edmund, though looking haggard with worry, had declared there was no logical reason he could see not to carry on as usual. Ferdie himself had even been putting a few hours in at the bank. In view of his father's intransigent attitude towards the paying of a ransom, should such a demand ever come, their necessary association there should have provoked loathing, could he have summoned up the energy. As it was, he was barely aware of his parent's presence. In between the time he spent there he had found himself walking aimlessly around the Regent's Park, peering into every pram he saw, until the hostile reaction of several mothers had stopped him. Since then, he had walked, or slowly driven his motor car around the streets in the same aimless and unprofitable way, sometimes even at night. The household had become used to him coming and going at ungodly hours.

Today, before setting out for the bank, he sat hunched over his toast and marmalade, going over the whole wretched situation, almost willing himself to believe that it was all a nightmare, that the new nanny must bring in his little Lucy as she routinely did each morning before he left, handing her to him for a cuddle, newly bathed and smelling sweetly of baby powder. He would spend ten minutes or so, ruffling her soft curls, playing with her, teasing from her a gurgling laugh and storing up memory that would warm and cheer him throughout the day. But then he realized that wasn't going to happen today. The meaningless day would go on, without him being able to think, despite the brave words he had first uttered, of any more steps that might lead him to Lucy.

Hewson, the parlour maid, getting on in years and bad on her feet, stumped in with the morning's post and handed it to him without a smile. No one in the house now seemed able to find occasions for smiling. It had become a sad little household. From being the happily unremarkable home of a privileged young couple with a solid background, just starting out to raise a family, with the first of them the joyful centre of everyone's existence, including that of most of the staff, it had become the centre of tension and fear.

Ferdie flipped through the letters. There was one addressed to Miss May Newcombe and the rest were for Violet – the usual batch of invitations, he could see, and two which he guessed were bills from her milliner which she put aside with a cluck, also a familiar-looking pink epistle from her dressmaker, an alarmingly high demand, he concluded from the way she bit her lip before thrusting it back into its envelope. There was nothing for Ferdie, but among the other, stamped and addressed envelopes was a note which appeared to have been hand-delivered, since it bore neither name nor address. It was in fact a single sheet of paper folded in half, then into three with one end tucked in to keep it closed. Ferdie opened it and sat staring blankly until Violet asked, 'What's that?'

'It's arrived,' he said. 'The ransom.'

She gave a queer, choking gasp and since he appeared incapable of saying more, jumped up, ran around the table, snatched the paper from his hand and read the large, scrawled block capitals. FIVE THOUSAND POUND OR ELSE. Nothing more, simply the five words. But it was enough to make Violet forget her resolution not to show temper. 'Five thousand pounds!' she almost screamed. 'What imbeciles! How do they expect anyone to have that amount?' It was indeed a staggering sum, one that might stretch even the resources of Martens Bank.

Ferdie found his voice. 'Violet,' he said in an oddly strangulated voice, 'never mind the money. Don't you realize this means Lucy is alive?'

'What? Well, yes, I do, of course I do! But it still means we shall have to get the money from somewhere, somehow, to get her back. And five thousand pounds!' Her fury had gone, but her voice still shook.

Ferdie made for the telephone with a speed he hadn't shown himself capable of since he'd first heard that his daughter had disappeared.

★   ★   ★

'They're attempting to unnerve you,' Gaines said when he arrived and was shown the note. He had asked to be told immediately, should the ransom demand arrive. It would, he had hoped, state terms and the means whereby the exchange would take place, all of which would enable the police to work out a possible intervention policy. But there was nothing in this note to suggest how or where this would happen.

'Unnerve us? If that's what they want, then they're succeeding,' Ferdie said. 'Because there's simply no question of being able to pay anything remotely like that. I've already telephoned my father and he's not prepared to cough up.'

'Your *father!*' Violet almost hissed. This monster hovering in the background who wasn't prepared to part with money even to save his own grandchild. Money that however huge a sum it might have seemed to the kidnappers, must be nothing compared with what he owned.

'He's convinced himself this is all a hoax, however ridiculous that is. He won't hand over any money at all, much less five thousand pounds, until it's proved otherwise. And how will that happen?' he asked bitterly. 'By Lucy being . . . killed?'

Gaines was quick to try and put this worst possible outcome from Martens' mind. 'You'll hear from them again. The note is simply an opening gambit, designed to frighten you. Will you let me take charge of it?'

In one way the missive was reassuring. It meant that the child had indeed been taken for money, not by a person who wanted to keep her for themselves, with no intention of ever returning her. He pocketed it, while knowing there was little to be gained from it. Fingerprints maybe, for which they would, however, need comparisons. The paper had been torn from a cheap exercise book, the pencilled message scrawled – perhaps in an attempt at disguise, but he thought not. It seemed to him much more likely to have been written by one not accustomed to writing, and possibly someone illiterate, unless it had been done in too much of a hurry to notice or bother about a missing 's'. *Five thousand pound,* it said, not pounds. A figure drawn out of the air. Five thousand pounds, a sum beyond the grasp of the imagination of those unacquainted with anything much more than a shilling or two. If an ordinary working man laboured for a lifetime such a sum would be unattainable – and yet such a person might well regard it as a drop in the ocean to people like the Martens, thinking they would regard it as a fair price to pay for their child. It seemed very much to him as though the perpetrator was an amateur with unrealistic expectations, but at least it was the first move in a game intended to start negotiations; it had broken the silence and made way for their next move. Instructions must follow, though it was by no means plain sailing yet.

No ransom must ever be forthcoming, but if the parents could be persuaded to cooperate and seem willing to pay, an exchange could be arranged, giving the police the opportunity to intercept the kidnappers. He didn't think it wise to say to either of them that, God help them, it was entirely possible, depending on who these kidnappers were, that if they thought there was any chance they might be caught, they would not hesitate to make specific that threat, '*or else*'.

Before he left, he urged them to speak of this latest happening to no one – no one at all, particularly the press. 'I won't mislead you. It's going to be tricky, whichever way it turns out, and publicity will only confuse the operation. We shall need your cooperation and the utmost caution.'

It was a pity the grandfather had already been told. Despite his uncompromising attitude, there was no way of knowing which way he might jump, if he thought the outcome was likely to affect him and his business in any way. Before returning to the Yard, thinking back to what Ferdie Martens had said, Gaines decided it was high time he bearded Martens père in his den, and that now was probably the best time, before Ferdie arrived – if indeed he would be able to bring himself to arrive at all that day.

He knew it was going to be a waste of time as soon as he was shown into Emil Martens' private office and saw him.

Dozens of people must have sat in this chair, facing him, many of them no doubt supplicants, and it didn't take long to see why it might arouse despair, possibly fear, though Martens looked less like an ogre, or even a bank owner, than one of his own clerks. He was a round, grey man just short of medium height, the roundness and greyness echoed by large steel-rimmed spectacles and a smooth, grey-haired head atop a body shaped like a rubber ball. A grey moustache bristled over a small mouth, but it was the eyes that did it. Behind round glasses that added another circular dimension, and through which he surveyed Gaines, they were chips of ice. Gaines, dressed in his outdoor clothes, almost shivered, and not because of the room's temperature. The private office was warm enough, heated by an iron radiator. He there and then absolved Violet Martens of any exaggeration about her father-in-law. It would be a big mistake to assume that any ball this man resembled would be one whit softer than a snowball with a rock inside it.

He waved Gaines to a chair, sat down behind his desk and folded his plump white hands on the desk in front of him, and though he knew why Gaines was here, waited expressionlessly for him to state his business. You wouldn't want to play poker with this man.

But Gaines had dealt with more formidable-seeming characters than Emil Martens. He reminded himself that the man's response to his son's appeal didn't necessarily mean that he would not, if it came to the sticking point, pay the ransom, only that he chose for reasons of his own not to let it be known that he would.

'I think you know why I'm here, Mr Martens.'

The banker inclined his head. 'I presume it's about that ransom note, so I'll tell you immediately you are wasting your time. Quite ridiculous. The whole thing is nothing but a hoax.' So that was how he was going to play it. 'To which I have no intention of submitting. If one gives in to blackmail of this sort, where does it end?'

He was Belgian, but there was no trace of accent in his speech. There was also no indication that he was prepared to be magnanimous and save the parents pain. Gaines thought of his own father, a sternly raised Victorian who had seen it as his duty to bring up his son, Gaines himself, in the same way, and then, in the hands of his grandchildren, had been like putty. However, regrettable as it was, becoming a grandparent, or even a parent, didn't automatically confer affection.

'I quite agree, Mr Martens, that under no circumstances must money be paid. But I would suggest it should be made apparent that it might be, that you are prepared to negotiate.'

'No. There comes a time when enough is enough. I have bailed my son out more times than I can remember . . . especially when he was younger.' He didn't add *before he had a wife* but that seemed hardly necessary. 'I don't believe I am ungenerous. Ferdinand earns a more than adequate salary here and when I retire he will take over. He needs to be taught a lesson. It will do him no harm to wait.'

Gaines was silent, wondering how far the punishment he was prepared to inflict on his son would go. Was he even willing to risk a baby's life, to make his point? Indeed, it was hard to think of him ever summoning up enough human emotion to lead to the fathering of a son at all, never mind one like Ferdie. Any parental resemblance in Ferdie must be to his dead mother.

There was nothing further to be said. Gaines brought the interview to an end, feeling he hadn't achieved much by coming here, but as he walked back to Scotland Yard, the words 'taught a lesson' continued to echo in his head.

Eleven

The next morning a hand-delivered letter was brought to David Moresby in his office at Westminster.

> *Dear Mr Moresby,*
>
> *I have something rather important to say to you and I wonder if we could meet? Somewhere we will not be interrupted? I know how busy you are, so perhaps you could suggest a time and place convenient to you? I can be available at any time. I hesitate to ask this, but I hope you will understand when you hear what I have to say.*
>
> *Yours sincerely,*
>
> *Alice Latimer*

David read the letter again and stared out of the window. A gang of feral pigeons jostled rowdily along the windows of an adjacent wing. They'd become such a nuisance lately, but no one had yet found a way of deterring them. Pigeons were survivors.

The formality of Alice's letter intrigued him as much as the obvious urgency of the request. *Mr Moresby.* He and Alice met socially, dined together, played tennis, had spent Saturdays-to-Mondays in various country houses to which both he and the Latimers had been invited. They were friends. He was normally 'David' to her, and he called her by her Christian name. He wrote back immediately – *'Dear Alice'* – suggesting a meeting the same afternoon in the Victoria Embankment Gardens.

He was there precisely on time and she arrived a minute later, dressed as he normally saw her, in the expensively smart clothes she wore with elegance, but always with a touch of impatience, it seemed to David. Today, it was a chic blue coat and skirt, its grey fur trim and the furled umbrella she carried both a challenge to the fickle April weather. As she came towards him with quick, decisive steps, he was concerned to see dark shadows under her clear eyes. 'Hello, David, it was good of you to come at such short notice.'

He was relieved she had decided to dispense with the 'Mr Moresby'. 'I hope there's nothing wrong. You're looking a little tired, Alice. Oh, forgive me,' he said, smiling, 'that's not the sort of thing one's supposed to say to a lady.'

'I'd rather have the truth than a facile compliment.' A return smile appeared and her hand was laid lightly on his arm. The grey suede glove was ruched about the wrist. A matching suede bag hung over it on a silver chain. 'Shall we sit?' He was surprised to feel the tremble of her hand through his sleeve. Alice was not a woman who trembled easily.

'The truth in this case *was* a compliment,' he said as they made their way towards a convenient seat. 'To the hard work you're doing at the clinic. Entirely admirable, of course, no one would think otherwise, but . . . one can overdo it, Alice.'

'So Edmund tells me. Yet he himself comes home so dog-tired it worries me – if . . . if he manages to get home at all, that is. All those late night sittings.'

David thought of the set of rooms, so convenient for Westminster . . . and for when Latimer was not inclined to undertake the drive home to Manessa House, though his dashing new Napier could easily make it in under an hour, even without exceeding the speed limit.

She raised her clear eyes to his. He could read no sign in them that implied anything other than exactly what her last remarks had said, but women were nothing if not adept at concealing what they really thought. 'Is that why you want to see me?'

'No. Of course not. Well, yes, in a way it is, though hard work is meat and drink to Edmund, isn't it? I'm afraid,' she went on, with the abrupt honesty that he'd come to know was typical of her, 'something is troubling him, and I don't know what it is. You see him daily and I thought . . . I've tried to talk to him but he won't discuss it with me. At first, I believed he might be ill, but it's not that.'

A melancholy toot sounded from one of the tugs on the busy Thames a few yards away, a reminder of the proximity of the never ceasing river traffic. All around were daffodils set in marshalled banks, a cheerful splash of colour against the grey buildings behind. The gardens' tidy, well-kept paths were flanked with beds where gardeners could be seen preparing for the riot of blazing colour they would be in a few weeks. The day was for the moment fine and sunny and the seats were full of office workers eating their lunchtime sandwiches. Some of them had even risked sitting on the grass.

'You don't need me to tell you what the situation is at the moment, Alice.'

The Prime Minister's recent introduction of the Home Rule Bill had precipitated a crisis and Parliament was at full stretch . . . the Opposition, many of whom had financial and land-owning interests in Ireland, were baying against it. The Lords, for similar reasons, were fuming at Asquith's successful curtailment of their powers to veto the Bill. And Ireland itself was in ferment: the mainly Protestant community of Ulster in the north bitterly opposed to a Catholic government by the rest of Ireland, while the Catholics themselves would not concede to government of Irish affairs imposed from Westminster.

'Yes, of course I know all that, but Edmund has coped with crises before. I feel it must be something more than that.'

He thought for a moment. 'There's no news about Lucy yet?' She hesitated, then shook her head. 'Could it be that he's worrying about that? It's a wretched business.'

'I'm not sure, but maybe . . . And yes, the last days *have* been wretched, awful in fact, especially for Violet and Ferdie, under such terrible strain. Everyone on edge, simply waiting for something to happen. But . . .' She hesitated. 'Yes, something *has* happened, David. We're not supposed to talk about it, but I know I can trust you. Somebody has sent a demand for money.'

'Have they, by Jove? But I don't suppose that's entirely unexpected?'

'No. Not really, it was always on the cards, and at least we know now why she's been taken. Not by someone playing games, or being cruel, nor some poor woman desperately longing for a child of her own.'

'So she will be returned once the money is paid?'

'If only it were so straightforward! Ferdie simply can't raise anything like the amount they're asking, and his father won't. He says the kidnappers are bluffing and they'll reduce their demands once they see the amount they ask isn't forthcoming. As if that is likely to happen!'

'That could be what is troubling Edmund,' David said slowly. 'If he's feeling morally obliged to find this money himself, for instance? I don't believe it's any secret how much he loves his little niece.'

'He does love her, yes – dearly. But they are demanding *five thousand pounds* – and Edmund's finances, I assure you,' she said wryly, 'aren't nearly so abundant as an outsider might imagine, or what he chooses to let people think.'

This was something David could believe, although without ever having given it much thought he had always imagined Latimer to be comfortably off. But he had given up a lucrative law practice for his Parliamentary career and now had expenses as an MP, which his junior minister's salary would not cover. Keeping up the social life, the entertaining and so on, that was expected of a man in his position, perhaps unfairly, was done at no small cost. Not to mention the high maintenance of such an establishment as the one at Manessa House, relatively modest as it was. The upkeep of David's own family home, a small, well-loved manor house situated in his Derbyshire constituency, which had been in the Moresby family for generations, at present lived in and looked after by his unmarried sister, was a constant worry to him. In a world where women were so often prevented from having a career the running of the estate suited his capable, strong-minded sister very well, and given his own inclinations he was happy enough with the situation, though finances were an ever-present worry.

Looking away, Alice went on in a low voice, 'You must think it strange that we can't speak of this, Edmund and myself, I mean. But if he's so against any discussion, I can't force him. Maybe he *cannot* tell me what's wrong. I can't be certain, of course, but I don't really believe it's anything to do with Lucy. But if I don't know what it is, how can I help him?'

David, normally a self-controlled man, felt momentarily utterly consumed with anger. She should be able to confide her worries to her husband and not have to turn to someone else for reassurance. Yet despite his anger, he felt overwhelming pleasure that *he* was that someone else, and when he thought of why that might be, his breath caught in his throat. He stopped himself. That was an indulgence he couldn't afford.

'You people are all under so much pressure,' she was going on, 'and he – Edmund – only occasionally talks about his work. It's something he finds very difficult to do, I know; he prefers to keep it separate from his life at home. I may well be entirely wrong, but . . . he's a very influential man, isn't he, and I've begun to believe someone might possibly be trying to persuade him in some way to – to do something against his principles. There are so many issues at present, goodness knows – all these strikes, Ireland and all the rest of it. Does that sound ridiculous?'

The mention of Ireland immediately brought that visit of Mona Reagan's to mind. 'Actually, no, it doesn't. We're all subject to pressures like that at times and we all have to face the sort of thing you're speaking about. Fortunately, I know of few who would succumb, especially Edmund.'

Yet he faced a dilemma. No one knew better than David how incorruptible Edmund Latimer was, or how firmly loyal he was to his Liberal party's policies. But just supposing Alice was right, that her husband was being threatened or coerced in some way . . . Supposing someone did have some sort of hold over him, what then? If so, David strongly suspected what that hold might be. But he was absolutely unable to say so – to Alice, above all people. To give her even a hint of his suspicions was impossible.

He had the greatest respect for Latimer, the statesman: for his political acumen, his steadfastness and tireless devotion to his work. In other directions, it was a different matter. He was loyal to Edmund where their work was concerned, loyal and correct. But he could not respect a man who led a double life. In fact, it was only lately he had come to realize that he did not actually like the man himself very much at all. Which was a civilized understatement to a murderously uncivilized rage when he thought of how this concerned Alice.

He managed with difficulty to stay calm and, he hoped, reassuring. 'I suppose it's quite possible he may be involved in some negotiations I haven't been informed about yet, possibly because they're so sensitive. Senior people like him are always vulnerable and as you say, it's a volatile time in politics at the moment – on several fronts. You've no idea how jittery we've become, nervous of saying, or doing, the wrong thing. Imagining intrigue where none exists. Why, only yesterday a young woman gave me a message for Edmund to be careful. Pure melodrama, I assure you, or simply an intention to unnerve, but you see what I mean. It does have an effect on some people, I'm sorry to say, but mostly we learn to take no notice, otherwise where would we be? Nervous wrecks, my dear Alice. Politics is a game, and not everyone plays fair.'

She had heard him out without interruption. Now she asked, quite sharply, 'A woman?'

Damn. That could have been more diplomatically phrased, or better still, not said at all. His intention to play down her fears of something worse by citing Mona Reagan's call on him had misfired. He was losing his grip.

'Who is she?'

'Only someone who works – worked – for one of the Irish Nationalists, in a menial capacity. I scarcely know her, in fact I've only met her once before.'

'Did you pass the message on to Edmund?'

'It's quite likely she spoke to him directly, as well as to me.' He hoped she didn't realize how unlikely it was that a lowly person like her would have access to someone in Edmund's position. Nor did he mention how frightened Mona had looked when she spoke.

He hadn't in fact spoken to Latimer because he needed time to think about it, to make discreet enquiries about Mona Reagan, and how valid the warning might have been, before passing it on. There was a man in Wee Joe Devlin's office with whom he often passed a friendly time of day and who was willing to talk, but he had gained little from him except Mona's address, though it had caused him to lift his eyebrows. The East End was not the sort of district where he had imagined a girl like her might choose to live, but he saw the point when Hogan pointed out that she would naturally feel more at home sharing the house of a man named Tooley with other Irish expatriates.

'How does she know Edmund?' Alice asked.

'I don't know that she does. She may simply know his name and have heard he's involved with some negotiations that might turn out to be tricky for him, that could perhaps backfire.' Not that Latimer had made David aware of any such negotiations, as he normally routinely did. 'She's leaving the country to go back to Ireland and perhaps it was just that there's something brewing with the Nationalists she thought he ought to be aware of.'

He tried to play down what he was feeling. The Irish were on the whole a quick-witted and good-humoured nation with a strong streak of romanticism, and while they might also believe in faeries and leprechauns, few Irishmen were averse to a fight. And the extremist faction among the Nationalist MPs were a powerful force in the British Parliament, holding as they did fervent convictions and unshakeable beliefs that it was the duty of every natural born Irishman to rebel against the centuries' old injustices inflicted on their people, and their inalienable right to join in the struggle.

Alice stayed silent for some time, circling the toe of her grey suede boot on the asphalt path while gazing unseeingly at Isambard Kingdom Brunel, one of the many statues placed around the gardens. 'I should speak to this woman. Can you find out where she lives? I'd like to meet her.'

Considerably taken aback, he said, 'Well, as a matter of fact, I happen to know. But you must not even *think* of going there, Alice. The East End is not where ladies go alone.'

She smiled faintly. 'You forget, it's where I spend a great deal of my time, David. Every day lately. Anyone might imagine I would be stepping into a den of iniquity.'

'That may not be so far from the truth,' he answered grimly. 'But there really isn't any point, anyway. She refused to say anything more than to tell your husband to be careful.'

'All the same, I must speak to her. Please let me have her address.'

The sun had gone behind a cloud and the sandwich eaters were beginning to disperse back to their places of work. He had learned never to rush headlong into anything and he was uneasy with the proposal, to say the least. He took refuge in prevarication. 'Miss Reagan is probably back in County Down by now.'

'In that case I shall have wasted my time, but I must at least try.'

'You could,' he ventured, 'always ask Edmund himself.' Before she could answer, he held up his hand, 'No, I'm sorry, that was foolish. I see that wouldn't serve, in the – er – circumstances.'

He now regretted even more the impulse that had made him mention Mona Reagan to her, especially when he saw the stubborn tilt to her chin. 'Very well. If you absolutely insist—'

'I do.'

'But only if you agree to me going with you.'

She smiled. 'David, don't be absurd. There's absolutely no need for that.'

'There's every need. Like it or not, I was the one she spoke to.

There's more likelihood of her talking to you if I'm there. Before we make any sort of move, however, I must try to find out a little more of what all this is about – if it amounts to anything at all, which I doubt – and then there might be no need to speak to her.'

She hesitated, but then she nodded. 'All right – and thank you, David. I would be glad if you'd do that.' She stood up. 'I must not keep you any longer. Thank you again for everything.'

'My dear Alice, it's the least I can do.'

'Goodbye for the present, then.' She held out her hand and as he took it she repeated, unhappily, 'He would never under any circumstances do anything dishonourable, I know.'

'Absolutely not.' If dishonour didn't include cheating on your wife, David reflected. It did sound as though she was trying to convince herself, and he suspected that confiding in him had cost her a great deal more than she was revealing. 'I'll see what I can find out. It's bound to be something trivial, that he doesn't want to worry you with. I don't know at the moment if anything will come of it, but I'm always happy to do what I can for you. I hope you know that.'

It was all he could offer, nothing more than a polite, conventional reply, but he felt something passed between them, a long, quiet moment of recognition, when they both realized something else had been said.

'Thank you, David. I'll remember that.'

He felt bad, letting her think she had convinced him to agree to what she proposed when he was damned if Alice and Mona Reagan would ever meet – or not if he had anything to do with it. His intuition told him it would be disastrous, why he couldn't imagine, but he had learned to trust that sixth sense which made him so good at his job.

He needed to proceed with caution. Latimer might well be headed for some disaster, for all he knew, but in his present capacity David was there to pick up the pieces rather than shatter the edifice.

They parted after arranging that he would let her know within the next couple of days what had transpired, and he went back to his office in the House of Commons where he worked like a man possessed until nearly midnight, until he was bone weary and the print on the papers started to dance before his eyes. Then he made his way to the small service flat within easy reach of Westminster which he occupied. It served him very well when the House was in session, though he liked nothing better when Parliament was not sitting than to travel home to Derbyshire, exchange his immaculate, formal suits for comfortable, well-worn tweeds and stride for hours over the hills, drop in at various pubs and keep in touch with the country and townspeople who made up his constituents, some of whom led lives of poverty and deprivation equal to any of those in the great cities. Going back was both a relaxation and a salutary reminder of why these people, for whom it was both duty and inclination to do his utmost, had elected him to be their representative in Parliament. Yet increasingly he knew his real life could never be wholly in Derbyshire. That lay here, in the corridors of power, among clever, ambitious and powerful people, where he had to keep his considerable wits about him in a busy and demanding environment, while never forgetting the real reason he was there.

At last he capped his fountain pen, shuffled papers together, closed files and then sat for a long time thinking about the problem Alice had faced him with. The only conclusion he came to was that he could do nothing for the moment except to put out feelers, then watch and wait. The longer they had to wait, the less determined Alice might be to carry out her intentions, though a wry intuition told him it would not do to be too hopeful about that.

He went to bed and fell asleep buoyed up by the memory of that brief snatch of conversation with her, when a line had been crossed into unknown territory and his world had suddenly gained another, brighter and yet infinitely more dangerous dimension.

Acquaintances in the smart circles she frequented would have been astonished to see the change in Mrs Fiore as she sat curled up on the hearthrug in front of the leaping fire in the room she called her boudoir. At that moment, she looked ten years younger than her age and scarcely recognizable as the woman Edmund Latimer had briefly spoken to at the Essendines' soirée. Relieved of the punishing whaleboning of her formal clothes that was essential to give women the sculpted, much admired hour-glass figure, she looked soft and yielding. She was wearing a Japanese kimono, peach-coloured silk lavishly embroidered with sprays of chrysanthemums and cherry blossom, and the leaping firelight cast a glow on to her cheeks and brought out the lights in her rich brown hair as she leaned back against Edmund's knee.

Turning her head sideways, she reached for his hand where it lay on her shoulder and pressed it to her cheek. They hadn't spoken for the last fifteen minutes or so, their long familiarity having no need of it.

'What must I do about all this, Connie?' he said at last. The firelight was not as kind to him as it was to Connie. It accentuated the lines and hollows in a face grown older even in these last few weeks.

'Won't you let me help?'

'You help me all the time, more than you'll ever know. But not this time, not in the way you mean. You know what I think about using influential friends. This is something I've brought on myself.'

'Indeed it is not! You must not castigate yourself, none of it is of your doing, and you must have faith that it will all come right in the end, if you do what you think is right.' Her voice was low and soothing. She had almost lost her American accent by now.

'Will it? I wish I could be as certain. One starts something, but one never knows where it will finish up. We fail to see consequences, for ourselves and for those dear to us. I never thought to find myself – or you – in a situation like this.'

'My dear, we do what we have to do. And you need have no worries for me. I can face up to whatever is necessary.'

'I have never doubted that you would, Connie my love. But I can't understand it. We have always been so careful.'

For a man of his intelligence and occupation, Edmund Latimer was sometimes incredibly naïve. How could he believe that their ten-year affair could have been kept in any way secret among those they knew? Herself, she was simply grateful that a blind eye was turned on such liaisons as theirs, as long as they were kept discreet – as it always had been, until now.

She believed he loved her in his own way, if it was only because she had forgiven him for marrying Alice, in a moment of weakness for which he now bitterly reproached himself. She had understood the reasons for a man in his position needing a wife, and had indeed approved, especially since she and Edmund could never marry. Mrs Fiore had not then, as she had allowed it to be generally understood, been a widow. Her husband, Alessandro Fiore, was still alive, but living in seclusion back in America, looked after by a devoted manservant who had been with him for forty years.

It had not taken her long after they were married to discover the truth. Her husband was drunk on their wedding night and scarcely sober for long periods afterwards and it was very soon evident he was fast becoming wholly dependent on alcohol. Long-term abuse was already causing liver damage, but he neither attempted nor wished to give up drinking, not even for the sake of saving their marriage. She was gradually forced to admit that the passing attraction between them had been just that – on her part, dazzled by the prospect of marrying into the sort of wealthy, self-made, entrepreneurial family so much admired in America, and on his perhaps fragile hope that it might pave the way to end his drinking. But that had never happened and it was clear to both that the decision to marry had been a huge mistake. Like the rest of the extended, closely bonded emigrant Fiore family, who made no decisions without the knowledge and approval of the whole tribe, Alessandro was strongly Roman Catholic, and there was no question of divorce. When she asked for a separation and an allowance that would allow her to live comfortably in Europe, a collective sigh of relief arose from within their ranks and a mutually satisfactory agreement was immediately drawn up. She had made an agreeable life for herself here in London, her arrangement with Edmund a suitable one for both parties while, contrary to what she had expected, the drink did not kill Alessandro, over in America. Until last year, when he had at last died and, to the fury of the Fiore clan, it was revealed he had failed to change the will he had made on their marriage, in which he had left everything he had to his wife.

Since then, Connie had made changes in her life, moved from the tiny apartment in St John's Wood she'd occupied to a larger one, began to have her clothes made in Paris, and made general improvements in her style of living. The only fly in the ointment was that Edmund was still married to Alice.

She steeled herself. 'I believe you should tell her, Edmund.'

'Tell her? Tell Alice? No! How can I? She is not at fault here. She married me in good faith and she has always played her part.'

She regretted having spoken. She was as much aware as he was of the consequences of such an act: divorce which meant social ostracism, his reputation for integrity in shreds, questions hanging over his political future.

It struck her suddenly how little she really knew him, after all these years of intimacy – quite possibly, how little anyone knew him, even, or perhaps especially, Alice, his wife.

Prosser Street, and what the devil was he doing here, David asked himself, for maybe the tenth time. How had he persuaded himself into doing something he positively knew was not a good idea? But he hadn't truly needed much persuasion and if he was honest, he was finding this mad escapade surprisingly stimulating, stirred as he had been to an uncharacteristic recklessness, a trait he didn't normally acknowledge he possessed. His only excuse was Alice. Sensible and independent-minded as he knew her to be, she was also inclined to be impulsive and he had little doubt she would have come here on her own if he had simply given her the address. On the other hand, if he hadn't supplied her with it, she was more than capable of finding it out for herself, and acting upon it. Every nerve had told him that would be the wrong thing to do.

The business of the day had left him with no choice but to make his plans, hopefully, for the evening, but in any case, where he was going wasn't the sort of district where you paid polite afternoon calls and left visiting cards. He was free at a reasonable hour, and as it became dark, he was able to get ready. It wouldn't do to stand out where he was going, so he donned the serviceable but well-worn tweeds and flat cap he wore in Derbyshire and added a muffler. It was the best he could do. It wasn't a cover-up that would stand up to any sort of examination, especially if his hand-made, well-polished shoes were spotted, but nothing better could be mustered up in the circumstances.

Having memorized the route from the map, he took a cab as far as he thought wise, and then walked. Plunging further and further into the dark heart of this alien part of the city, he became even more shocked than he had been when he first learned that Mona lived here, a girl accustomed to the soft, clean air, the green hills and the fresh winds of County Down. No wonder she wanted to go home. He was appalled that anyone at all should be forced to live here, among these noisome courts and crumbling tenements, everything overhung with the stink of poverty. Perhaps that was why so many of them took to the streets. Despite the lateness of the hour a vibrant outdoor life was still being lived there, people thronging the pavements where smells from the stalls of the food sellers mingled with the distinctive, unpleasant odour of the naphtha lights flaring above them. Women shopped for cheap, tired, end-of-day vegetables. Dirty and ragged children who should have been tucked up in bed long ago swarmed around in rowdy gangs. As much as possible he kept circumspectly to the shadows, aware that if he drew the attention of any of the unsavoury characters hanging about outside the pubs or on the street corners he could be relieved of the money that was in his pockets and maybe the clothes off his back. He didn't allow himself to think of the possibility of having his throat cut. And thankfully, it was still a bit too early for the night-ladies to be out and about, ready to hang on to his sleeve and offer an invitation.

It had never been part of David's plan to allow Alice to seek out Mona Reagan. Even as he had promised to find out more, he knew he would find some way of preventing contact. He didn't admire himself for allowing her to think he would, but it had not been one of his finer moments when he had revealed to her his last encounter with that young woman, and he still tingled with mortification at having done so. As soon as it had passed his lips, he had known it was a blunder ever to have allowed the woman's name to be mentioned. True, he was more accustomed to dealing with men than with women, but all the same, he ought to have known that any woman was likely to show some reaction when her husband's name was coupled with another's, however innocent the context. God forbid that she should ever find out the real truth about Latimer.

And then he'd also made matters worse by promising to accompany her when all the time he suspected the mission would be futile. Either Mona would already have left the Prosser Street house and gone back to Ireland, or she'd refuse to say anything more than she'd said to him. What was it about Alice that made him act so out of character, to want to protect her? She was a self-reliant woman who had no need of that. All the same, he had a gut feeling it would be a disaster to let her get involved in what was probably nothing more than a young woman's casual reference to something quite unimportant, but might well, in the volatile world of politics, turn out to be something very nasty indeed. He fully intended none the less to get to the bottom of what it was about Latimer that worried her so much, while proceeding with caution. Nothing would be achieved by rushing.

While trying to decide what to do, he had meanwhile put out a few more feelers, with not much result. He had learned only that Mona Reagan had ceased working for Wee Joe Devlin, which didn't mean she had necessarily left London. At first, it had been no more than a fleeting thought, but the idea of finding out whether in fact she had left or not grew quickly and he had acted before he had time to let mature consideration take over. He still wasn't quite sure what was making him do this, except that all at once, he'd felt that he'd spent too many years being cautious. He didn't want to go into middle age as a man who had never done what he wanted rather than what he ought. Recklessness had begun to have a certain appeal. He hadn't felt like this since he was a schoolboy. Still, here in the dark, on Prosser Street, hiding in the shadows, he couldn't help feeling he was a fool, and that he was going to live to regret his decision.

Beyond the main road, in contrast to the teeming streets he'd just left, he had passed into this relatively quiet area, disturbed only by the occasional passer-by on this cold and moonless night. A few of the gas lamps had escaped the vandalism of street urchins and still had some of their glass or mantles intact, but the yellow light they offered was insufficient and the spaces between were pools of black shadow. A seedy street, but better than what he'd left behind. One side of the once respectable but now run-down Prosser Street was a row of flat-faced, three-storey terraced houses with steps leading to the front doors, black iron railings guarding more steps to the basements. It was a short street with houses on one side and on the other an ornate yellow brick building that announced itself by a sign carved into the stone above the main door as the Municipal Baths and Wash House. It was into the dark, recessed doorway of the one marked 'Women' that David pressed himself while he made up his mind what to do. No sounds of Irish conviviality issued from the tall, thin house opposite on which his interest was focused, though there were lights in nearly all the windows and multiple shadows moved constantly behind the thin curtains on every floor. Those living there must be crammed in like herrings in a barrel.

Reluctant to cross the street, he stood for some time while an intermittent drizzle blew into his face. The almost eerie feeling about the street began to give him the creeps. What had possessed him to come here, what on earth did he hope to find? He had intended nothing more than knocking on the door of the house he sought and asking for Mona, but now that he was here, the idea was cut short at birth. She would think he was spying on her – and of course that's what he was doing, but only because he couldn't dismiss the persistently queasy feeling this whole business was giving him. He knew only too well he wasn't brave or cut out for this sort of thing, but if Latimer – and therefore Alice – was involved in something underhand, then he would have done much more.

He stood where he was for ten, fifteen, twenty minutes before finally beginning to admit the futility of his mission and was on the point of abandoning the whole project when something stopped him. As two men approached the house and then went down the area steps, he pressed even closer back into the doorway. In a few minutes, they were followed by others in ones and twos. All of them appeared to be working men, shabbily dressed. Seven or eight he counted. Then two more came.

If he hadn't already been pressed into the baths' doorway, he would have reeled back in shock at the sight of a man he had never, in a million years, expected to see there.

Twelve

Rain beating a tattoo on the windows woke Alice. After her meeting with David, she had slept better and this morning felt rested. Although she hadn't heard from him since then she had felt a distinctly encouraging lift to her spirits in knowing that she was no longer alone in worrying about Edmund. She'd had serious doubts about consulting him, but she was glad now that she'd done it. The name of that woman, Mona Reagan, wouldn't erase itself from the forefront of her mind, but now she had convinced herself that the connection with Edmund must be some easily explained triviality, though she didn't yet feel it was something she could approach him with.

The rain ceased abruptly, and immediately afterwards the sun came out, making sparkling diamonds of the raindrops on the window panes and sending sharp, reflected light into the room, April living up to its reputation. Should she risk a soaking by being caught in the showers while cycling to and from the Dorcas? Public transport from here was a tedious business, and summoning a cab to Spitalfields to bring her home always seemed like an affectation. She had learned not to excite comment from those who might wish to believe her voluntary work there was a form of condescension: if people got the idea you were lording it over them and patronizing them by offering free medical attention then trust would be lost. It would have to be Lowther. She sighed, but she would suffer him rather than forego her day at the clinic. Everyone seemed to think that carrying on with her duties at the Dorcas on a daily basis was admirable in the circumstances, when it was in fact therapeutic. Even at normal times, it was only there that she felt truly herself, something she rarely admitted but was always conscious of at some deeper level. Now, she was only too glad of it. Doing something useful and practical was always guaranteed to put things into perspective for Alice.

Half an hour later she was waiting inside the open front door for Lowther to bring the car from the old coach house round the back where it was garaged, but instead of the car appearing, it was

Lowther himself who came rushing into the hall, out of the door which led to the Martens' side of the house. She was aware of a commotion he'd left behind him as he almost shouted, 'The baby's back, Mrs Latimer, madam!'

'What?'

'There in her pram, just outside the back door, nice as ninepence!'

She rushed past him and into the room where breakfast had been laid out for Violet and Ferdie. Only Ferdie was there, half-dressed, in shirtsleeves and braces, his normally brilliantine-disciplined hair as yet unbrushed, looking as though he hadn't slept, as he always did nowadays. But he was transformed. He was pacing about, cradling the bundle that was Lucy in his arms as carefully as if she were a fragile piece of Edmund's Dresden china that might crumble into pieces if he did more than draw breath anywhere near her, almost as though by simply breathing his heartbeats might shatter her into pieces. The child lay still, deeply asleep, tightly cocooned in a shawl, only her sleeping face and her golden curls visible. She didn't wake, even when at that moment Violet flew into the room, her arms held out towards her child. It was a moment or two before Ferdie could be persuaded to surrender his precious daughter.

'Oh, my baby!' Violet held Lucy on her knee and sat staring, almost stunned with disbelief, at her calm, sleeping face, eyelashes fanned out on the cheeks,. But after a while she said, almost defiantly, 'You see, I told you she would come home to us, Ferdie.'

'So you did, Violet, so you did.' He cradled his baby's hands in his. 'And you were right, weren't you?' he added after a moment.

No one yet was asking why or how this miraculous return had been brought about. Alice thought that perhaps they were all, herself included, only too thankful that the waiting, watching, praying was over. It wasn't possible the ransom had been paid, since no instructions had been received for paying it. They had been waiting on tenterhooks to hear how and why this was to be carried out ever since the demand had arrived, but in fact there had been no further communication after that first one, nothing at all. Unlikely as it seemed, the kidnappers could only have had a change of heart.

The room, its silence undisturbed ten minutes ago save for the ticking of the mantel clock and the crackle of the newly lit fire as it got going for the day, was suddenly full of people, everyone talking once. Hewson, who'd been on her way with the breakfast bacon and sausages in a hot dish under a silver cloche, plonked it down on the sideboard and stayed where she was, struck dumb, her middle-aged legs apparently having lost the power of motion. Mrs Lowther was next into the room, exclaiming, followed by Emma, who ran over, beaming, to look at the sleeping child.

'Shall I put her in her cot, Mrs Martens, till she wakes up?'

'What? Oh no, Emma. Best to let her sleep here on my knee.'

It was Lowther who had first spotted the perambulator, on his way to get coal in for the kitchen range before driving Alice to the clinic. It had rained heavily during the night and the flagstones on which it stood were still wet, but the waterproof apron had been fastened tight, the hood raised and Lucy in her blanket was perfectly dry. She must have been left there earlier that morning. The wickerwork of the pram was not sodden as it would have been had it stood there all night.

Suddenly, Violet said, 'She's awfully pale, isn't she?' Her voice began to tremble. 'What have they been doing to you, Baby?'

'Nothing to worry about, I'm sure, ma'am,' Emma said soothingly, 'but maybe Doctor Latimer should take a look at her?'

Alarm sparked in Violet's eyes. 'Do you think so?' She looked up, all at once aware that Alice, who had been silently watching, consumed with delight but unwilling to interfere, was in the room, too. She held the baby jealously to her for a moment, but then she said, 'Of course, yes. Yes, Alice, please do.'

'I'm sure Emma's right, there's no cause for worry,' Alice replied, 'but I think I should check her over.'

Lucy was relinquished to her and she sat down with her on her lap. She still didn't wake, even when the cocooning shawl was removed and Alice began gently to undress her.

'*Look* at what she's wearing!' Violet exclaimed suddenly, but not with indignation for a Lucy clad in a plain flannel gown, bereft of all her usual, embroidered cotton flounces, rather was it annoyance at the sight of the little bracelet that had been clasped round her chubby wrist. For a moment, it looked as though she would have snatched it off, but at the sight of her peaceful child, she checked herself and gently eased off the offending object.

It was the sort of present, Alice saw, often given to baby girls at their christening, made to expand as the child grew, but still ridiculously big for Lucy. It would not have stayed on her wrist at all had it not been bent out of shape a little. It was obviously not new and had perhaps been worn by some other little girl. Maybe it was that which had caused Violet to show such extreme reaction towards an object there was no reason at all to dislike. It was quite pretty, a slender twisted design in silver, ornamented with a tiny cluster of leaves, enamelled in green. 'Don't you think it ought to be shown to the police?' she asked, as Violet thrust it into her pocket.

'Oh, there's no need for that. Well, yes, I suppose so, though what it will tell them I can't think. I'll give it to Inspector Gaines when I see him.'

'He'll be so happy to know Lucy's back,' Alice said.

'I'm sure,' Violet said carelessly.

'I'll let him know,' said Ferdie, but he made no immediate move.

'She's pale, and she must have been given something to make her sleep like this,' Alice was able to say after a gentle examination which still didn't wake Lucy. 'But she seems perfectly all right, Violet; she's clean, well fed and cared for. Quite unharmed and healthy. She's even sprouted another tooth. It's probably some sort of mild sedative she's been given, but it shouldn't harm her. Don't try and waken her, just let her sleep until she wakes naturally. If you like,' she added, 'I'll stay with her until she does.'

In fact, Lucy slept for another couple of hours, then woke, beamed round at everyone and immediately tried to sit up, crowing with delight over her disreputable rag doll that Emma gave her. Between them, Emma and her mother let her splash in her bath, powdered her, gave her some breakfast and dressed her once more in her rich-little-baby garments. It was a wonder to everyone, but she appeared to be quite unaffected by having been looked after by people she wasn't accustomed to. But who would know, with a baby who couldn't speak? Had she cried, sobbed for familiar faces and loving arms, for being left uncomforted by her nanny, who was (though Violet would not have liked to hear this) more important at this stage than a mother who only saw her once or twice a day? Was a baby of that age still young enough not to have known what was happening, too young to be afraid, too young to have felt abandoned by those who loved her? Lucy was a sunny-natured child who would go willingly into outstretched arms, respond to kindness. And that was, after all, the best hope they could cling to.

* * *

'Somebody must have paid up,' Inskip said, when the great news of the return of the Martens baby was relayed to Scotland Yard, to much jubilation from every man in the place. The awareness of what had been happening had had a sobering effect on everyone, from those who were husbands and fathers down to the youngest constable.

But it would seem not, as he and Gaines discovered when they arrived at Manessa House.

'You're sure no money was handed over?' Gaines asked.

'Absolutely not,' said Ferdie. He was predictably brimming over with *joie de vivre* at the return of his precious child. The days without Lucy had changed Ferdie Martens into a shadow of himself, someone scarcely recognizable, but he had magically reverted to his usual cheerful, optimistic self. Whereas Violet Martens looked bemused, slightly stunned with disbelief, as if unable to convince herself that present-day miracles did actually occur sometimes.

'And you say Lucy was simply left outside? No note, or any indication of why she'd been taken?'

'Nothing, Inspector, but we're not complaining,' Ferdie said buoyantly. He was not the only one who was happy. An altogether different atmosphere from their previous visits prevailed throughout the household. Lucy's homecoming had miraculously lifted the gloom and apprehension that had lain over it like a pall. 'Damned funny business if you ask me, but what does it matter? Don't suppose we'll ever know the truth, but I for one don't care, as long as she's unharmed, safe at home where she belongs.'

'It's over, and we can forget it,' Mrs Martens said.

It took Gaines' breath away, that she really seemed to believe that. Well, thankfully, it *was* over. If not in the way he wanted, with the culprit behind bars. He too should be feeling relieved that it was a happy outcome which left him free to concentrate on his other case, the murder of Lennie Croxton, where lack of progress was beginning to be worrying. But how and why the kidnapping had taken place at all still remained as much a mystery as ever and if her mother did not want to know the details, Gaines did. He couldn't be satisfied with such unfinished business. It was an anticlimax which left behind too many unanswered questions, and a nasty, if undeserved, feeling that they, the police, had been left wanting, the chief question being why had she been returned, without explanation, and the demand for money dropped. Yet the unlikely possibility persisted of Emil Martens having succumbed and paid the ransom, having taught his son that lesson he thought he deserved. 'There's no chance that the money was paid?' he asked.

'How could there be when we don't know who was demanding it? We've had no communication since that first note,' Ferdie reminded him.

It still made no sense. Maybe the whole operation had indeed been nothing more than a spiteful or malicious act, specifically designed simply to cause worry to the Martens, and not to gain money. That in itself was a nasty thought. The fact remained that the perpetrator had wasted valuable police time and resources, caused untold grief and agony, and they were no nearer finding out who that could possibly have been.

Yet if the intention to return Lucy had been there all along the ransom note had been pointless – although not if it had been sent by someone other than the kidnapper, someone who wished them ill taking the opportunity to frighten them. There were such people around, plenty who were sick enough to do even that. Gaines didn't think it wise to voice his thoughts, though the attitude of both parents, Ferdie's blithe disregard of the still unanswered questions and his wife's inability, or unwillingness, to face them, was oddly disconcerting, in a way he couldn't put his finger on.

Lucy herself, now bouncy and active in the arms of a cheerful Emma, who had already seen off two reporters and a press photographer wanting to take a picture of Lucy after the news of her homecoming had somehow already leaked out, was brought out for their inspection, together with the clothes she'd been dressed in on her return. These would be sent for forensic examination, but there was little hope of gaining anything from them. 'They're a poor exchange for the clothes she was wearing,' Violet roused herself to say, wrinkling her nose in distaste. 'I suppose they're clean enough, but I'm surprised she hasn't developed a rash, with that rough woollen vest next to her skin.'

'Where's the bracelet? I don't see it here.' Alice was putting the little garments together, ready to be parcelled up.

'What?' She looked vague. 'Oh yes, the bracelet. It had slipped my mind.'

'I think the inspector would like to have it, Violet.' Alice explained how the bracelet had been found on Lucy's arm when she was brought back, left there by whoever had been keeping her.

Without much interest Violet said she didn't see how it was going to be any help. 'It's only a cheap bauble, after all. To tell the truth, I don't know where I put it . . . I'm not actually sure I didn't put it with the rubbish to be thrown out.'

'If you would take the trouble to see if you can find it, Mrs Martens, I'd be grateful. It might prove useful.'

'Go and have a look for it, Violet,' Ferdie said quietly. She threw him a quick glance from under her eyelashes but, meeting his look, reluctantly left the room, giving no indication that she would be in any hurry to return.

Lucy became once more the centre of attention, loving it and giving out toothy beams and chuckles in return. Everyone wanted to pick her up and give her a cuddle. She was a bonny baby, the sort anyone would love, Gaines thought as he chucked her under the chin. Fat little hands like starfish reached up to grab his moustache.

Eventually Mrs Martens came back and handed over the bracelet. Gaines didn't think it worthy of her scorn, being neither tawdry nor cheap-looking to his eyes. Made of silver, it consisted of two narrow strands twisted together, delicate enough to have been flattened slightly out of shape, presumably to keep it on the baby's wrist, with a tiny central trefoil in green enamel decorating it.

'That's a St Patrick's symbol, a shamrock,' Alice pointed out. 'It was a christening gift, I should think. Little girls are often given something like this, or a silver locket, aren't they?'

Inskip said, 'St Patrick? It's Catholic, then, is it?'

'Not necessarily, but possibly,' Ferdie put in.

'I notice it wasn't listed among the items she was wearing when she was taken. You're sure she didn't have it on then?'

Gaines addressed the question to Emma, who shook her head, but it was the mother who answered. 'No,' she said, very sharply, and repeated her mantra. 'Why would I let my child ever wear a thing like that?'

There was obviously little more required of the police here. It was farewell to Manessa House and its occupants. Alice accompanied them out of the room when they were ready to go. Outside the door she paused, evidently wanting to say something, but seeming unusually hesitant. Making up her mind at last, she said, 'Inspector, may I speak with you both, if you could spare a few more moments?'

'Certainly.' He wondered what it was that couldn't be said in front of her in-laws as they followed her into what was evidently her own part of the house, where everything was in complete contrast to the apartments they had just quitted. Well kept, last-century solidity. Weighty, gleaming mahogany, stiff dining chairs, plush-covered sofas, heavy, gilt-framed pictures – although apart from rather too many of what looked like valuable pieces of porcelain, there was a merciful absence of Victorian knick-knacks, and only a few pictures and photographs. Gaines thought the furnishings unlikely to be due to Alice Latimer's personal taste, but rather to her husband's – or more likely, he amended on further reflection, that of his parents.

'I have something you might like to see. Please take a seat while I fetch it.'

Inskip, congenitally incapable of sitting unoccupied for more than a few minutes at a time, wandered around looking at the various photographs while she was out of the room. One photo in particular held his interest for several minutes. He picked it up to examine it more closely and was still looking at it with a puzzled frown when Alice returned, holding a small brown paper parcel. She raised her eyebrows when she saw him with the photograph in his hand.

'Forgive the liberty, Mrs Latimer. I was only wondering where I'd seen this man before. A fine-looking man. Funny, isn't it, but I have a feeling I might know him.'

Alice sat down and smiled. 'I don't think so. That's my father. He died some years ago and he never moved far from Herefordshire, where he lived most of his life, so it's unlikely you ever met. Do sit down, Sergeant.'

Inskip replaced the photograph and took his seat as she asked. But he was sure now. This man looked out of the frame with the same humorous regard as when he'd been captured standing at the edge of that other picture, smiling and watching those being snapped. He tried, without much success, not to let his excitement get the better of him and shrugged as if it was of no account. 'Maybe I was wrong then. But . . . do you by any chance know a young man by the name of Leonard Croxton?'

Surprised, Gaines frowned and shot him a warning glance but Inskip was fired up and couldn't have stopped now even if he had seen it, which he didn't. Seeing this, Gaines allowed him to carry on.

'It's not a name I recognize. Why do you ask?' Alice smoothed down her skirt. There was a vase of lilies on the window ledge. The warmth of the sun had brought out their perfume, heavy and cloying. 'Do you mind if I just move these? The scent's overpowering sometimes.' She moved the vase to a far corner of the room.

'You don't remember your Nurse Peg talking about him when you were attending to my face?' Inskip asked when she came back.

She said carefully, after thinking for a moment, 'Are you speaking of that poor man who was murdered?'

'Lennie Croxton, yes. And I have an idea, more than an idea I should say, that I *have* seen this man here – your father, you say he is – in another picture that was in Croxton's possession, taken when he was a child – himself, his mother and his sister in a garden. Can you explain that?'

She had gone pale. 'Well, I do have a photograph that sounds similar to that. It's in an album somewhere.' She waved a hand towards a built-in cupboard in one of the fireplace alcoves, but made no immediate move towards it.

'Perhaps we should see it.'

She hesitated, then went to the cupboard and brought back a velvet-covered photograph album. After turning the pages slowly, she at last came to the one she wanted. 'This is the one I'm thinking of, but there must be some mistake; it can't possibly be the same one as you say this man Lennie Croxton had. That's my father, there.'

'And who is the boy?'

'He's my cousin, Dudley Nichol.'

A minute elapsed, allowing Gaines to interpret Inskip's nod that this photograph was identical with the one Lennie Croxton had left behind. Somewhere in the house, the telephone gave a dozen rings, then was silent. Alice looked from one to the other.

Gaines said, 'It seems we'd better have a word with your cousin, then, if you can tell us where we can find him.'

'I would if I knew where he is. He was staying with us for a while until he left – quite suddenly, actually. He didn't leave a note explaining why and I suppose we probably should have reported it before, but he'd taken all his things. There was no reason to think—' Her voice betrayed her. She stood up abruptly and walked to the window, looking out until she gained control of herself.

Inskip again exchanged looks with Gaines and with an effort of will restrained himself from punching the air. Both of them recognized that this might very well be what they had been waiting for, another one of the pieces in the two enquiries that were all presently scattered around like bits of broken china. With a bit of luck, and more investigation, it could turn out to be the one key piece that enabled the others to fit together.

Alice at last turned away from the window and came to sit down again. 'I'm sorry. It's no use pretending, is it?' she said shakily. 'I think I've known ever since . . . since Nurse Peg mentioned the glasses he wore, and you said you'd found them. They were really awful, held together with sticky tape. I don't know where this man Croxton comes into it, but it's Dudley who is dead, isn't it?'

'It's flimsy evidence yet to draw firm conclusions on,' Gaines said, though he had no doubt she was right. 'To begin with, it would seem as though he might have been living in the district where you work, as Leonard Croxton. Either that, or Lennie Croxton was pretending to be your cousin.'

'No, that can't be so. He was my cousin Dudley, without any doubt. Even though I hadn't seen him for so long, I'm certain it was him. He had the Nichol nose, for one thing,' she said sadly. 'And he knew all about the family. I should have spoken to you before, but I kept telling myself it couldn't be true. Then today, you being here . . . well, that's why I brought this.' She waved towards the little parcel which was still on the small table where she'd put it, but she sat with her head bent, making no move to pick it up. Tears did not seem far away.

Inskip glanced at the photograph again. If they had needed further confirmation, the Nichol nose, now that she'd mentioned it, was evident in the profile of her father that was turned to the camera, the same rather beaky nose which had been the only distinctive feature on Croxton's otherwise unremarkable face.

'Mrs Latimer, could you give us a little more to go on?' Gaines said. 'You could start by telling us more about your cousin.'

'There isn't a lot I can tell you. I didn't know him well, in fact

I hadn't seen him since we were children. That photograph . . . it was taken at a family wedding and I believe that must have been the last time I saw him, until he came here unannounced several weeks ago. He stayed with us and then he packed up and left us, quite suddenly, without a word, for no apparent reason.' At last she reached out to the table for the parcel and unwrapped the brown paper to reveal a red leather prayer book, which she passed to Gaines. 'This is his missal, which he left behind when he went away. I kept thinking he would come back for it because his mother had given it to him and I know she meant a great deal to him. But he never did.'

Gaines opened the prayer book and read the inscription inside. '*First communion.* Was he by any chance Irish?'

'No. His father was my father's cousin. The Nichols are country folk from Herefordshire, farmers mostly, and solidly Protestant, all of them.'

'But with a Roman Catholic prayer book?'

'Well then, perhaps he was a Catholic. Maybe his mother was Irish. She may have been, I don't remember much about her. I was a child when I last saw her or my uncle, in fact I only ever met them or either of my cousins on family get-togethers such as that wedding where the photograph was taken. As I said, I don't think I ever saw Dudley again after that until he turned up here, nor Phoebe – his sister. She died young, of diphtheria, and their father had died before that.'

'I'm sorry, Mrs Latimer, but I'm afraid we may need to ask you to identify him as your cousin. It may be very upsetting for you.'

'You forget, I'm a doctor.'

'This is different. Someone close.'

'I've told you, we weren't close. It *is* upsetting, naturally, that he has died, especially so horribly. I suppose I'd grown fond of him in a way while he was with us, but I never really knew him.' She stopped, looking troubled. 'But I did blame myself when he left so suddenly. I thought I'd hurt him by showing my feelings all too clearly. You know what I mean – it's one thing to have a guest staying, but when it seems as though they're beginning to regard themselves as a fixture . . . I'm sorry I wasn't kinder.'

'Guests who outstay their welcome, I know . . . What brought him here in the first place?'

'To be truthful, I have no idea about that, either. I gathered that since his mother died, he'd been all over the place, trying various jobs – he wasn't qualified for anything, so he'd just taken what he could get – a bit of clerking here and there, and I think he'd once worked in a circus, though as what I can't imagine. He was actually quite intelligent, but full of wild ideas about what he might do – some day. I – we – were sorry for him. You couldn't help being, because he obviously hadn't two pennies to rub together and he was . . . without a rudder, as you might say. He was still a boy, I think, in many ways. He had no idea how to run his life. I had the impression his mother had been an extremely controlling person and he'd relied on her to tell him what to do next. But he worshipped her.'

'What was his mother's name?

'Her name?' The question surprised her. 'Oh, it was Mary. My Aunt Mary. I don't know what her maiden name was.'

'Did he ever mention a friend called O'Rourke? Daniel O'Rourke?' Inskip asked.

'No. If he had any friends at all he never spoke of them.'

'Or a man named Tooley?'

She shook her head. 'I'm sorry, I've never heard either name. Why do you ask?'

Gaines avoided a direct answer to that. 'It seems your cousin had been living as Leonard Croxton in the same area where you work, until he came to stay with you. We haven't discovered why he should have come here, but afterwards, he went back. Not much was known about him in the district although he attended the Catholic church – which is how your Nurse Peg knew him, but otherwise he seems to have kept to himself.'

He stood up ready to leave and held out the prayer book, but she hastily drew back. 'No, I don't want it. You must keep it.' He had let go of the book too soon and it fell to the floor between them.

Apologizing for his clumsiness, he bent to retrieve it, and picked up the now disintegrating pressed leaves which had fallen from between its pages. 'Looks like a four-leaved clover, or did once. Pity it didn't bring him luck.'

'No, I think they are probably shamrock leaves.'

Thirteen

It was barely eleven o'clock and yet the day had already been filled with so many happenings, Alice was left with a turmoil of emotions she could scarcely identify: joy mixed with perplexity at Lucy's return, the shocking news about Dudley, but most of all, incredulity on both counts. It was almost as though she had to reassure herself that the miracle which had brought Lucy back really had occurred and had not been a dream, she thought, finding herself telephoning the Dorcas, and afterwards feeling the same compulsion to call David Moresby. She told herself David would be as delighted as Sam Weston and the rest of the staff at the clinic had been to hear the good news, but she knew the real reason for her call was that it might act as a reminder that he hadn't yet given any indication of how his enquiries about the woman Mona Reagan were progressing. Having heard nothing from him, she had told herself briskly, several times, that her worries over Edmund had been exaggerated, her usual common sense had been overridden, that she was guilty of letting a very small molehill assume the proportions of a mountain. Edmund, after all, was more than capable of coping with the sort of problems that faced every man in his position from time to time. More so than most, in fact. Now that Lucy was safely home again, she ought to be able to stand back and see things in better perspective.

Which might have been possible, had it not been for what she'd learned about Dudley, now that what she had at first felt to be a minor anxiety about her missing cousin had turned into something so appalling she hadn't yet fully taken it in, even though she had been almost certain since that time at the clinic when Nurse Peg had spoken of him. Dudley, murdered! How truly awful. And she had an unaccountable, sinking premonition that worse was to come.

David heard what she had to say about Lucy and was predictably pleased. Then he said, 'I was about to send you a note. We should meet again, Alice.'

He sounded strange. The line, as so often, was not particularly good, but could that have been urgency she detected in his voice? 'You've found something.'

'I've *seen* something. Or someone rather, who might or might not be important . . . important to what we were talking about, I mean. I don't want to worry you, but I think we should talk. Not over the telephone, though. Are you free by any chance? If so, I could take a taxi and be with you within an hour . . . if that's agreeable to you?'

'I was on my way to the Dorcas but they're not expecting me after what's happened here so, yes, I'm free. But don't come to the house.'

'Of course.' His suggestion had been tentative and he didn't need her to explain what she meant, that his coming to see her might arouse unnecessary comment. 'Shall we meet in the same place as before?'

They arranged a time, and it was she who took the taxi there. The day had turned grey and sunless with a sharp breeze blowing from the river, and he immediately suggested walking further along. 'It's too cold to sit here for long. Let's find somewhere out of this wind. We can talk as we go.'

She agreed but he didn't seem anxious to start a conversation as they walked further along the Embankment. They met several well-dressed strangers on the way and she was conscious of not having changed from the clothes she had dressed in for a day at the clinic, a cream blouse under a plain dark blue barathea coat and skirt, decidedly not new, and hastily made apologies for it. 'This is my working garb.'

'No need for apologies,' he said with a smile. 'It suits you.'

She didn't think he was paying what she had previously, regrettably, called facile compliments. She knew instinctively that she looked better, and felt more at ease in the plainly cut costume, rather shabby as it was, than in the frivolous and expensive clothes demanded by the overdressed occasions where they usually met. At least her felt hat, though unadorned, was softened by a curving brim that she couldn't help knowing was becoming.

'I expected to see you full of smiles, Alice. What is it? Nothing about Lucy, I hope? Nothing gone wrong?' What he could see of her profile was pale and his heart misgave him at what he had to say to her.

'No, thank goodness. Nor likely to, with Ferdie watching over her like a guard dog. I doubt he'll be persuaded to let her out of his sight from now on.' She hesitated, then said quickly, 'I haven't yet told anyone else about this, not even Edmund, I haven't had the chance – but something else has happened – something quite dreadful. To my cousin, Dudley Nichol. You never met him. The police were there, at the house, because of Lucy, and I've just come from them. . . . David, he's been murdered.'

'What?'

'It's true, I'm afraid.' She was trying to speak calmly, but it was impossible to hide her agitation. They had walked rapidly and had reached a point where the curve of the Embankment shielded them a little more from the wind. It wasn't really a feasible proposition to talk properly while walking side by side and despite what he had said earlier about it being too cold to sit, he led her to a seat. There was a coffee and tea stall not far off. 'Wait here.' He left her sitting while he brought back two cups of tea. 'Brandy would have been better, but at least this is hot. It'll make you feel warmer.' It was scalding, and had sugar in it, which she never took, but she drank it gratefully, nonetheless.

'That better?' he asked presently.

'Thank you, yes.' What had happened in the last few hours had been more of a shock than she had admitted. As the hot, sweet tea began to do its work, she felt a return of energy and a grateful warmth in her hands where they had wrapped around the cup. Even the wind seemed less chilly. After he had returned the cups to the stall, she was able to tell him calmly enough what the police had told her about Dudley. He was a practised listener and let her go on without interruption until she'd finished.

'Good God,' he said quietly, 'it's worse than I thought.'

Alarm flashed across her face. 'Worse – whatever can you mean?'

'I'm sorry, I didn't mean to scare you. That's dreadful news for you, about your cousin. But you say this policeman asked about a man named Tooley?'

'Yes, and someone named O'Rourke.'

'I don't know about any O'Rourke, but Tooley—' He fell silent for a while, as if bracing himself for what he had to say. 'It's either a very great coincidence or— Well, here goes. Last night, there was a meeting at the house where Tooley lives. That's what I wanted to tell you. I was there – not at the meeting, but I watched people arriving.'

'What? Where was this? You mean this Tooley is that "someone" you said might be important?'

'No, that was . . . another man.'

'Another? You're being terribly mysterious.'

He knew he was mysterious and without doubt annoying. 'Alice, please listen. I can't tell you who this man was for very good reasons. For your own sake, and for his, we must not, I think, probe too deeply into Edmund's affairs.'

She grew very still. 'I think that requires some explanation.'

'Oh Lord, yes, it does. But I believe, when you've heard what I have to say, you'll agree with me.'

For there was no other way, after all, than to tell her, right from the beginning, how and why he had found himself in Prosser Street. It was a lame story, no one knew that better than he, and the cloak and dagger methods he'd used seemed rather more ridiculous now than they had even then – and even dangerous in view of what he now knew. He had to make her believe how serious this was and that, on reflection, made him change his mind about not telling her who it was he'd seen going into the house. She was incredulous.

'But I know him, at least I've met him. I would hardly have associated him with people of that sort. He's rich, and clever and . . . What was he doing there?'

'Alice, Erskine Childers makes no secret of where his sympathies lie. He's a decent and mild-mannered individual, but it would be naïve to rely on that. There are those who even believe him to be dangerous – simply because he's capable of stirring up the same strong feelings he has himself. He isn't troubling to hide the fact that his opinions are becoming more radical. He's been addressing meetings all over the place, trying to drum up support, though with varying degrees of success. And I suppose a house like Tooley's is no better or worse than a draughty meeting hall with half a dozen in the audience.'

It shouldn't have occasioned surprise that Childers should present himself at what had seemed to David to be a meeting of ordinary working men. He took his opportunities where he could and spoke to anyone who was prepared to listen to his impassioned pleas, to gain support where he could for his idealistic and single-minded commitment to self-government for the Irish, addressing meetings and going so far as to state that anyone who was not for Ireland being ruled solely by the Irish was, in his own words, 'against the light'. Indeed, he had resigned his lucrative and prestigious appointment in the House of Commons to work for the Irish cause. He continued to write his books – though there had been no more best-selling spy novels – and in his most recent publication he had drawn up what he saw as a reasoned framework for how Irish self-government could be achieved, not by coercion, repression or violence, but by peaceful means and compromise. If Ireland was disorderly and retrograde, he had demanded, how could she deserve freedom? He cited the great Daniel O'Connell on achieving religious freedom for the Catholics without resorting to the gun or the sword. Why should the two opposing sides not similarly reach an agreement on self-government?

Such moderation didn't satisfy everyone. Even here in England the belief was growing among those with Irish connections or sympathies – with the width of the Irish Sea to protect them – that aggression was the only answer. Both sides were well on the way to resisting opposition to their views by force of arms. Committees here were being set up to raise funds, but it was difficult to find someone with enough money and who was willing to fund any of the large-scale operations envisaged. Childers was rich, and his own advocacy of diplomacy as the only way to achieve a solution was reputedly wavering. So how far would his passionate belief in Home Rule take him? How far had it already taken him?

David thought it unlikely, however, that the meeting in Tooley's basement could be for raising funds, and even more unlikely that an astute politician like Edmund would jeopardize his career by getting himself involved in anything so damaging. And yet . . . how to account for Mona Reagan, whose warning had taken him to Tooley's house? That whole business was beginning to look more ominous than he had first been willing to own.

He could see that Alice was stunned by what was being uncovered, and struggling to see where, if anywhere, Edmund fitted into the pattern. He said, 'Alice, my dear, the best piece of advice I can give you is to leave this alone.'

She found herself unable to answer for a moment. 'This is my husband we're talking about,' she said eventually, and her voice was cold. 'How can you believe I would do that?'

Was she trying to believe it was her duty, or was that simply wishful thinking on his part to think she was? It scarcely mattered. She would continue to be a loyal wife, come what may . . . until, or if ever, she heard about Connie Fiore. That might be a different matter.

He turned to face the river, giving himself time to think. The wind lifted his hat but he grabbed it in time and kept it in his hand. 'It's a matter of trust, Alice,' he said quietly, turning round to face her, still holding his hat, his hair ruffled. 'I must ask you to trust me. We don't know that this has anything to do with Edmund at all, or Mona Reagan, come to that, except that she lives – or lived until recently – at that house, with other Irish expatriates.'

'This man . . . this Tooley. Why did Inspector Gaines ask me about him when he told me what had happened to Dudley? What has Dudley to do with what you've just told me?'

'I don't know, but that's out of our hands. No, listen, Alice, please! None of this is a game for amateurs, believe me.' He gave his words all the seriousness he could. That impulsiveness of hers, though he had always thought it somewhat endearing, was less so when he thought of how easily it might plunge them both into disaster. At this moment, however, she was also very angry, and with him, that he should dare to suggest she must not dabble in Edmund's concerns. He could understand it, but she really shouldn't. 'Whatever it is you think may be bothering your husband, by interfering in things you don't understand you could make everything worse.'

'Things I don't understand? Interfering? I'm sorry I asked you.' She stood up and began to walk away.

He followed her and put his hand on her shoulder to turn her to face him. 'Don't let us part in anger, Alice.'

She stood where she was, frozen. 'As you rightly observe . . . I don't understand.' He opened his mouth to answer but she said, 'No, don't say anything else.' She backed away, then began toying with her gloves. At last she sighed. He saw himself reflected through her eyes: uncertain, hatless, and with his hair ruffled. Feeling utterly at a loss. 'I'm sorry. That was uncalled for on my part, David. I know you only mean well.'

He almost choked. Was this what his desire to protect her amounted to – Alice feeling that he 'meant well'?

'What I'm trying to say is that I was wrong. You are in a far better position to know about these things than I shall ever be. I can see I don't have any option but to do as you advise.'

That was not how he wanted her to see it. He didn't want the reason she was agreeing with him to be simply because she had no alternative. But the implications of what might be happening lay heavily on him. Latimer must be into something suspect, otherwise Mona Reagan's warning made no sense. He didn't know her at all, of course, but by what he had seen of her he didn't believe she would have found that an easy thing to do. Yet Latimer, and what happened to him, was surely nothing to her – so why had she felt compelled to say what she had? Perhaps, he tried to tell himself, it had been a kindly gesture on her part towards David himself, knowing how closely he and Latimer worked together – on the principle that mud sticks. He singularly failed to convince himself of this.

Whatever was at the bottom of it all, he had no intention of letting his dislike of Latimer and what had passed between himself and Alice about him cloud his judgement. For one thing, he did not believe Latimer, in any capacity, would do anything he had reason to be ashamed of and like Alice, he could not seriously believe he was being blackmailed over his niece's kidnapping. On the other hand, he thought it quite possible he was being black-mailed over *something*. Unlike Alice, he was in a position to make a calculated guess as to what that was.

'Should the police not know of what you saw?' she asked suddenly.

'There's no point telling them what they probably know already . . . and there's nothing illegal in what I witnessed.' If the police were brought into this, they would want to know why he was there, and that would mean explanations involving Latimer which might bring unwanted attention and even suspicions on him, and for every reason he could think of that was something he was loath to do. 'I'm not going to fob you off. Edmund may well have good reason to be worried, although one thing I am sure of: if he is, it's for some simple and rational reason. I promise I will let you know what I can find out by the end of the week. By then it will prob-ably have all blown over. But Alice—' He hesitated. 'Whatever comes of it, remember, you are a strong woman. Hold on to that. And you are not alone, my dear.'

Inskip made it in his way to go to the Nag at a time early enough in the morning to feel there was less chance of the free-fisted clientele he had previously encountered having made their way there. When he pushed open the door, apart from the landlord, who was damp-mopping the tiled floor and not looking happy about it, the public bar was empty. The doors and windows were wide open but the place still reeked of the previous day's beer fumes and tobacco smoke.

'The woman's taken sick with the flu,' Corrigan explained when he saw him and added sourly, 'Or too many free drinks in her last night . . . "*Have one on me, Maureen. Well, I don't mind if I do!*" And now me having to mop me own floors, for God's sake. All right, what can I do for you?'

'Anything for me on O'Rourke yet?'

Corrigan squeezed the mop out for the last time and propped it against the bar. 'Sit down and take a drink.' He waved to a scrubbed-top table. 'Mind how you go, the floor's still wet. What'll you have?'

'Too early for me, Michael. I've only just finished my breakfast.'

It was never too early for an Irishman, but Corrigan himself was abstemious and Inskip waited while he went out to the back, returned with a teapot and joined him at the table. The landlord had quickly recovered his usual good temper but he was serious when he pushed across the sugar and said, after a minute, 'That murder, that's what all this amounts to, right? That young fella, the young chap that lodged with Mrs Maclusky, with your Auntie Orla. It's what you'll be wanting O'Rourke for?'

'It is. What have you to tell me about him, Michael? O'Rourke, I mean, though maybe you knew Lennie Croxton as well?'

'Never laid eyes on him. He didn't come in here. O'Rourke? The word is, he's away back to Dublin.'

'Back to Dublin? Is that right?'

Corrigan shrugged, then got up and closed the nearest window, as if there might be some eavesdropper lurking outside. He came back and sat silent, drumming his fingers on the table top until at last he spoke. 'Believe that. But if you want to know more, take yourself to Kindler Street at nine o'clock tonight. There's a woman, Shelagh Quinn, she'll meet you there.'

'Kindler Street, huh? And how will I know her?'

'She says she saw you once, when you were looking for Tooley. And it would be hard to miss a woman of the likes of Shelagh. She has hair the colour o' them ox-blood tiles on the bar and a manner of looking at you that you wouldn't mistake.'

Kindler Street was notoriously well known in more ways than one and Inskip had no difficulty in imagining the bold-faced redhead he'd seen leaving Tooley's house would not be out of place there. It was a pity, he thought, that it wasn't going to be the dark-haired one with the white skin he'd be meeting.

'The church of Our Lady, inside,' added Corrigan. 'She's a regular communicant.'

'Oh,' said Inskip, adjusting his uncharitable thoughts somewhat.

It was going to be a nasty night. He turned up his collar and headed into the drizzle, towards Kindler Street and the church of Our Lady. As he pushed open the heavy door, he was taken back to his younger days by the familiar, lingering aftermath of incense, a dimly lit interior and the red light of the sanctuary lamp winking near the altar. As his eyes adjusted to the dimness, he saw she was already there, kneeling in one of the pews near the back. He took his time, brushing off what rain he could from his jacket, blessing himself with holy water, and afterwards obeying an old instinct that rather took him by surprise, to light a candle and offer up a prayer of thanks for the safe return of little Lucy.

She must have heard him come in, but he had slipped into the pew and sat beside her for several minutes before she finished her prayers and sat back. It was only then that he saw she was not the redhead he was looking for, but a young woman with white skin and blue-black curls escaping from under her hat. She was respectably clad in a dark coat and skirt, her gloved hands held a prayer book and the face she turned to him was serious and unsmiling.

'I'm sorry to disturb you. I seem to have made a mistake. I was looking for someone else.'

'No, you have the right person. Shelagh Quinn, she's changed her mind so I've come in her place. I'm Mona Reagan.'

'We've already met, briefly, Miss Reagan, haven't we?' He gave her his name.

'Yes, I remember you, Sergeant. You were looking for Paddy Tooley.'

'I wanted a word with him, but it was Daniel O'Rourke I was looking for. I think there's something you want to tell me about him?' The church was empty, except for themselves, but she looked round nervously. 'O'Rourke?' he prompted. 'We're anxious to talk to him, Miss Reagan.'

'Mona,' she said with a little smile, something more like the laughing girl with the disobedient umbrella, but it was soon gone. 'I don't know where you'd find him. He comes and goes.'

'I did hear he's back in Dublin. But I'm thinking maybe that's just a rumour, and he's really still in London?'

She shrugged. 'Maybe he is, but I don't know where.'

'You might make an educated guess, I suppose?'

'I might, but I won't. I value my own skin too much.' She kept her voice lowered. 'I'd tell you if I knew.'

If she wasn't going to talk, why had she agreed to meet him here? He kept a hold on his patience, trying to believe her, though the way she'd answered, he knew she wasn't telling the truth. He decided to change tack. 'Miss Reagan – Mona, what can you tell me about Lennie Croxton?'

'Lennie who? And who might that be?' She was unconvincing. Her hands tightened on the prayer book she was still holding.

'He was that young fellow who was knifed in a taxi, you must have heard about it, and the person who's in the frame for it is O'Rourke.' He was taking a chance, telling her that, but he thought it might shock her into an admission. He had underestimated her stubbornness, though – or was it fear that was stopping her? She still didn't reply, so he said, 'It's guns, isn't it? That's what it's all about?'

'Shhh, not so loud!' Again she darted a scared look back over her shoulder, but she didn't deny it. Then, gaining confidence, she said, 'And where would he get the money for that, the likes of O'Rourke?' She'd been nervous before, but not now: the scorn in her voice would have scalded the skin off a rhinoceros. He wondered what Daniel O'Rourke had done to her.

It had always been on the cards, inevitable perhaps, as soon as

O'Rourke with his recent Irish connections had entered the scene, that guns were at the bottom of it. It would have taken something like that to bring him back to England, where he faced consequences from more than one source for his past misdeeds. Given what he was, it wouldn't have taken him long to find his place in Ireland when he'd fled England and arrived over there. If you wanted trouble, you didn't have to look far. And trouble there was aplenty by way of the bad boyos who were prepared to do anything they thought necessary to those they considered the enemies of Home Rule, that miracle which, if it ever came into force, was going to change everyone's lives for the better. But for what they needed to do, it was vital they had weapons to replace the spades, shovels and pickaxes which was pretty much all they could muster at the moment. And before that, needless to say, the money to buy them. Machine guns were what they needed most, and in quantity, to buy from abroad, and for that money was needed.

She was right in saying that raising funds was hardly in O'Rourke's line, but getting hold of at least some of the guns the insurgents were so desperately short of wouldn't be beyond his capabilities. Not the machine guns, that would be beyond him . . . but nothing was despised. One here, another there, anything was welcomed. No matter what sort – shotguns, rifles, pistols, revolvers. Old souvenirs from the Boer War that might explode in your face if you tried to fire them, anything. Stolen, bought for a song, donated by those who mistakenly sympathized. Pathetic, in view of what was needed, but all grist to the mill. A scenario that fitted O'Rourke like a glove, but he still couldn't figure out where Lennie Croxton/ Dudley Nichol came into it.

'So what is it you have to tell me, Mona?' This was getting nowhere and he was growing restive.

The door opened and three elderly women entered, bringing a draught with them. She bent her head as they presently walked towards the altar, bestowing curious glances on the pew where they were sitting. One of them carried a bunch of flowers and when they reached the front, they sat together in a row.

'They've come for a vigil,' Mona whispered. Belatedly, he saw a draped coffin and more funeral flowers at the foot of the chancel steps. 'There'll be more coming . . . and I think they recognized me. I have to go. I'm sorry, it wasn't my idea to come here and I should never have agreed to it, it was a mistake.'

What had made her change her mind? Not just the three old women, surely? Had he unwittingly said the wrong thing, or not asked the right question soon enough? Whatever it was, he cursed himself for having alarmed her into having second thoughts, but this environment was in any case scarcely conducive to getting the sort of confession he wanted from her. 'Let me take you somewhere we can get a cup of tea and talk more comfortably.'

She wasn't listening. She had taken fright and stood up ready to flee, and he had no option but to remove himself from the pew and stand aside so that she could leave. He followed her hurrying figure outside and for a moment she turned to face him. 'You need to look further than O'Rourke,' she said breathlessly. He put out a hand to detain her, but she pulled away, broke into a run and left him standing looking after her in frustration.

It was lunch time and the pie-and-mash shop was busy, full of hungry customers. It was a good place for a talk, a place with high-sided booths where you could have a private conversation. Moreover, it had a licence to serve ale.

'So O'Rourke's still in London?' said Gaines, as a harassed waiter left after dumping their food anyhow on the tiled table. Inskip pushed Gaines' abstemious shandy towards him, his grimace making it obvious what he thought of it. How could he drink the stuff? Lemonade spoiled, and an insult to good beer. A pint of it! Inskip himself had a half of mild, the best thirst quencher he knew, and a plate of jellied eels. Gaines saw him looking, raised his glass and smiled slightly.

'I would say the bastard's still here, though Mona Reagan wouldn't. Or couldn't.'

'Tell me exactly what she said.'

'She'd braced herself to tell, but suddenly she got scared, wouldn't say yes or no, though I'd bet my last tanner she knows, right enough. She could have saved me going out in the rain last night. The only thing I got from her was to tell me to look further than O'Rourke.'

Gaines cut his pie into eight precise portions and ate one of them with a forkful of mash. 'I'm not happy about that. Look further, where? And who for?'

'I'm not over the moon about it, myself. It's O'Rourke we want. He's committed murder, so who else should we be looking for?' In his own mind there'd never been room for any doubts whatever on that score. It was clear as crystal to him they'd have to look no further for Nichol's murderer than O'Rourke – when they eventually caught up with him, which he had to believe they would, sooner or later. The odds were stacked against it being anyone else. He had no problem with believing it and said so at length.

Gaines allowed him to continue in full flow while he sopped up the green parsley-and-eel liquor that had come with his pie. He put down his knife and fork and rested a long, speculative gaze on Inskip. Then he said steadily, 'Just you hold on a minute and listen to me. Has it ever occurred to you that you're letting this get out of hand?'

He hadn't raised his voice and had it come from anyone else, Inskip wouldn't have paid it any attention, but coming from Gaines, who rarely spoke heatedly and never pulled rank, it silenced him, momentarily at least. Yesterday, when he'd judged the time right, he'd made a clean breast of it to Gaines – not to tell him how he felt about O'Rourke, or what his feelings towards Cathleen had been, but to give him the facts of what had happened to make him scarper off to Ireland or wherever he'd been holed up since. Looking at Gaines' face as he spoke, he realized why he hadn't told him the whole of it in the first place, and now wished he hadn't mentioned it at all. The old devil had guessed he still hadn't been told the whole story – and then no doubt he'd done some digging afterwards and found out a bit more on his own account. 'It's time you remembered that you can't afford to let your feelings get the better of you in this job. You may have a personal score to settle with O'Rourke, but – just forget it, Sergeant. Forget it. Is that clear?'

'I was just saying, sir.'

Inskip braced himself for more. But Gaines was never one to labour a point. 'All right, Joseph.' Having delivered himself of what he had to say, he changed the conversation. 'Well, never mind Mona Reagan for the moment. Let's go back to what Mrs Latimer told us yesterday about that cousin of hers, Dudley Nichol, and why the devil he was calling himself Lennie Croxton and living as your aunt's lodger.'

'Or vice versa, as you pointed out.'

'Oh, I shouldn't think there was any doubt about him being her cousin. What I do question is why he arrived there at Manessa House without warning and then disappeared just before the baby's kidnapped.'

'Coincidence?' Inskip said doubtfully.

'If such a thing exists. There's always a rational explanation, if you can find it.'

'Which we haven't done yet.'

Gaines put down his knife and fork again, and began to lay out facts as if he were dealing out Patience cards, slapping his hand on the table with each one. 'Nichol mysteriously leaves the Latimers, as mysteriously as he'd come into their lives. Next it's the baby who disappears. An outrageous ransom is demanded. Nothing is forthcoming, but no further demands are made . . . and then she's returned, unhurt. With no explanation. Why?'

'The kidnappers got cold feet when they realized there was going to be no cash?'

'How did they know that? As I've said, no further communication.'

Silence for a while. Inskip watched while a tingalary man wheeled his machine up to the window outside and wound it up, hopeful that its jangling tune wouldn't be lost in the noise outside. No one seemed to be taking much notice of his music. 'Because the person asking for it no longer needed the money,' he said. 'Because Dudley Nichol was dead. But he died before she was taken.'

'Right. Then who did take her? And who has been looking after her? Someone who didn't expect Nichol to be killed and didn't rightly know how to deal with the situation when he was?'

Silence fell between them again as they thought it over, until Gaines said, after polishing off what was left of his pie and pushing his plate away, 'Wouldn't you have thought someone in that family, at some point, might have made a connection between this chap who'd been living in the same house with them for weeks disappearing from their lives like a puff of smoke, and the baby's disappearance the very day after?'

'Mrs Latimer? Nothing much escapes her, I'd say, but maybe it was just a bit too hard to credit, especially if he had as little get-up-and-go as she seemed to think.'

'Possibly, possibly. He was her cousin, after all, but there's a lot that worries me there, too. Like why she didn't report him missing earlier.'

Inskip took a drink. Wiped the froth from his lips. 'What she said – she only started to make connections when the baby came back, and that's why she decided she ought to tell us.'

'And what about Edmund Latimer, hmm? Where does he come into this? After all the fuss he created at the beginning, he's been mysteriously quiet since then.'

'I expect he's had other things to distract him. All this Irish business and so on. Anyway, we ruled him out from the start for obvious reasons, being so busy and all that.'

'Too busy to be distracted from his supposedly adored niece's disappearance? I doubt if it works like that with politicians. They're used to juggling those sort of problems. Keeping the homes fires burning with the other eye on their careers. A bit like policemen. But let's not forget that Nichol had Irish connections, and Latimer is very much in the thick of Irish politics at the moment.'

'It wasn't him that received any ransom demands.'

'We don't know that he didn't. Do as we say . . . or else. Political blackmail.' But he sighed. 'What the devil's going on, Inskip? Blessed if *I* know.' He sat silently for some time, then pulled the silver bracelet from his pocket, where it had resided ever since it had been tested for fingerprints, none of which had shown up, apart from those of Violet Martens.

'Pretty little thing, isn't it?' he said, looking at it lying on his palm.

'Yes, but what has it to do with anything?'

'I wonder why Mrs Martens took such exception to it?'

'Easy. She wouldn't take to the idea of her daughter wearing something second-hand, would she? And it's obviously not new.'

'What do you make of her?'

'Violet Martens? Oh, half the size of a walnut and twice as hard, as my old Nana used to say.'

Gaines laughed. 'And Ferdie Martens?

Inskip shrugged and spread his hands eloquently. Gaines signalled for the bill. The café noises went on around them and the tingalary man, who didn't seem to be getting much custom, finished his latest tune and moved on while they waited.

As Gaines pushed away his plate, ready to leave, and fumbled in his trouser pocket for a tip, Inskip blurted, 'Sir. What you said.

About O'Rourke – and me. I'll admit I can't abide him' *(I hate his guts was what he would have liked to say)* '– it goes back a long way, but I won't let it get in the way.'

He was met with a steady look. 'Right. Mind you keep to that. You could be in this job a long time yet. Don't go ruining your chances.'

He put a sixpence on the table, finished his shandy with every appearance of enjoyment, wiped his moustache and stood up. His glance fell on Inskip's plate where nothing of the jellied eels remained except a bit of central bone and a few tiny, pathetic ones, swimming in vinegar. 'Strewth, that looks disgusting.'

Inskip grinned. All right. Maybe the boss was entitled to a bit of a dig, after the look Inskip had directed at his shandy.

Part Four

Fourteen

It was a classic, the victim's body slumped across the desk in his own study, blood pooling under his head, one arm dangling and the gun dropped from his lifeless hand on to the carpet. A suicide note under the other hand, arm stretched across the desk.

The only surprise was that this particular suicide was that of the Right Honourable Edmund Latimer, MP.

After twenty years in the Force Gaines was not easily taken aback, but the last person he would have expected to take this step was Latimer, a successful and respected man at the height of his career, a man tipped for even higher office. He stood by while the police doctor examined the body (it was Fenton, the same man who had been called to the scene of Dudley Nichol's murder), waiting for what he had to say, though there were going to be no more surprises. Apart from why Latimer should have done it at all.

Why? Always the first question to be asked. Money troubles? Secret gambling, women? Unorthodox sexual proclivities that left him open to blackmail? Anything was possible, but there was no point in speculating. They would know soon enough, directly the body had been removed and they had that note in their hands.

Gaines had seen too many suicides for comfort, from every spectrum of society. Members of the church where he was a deacon were inclined to regard what they termed self-murder to be an unpardonable sin against the Almighty. He thought it might cause them to have another think if they ever had to look into the desperate lives, as he did, of those who'd removed themselves from an intolerable existence the like of which more fortunate people had never dreamed. Gaines had never found anything to blame those despairing souls for, and he hoped and prayed the Almighty felt the same. But he could not, as a rule, find it in himself to waste much sympathy on folks like Edmund Latimer, those who took a cowardly decision that left others to deal with the chaos they left behind. For them, Gaines couldn't help feeling, there must always have been another way out of their difficulties, which were invariably the result of their own actions. Money and influence had the effect of providing escape from almost anything.

'All right, he can be moved. Dead about eight hours, to save you asking. I'll give you more details after the post mortem but for now, the bullet went in here' – the doctor indicated a small round hole in the right temple – 'and exited behind his left ear.' He stood back, carefully avoiding the desk lamp which had toppled on to the floor, and removed his rubber gloves, looked around and sadly shook his head. 'Lord, what a shambles these poor devils leave!'

There would be no difficulty in finding the bullet. It had smashed into a small, heavily framed black-and-white etching, the subject of which was now indistinguishable, and gone straight through into the wall behind, leaving a scattering of glass on the polished floor surrounding the carpet below and a sloppy mess of blood and brains along the way.

'Thank you, Doctor.' He turned to Inskip, who had just re-entered the room after speaking to the staff. 'Where's Mrs Latimer? She found him herself, I understand. I'd like to have a word with her – if she's in any fit state to talk.'

Fenton looked up from reassembling his medical bag, eyebrows raised. 'I'm acquainted with Doctor Latimer, and I think it's unlikely,' he said dryly, 'that she'll have gone to pieces.'

'No, of course. You're right, I daresay she won't.'

'She's in her sitting room, sir,' Inskip said. 'With Mrs Martens and her husband.'

Not good news, that. Dealing with Violet Martens' histrionics again wasn't a prospect Gaines relished, but she had after all been the dead man's sister. He braced himself for the encounter.

When the call had come in and been reported to the detective superintendent, the name of Edmund Latimer had immediately set alarm bells ringing in Renshaw's head. A senior politician committing suicide was enough trouble on its own, but coming on top of the kidnapping Latimer had made such a fuss about, plus the further revelation that the chap in the ongoing taxi-cab murder investigation was actually the cousin of Mrs Latimer, Renshaw's nose had begun to twitch in alarm. Of course, this sort of thing happened all the time: misfortune was no respecter of persons and some families seemed destined to suffer one tragedy after another, but in this instance, it needed handling with kid gloves.

He had no difficulty in shying away from responding personally to the call, despite its high profile. A man with greying hair, nearing retirement, he was a respected and experienced senior officer, stolid and unimaginative, and one of the few who didn't object to the desk work that inevitably came with promotion. Most people thought that was all to the good. He'd been right enough in his day as a hands-on copper, but that day was long gone and it had to be said, he was in fact better as an administrator than he'd ever been as a detective. It didn't take him long to choose Gaines, along with his able sergeant, two of his best officers, but more importantly who were already only too familiar with Manessa House and its occupants. 'Tread softly on this one,' he'd warned. 'Going to be a hot potato, so don't put a foot wrong,' he'd added, never one to despise a mixed metaphor.

Violet Martens was not with her husband and Mrs Latimer, though someone else was. A well-brushed, well-dressed, correct and polite young man who was introduced as David Moresby, a colleague of Edmund Latimer's, a fellow MP who had worked closely with him. They were all standing up, like people after a funeral, not knowing what to say. Alice, by the fireplace, was white and shocked, but she was in control of herself. She hadn't taken it in yet, Gaines thought. Not fully. When she did, that was when it would begin to hurt.

Martens stood by the window, looking out, his hands clasped behind his back, but he turned round when Gaines and Inskip entered. He looked appalled at what had happened. Then he found his voice in order to make murmured apologies for his wife's absence. Didn't feel well . . . all this, you know . . . given her a headache. 'She's gone to lie down with an aspirin,' he finished, looking mightily as though he would like to do the same.

There was likely to be little help for Alice from that quarter. 'You don't need to stay, sir. We can see you both later, if necessary.'

Ferdie threw a wavering glance at Alice. 'Yes, Ferdie, you go to Violet. She needs you.'

For a second or two he stood, indecisive. Then, 'Not as much as you might think, Alice,' he said, and with a quick kiss on her cheek, he left the room. Gaines threw a sharp look after him. Not for the first time, it struck him that Ferdinand Martens might sometimes have more oil in his lamp than he was given credit for.

Alice, too, watched him make his escape. Good-hearted, easy-going Ferdie, red-faced at any show of emotion, who nevertheless had managed to cast embarrassment to one side and given her a warm, if brief, embrace – but now, as usual, didn't know how to react to a difficult situation. Violet hadn't been any use at all, either. But she was suffering her own misery over the brother who had, because of the disparity in their ages, been more like a father to her.

'This is very distressing for you, Mrs Latimer, for you all, but—' Gaines spoke briefly of what was to happen next. 'We don't have to trouble you at the moment. We'll need to talk to you later, of course, there will be questions asked at the inquest and you might like to be prepared—'

But Alice wanted to talk now. She indicated seats to the others and took one herself on the sofa. The horror of what she'd seen and found when she had gone into Edmund's study that morning would be with her for the rest of her life, she knew, crouched, ready to spring at any time, but for now she had to face whatever needed to be faced. Pushing it into one of those mental compartments labelled 'later', locking it away, wasn't going to help this time. 'Please, anything you want to know . . .' She followed his glance. 'There's nothing I want to keep secret from Mr Moresby.'

Moresby had half-risen to leave when Gaines had spoken, but now, after exchanging a look with Alice, he sat back again, crossing one elegantly trousered leg over the other, assuming a detached expression which didn't lessen the impression Gaines had, that he would not allow much to escape him.

'If you're sure you want to go on? Then perhaps you should see this letter. I'm afraid it may be rather painful.'

Alice looked at the single sheet of paper held out to her. Before he told her where it had been found, she knew what it was and instinctively she shrank. But she took a breath and accepted it.

She hadn't noticed this, or didn't recall seeing it, when she had opened the study door and seen Edmund slumped across the desk. Her only memory of that moment was fixed, static: Edmund, indubitably, unquestionably dead. Blood. White shirt. Head resting on the desk as if he were asleep. Hair falling forward and a bald spot on his crown that she'd never noticed before. More blood, and worse. No screaming from her, only an inability to move, a red mist swirling in front of her eyes. After that, she only remembered Hewson, dear, kind old Hewson, her own body trembling as she led Alice away.

She held on to the letter as Gaines put questions she might have anticipated, had she been in any condition to think that far ahead. Had she heard the gunshot or any other disturbance during the night? How had her husband seemed yesterday? What had been his state of mind lately? Perhaps he had been in financial difficulties? Had he ever given any indications that he might do this sort of thing?

She shook her head. 'Of course not, no to all of that.' But she hesitated, glanced quickly at Moresby and then away again. 'Though Edmund – well, he hasn't been quite himself, I suppose, for some little time. I can't be more specific than that – but I never imagined it was anything as bad as this. Nor did I ever dream he had a gun.'

A gun. So absolutely unlike Edmund, just another part of this terrible, unanswerable situation. Edmund, shooting himself! Her resolution to carry on almost faltered. She had seen death many, many times, in most of its manifestations, but never like that. She had comforted relatives, helped them to find reserves of strength. But when it happened to yourself, she now found, it was overwhelmingly different. How was it she had never realized this before?

She hadn't been aware of David getting up and crossing the room, but he must have done, because he was now sitting on the sofa close to her, his hand a brief touch on her arm, the warmth of his body communicating itself to her.

The inspector was speaking. 'If you feel able, Mrs Latimer, perhaps you would read the letter? Or I can leave it with you if you would rather, and discuss it later.'

'No, I'm quite all right.' And she was, or would be. She was not in the habit of going to pieces in a crisis, and she wouldn't let go, especially now. There might be no simple, rational explanation for Edmund's uncharacteristic unease lately, what his death might mean, but . . . She began to read the written scrawl she barely recognized as his normally careful, rather elegant script, without anything in it meaning very much. The inspector had called it a letter but it was hardly that, rather a collection of disjointed phrases, not addressed to her as she had expected, or indeed to anyone. Nor would it be, she thought, understanding belatedly that it was obviously only the first draft of a letter of resignation which would, as a fair copy, have been addressed to the Prime Minister. Her breathing became very fast as she tried to make sense of that and began to realize that those nebulous fears for Edmund which had haunted her lately had not been so groundless after all. Something bad must have happened to him.

Several starts at the letter had been attempted but all of them were crossed out and in the end it had never been coherently put together at all. Separately, the phrases made no particular sense, though together their meaning was plain enough: '*Circumstances have made it necessary for me . . . increasing grounds for concern . . . resignation . . . very great regret . . . always an honour . . .*' One partially completed phrase in particular stood out, coming at the end of what he had written, still readable though it had been heavily scored through: '*I will continue to support . . .*'

She felt the inspector watching her keenly as she read those particular words over and over again, disbelievingly, but they still didn't make sense. That was not the sentiment of a man who was intending to commit suicide. Obviously, Edmund had not been thinking very clearly. When it had come to the actual writing of the letter, had he begun to suffer doubts about his ability to carry out that final, terrible act on himself? Or had he never intended to kill himself at all, but had then been overtaken by a sudden despair which had made him do it? Almost as if he'd suddenly asked himself what the point was in carrying on. But nothing of that was like Edmund. He made considered decisions and never went back on them, once made, however painful. She preferred, however hard that was to accept, to believe his intentions had been clear-cut all along, despite the uncharacteristic false starts.

She passed the paper back to Gaines as if it were something unclean. This letter was not meant for her. If he had lived to complete and send it to Mr Asquith, the person it was meant for, she would never have seen it at all. On the other hand, if it had been his intention all along to kill himself, perhaps he would have left something for her eyes only . . . but she was capable of analysing none of this at this particular moment. It might hurt in future that he hadn't considered her, but just now it didn't matter. Those final words, maddeningly inconclusive, and impersonal in a way that revealed nothing of the torment he must have been feeling, were not something she would ever want to look at again, but in any case, she knew they were indelibly engraved in her memory.

Gaines said, 'With your permission, Mrs Latimer?' He was holding the letter out to David. 'I think Mr Moresby might like to see this, too.'

'Yes. Yes, of course. Please read it, David.'

It took him no more than a minute to read. When he looked up his face was grim. Then he folded it and handed it back to Gaines.

She had already, that morning, received messages of sympathy from many of Edmund's colleagues, and a brief, kind letter from the Prime Minister, written as soon as the shocking news had burst upon Westminster and delivered by hand, together with a characteristically eloquent but more personal and sadder one from Winston Churchill at the Home Office, where Edmund's responsibilities had lain. David himself had arrived within the hour, and she had never been as glad to see anyone in her life.

You are not alone. The words he'd used on their last meeting had come back to her in those first moments after her shattering discovery this morning, but it had immediately been followed by the realization that dealing with any questions the police might have would put an intolerable responsibility on him, when he must already be swamped with all the aftermath of Edmund's affairs. Things were likely to be in turmoil at Westminster. Edmund's death could not have come at a worse time, when the Government was in crisis over Irish affairs. Asquith would be seeking a replacement for Edmund, there would probably need to be a Government reshuffle, and David would be in the thick of it. She had closed her eyes, trying not to think of the upheaval it was going cause, of all the publicity the press would give to it . . . Utterly grateful as she would be for David's support, she couldn't ask for his help, couldn't place extra weight on his shoulders.

But he had arrived, unasked, and she had felt as if a lifeline was being thrown out to her.

Gaines was now saying, 'I'm bound to ask this, Mrs Latimer: had your husband ever spoken of the possibility of resigning his office? It seems, from the letter he left, that he obviously had some concerns about his position in the Government. Can you throw any light on that?'

She looked down at her hands, clasped on her lap. 'I can't even begin to think what any of this means. As I've said, he had seemed – a little worried lately, but that's hardly surprising, given the import-ance of what's happening in the country at the moment. In any case, he often had weighty problems on his mind, but he was more than capable of dealing with them. He wasn't in the habit of discussing his work with me, but I'm sure there was never enough to cause him to . . .' After a second or two her chin lifted and she said more firmly, 'Edmund was absolutely the last person to take such a step.'

Gaines gave no indication that he'd noticed any ambiguity in what she'd said, though she'd noticed it herself, immediately. What step had she been talking about? Resignation? Or suicide? Either seemed beyond credibility, and yet Edmund had at the very least been contemplating the one, and had in the end acted upon the other. Yesterday, she would have been prepared to swear to the impossibility of either but now, having seen with her own eyes what he had done and what he had written, it came to her that there must have been some dark shadow in his life of which she had been unaware. Which was to admit she had not only walked into her marriage blindfold, she had remained so ever since.

Gaines had now turned his attention to David. 'Mr Moresby? Since you worked so closely with Mr Latimer at the Home Office, as I understand it, maybe you could throw some light on any problems there might have been?'

'I could make a guess at any of a dozen subjects that are of concern to anyone in Parliament at the moment. None of them enough to warrant what has happened.'

He rose and walked towards the fireplace and stood with his back to it, one elbow resting on the corner of the mantel, the other thrust into his trouser pocket. Not quite the smooth, correct young man presented by the starched shirt and the Savile Row suit that he had first seemed, the confident sort who would get straight to the point. He looked uncertain. Something was bothering him now. Gaines waited to hear what it was.

Eventually, Moresby looked at Alice and some question and answer seemed to pass between them. 'Inspector Gaines, I don't know how relevant this is . . . or even if it's relevant at all. But I understand from Mrs Latimer that you are interested in a man named Tooley?'

Inskip looked up from his notes, pencil poised, suddenly alert.

'That's right,' Gaines said, 'I asked if the names of Paddy Tooley and Daniel O'Rourke meant anything, but you knew nothing of them, Mrs Latimer, isn't that so? But I take it you know something of them yourself?'

'No. No, I don't *know* either of them. But I have heard the name Tooley.'

'In what connection?'

'I recently had reason to contact someone who used to live at the same address. I needed to speak to her and I went to a house on Prosser Street, which I believe belongs to that man, but I left without seeing her.'

'A woman?'

Again he glanced at Alice before answering. 'Mona Reagan, her name is. She's someone who used to work for one of the Irish Nationalist MPs, Joe Devlin. That's a name you're likely to recognize.'

'It's familiar,' Gaines said dryly. 'Go on.'

'I believe Miss Reagan's probably back in Ireland by now, but . . .'

He was listened to attentively as he recounted the story of why he'd gone to Prosser Street and why he had left without attempting to speak to Mona Reagan. The name of Erskine Childers caused a certain frisson but elicited no further response from either policeman. 'And that's it,' he finished. 'Mrs Latimer, by the way, knew nothing of my visit.'

The clock on the mantelpiece went on fussily ticking its way about its business in the silence that followed. Eventually, Gaines spoke. 'You haven't said why you wanted to see Miss Reagan in the first place.'

'It wasn't anything important.' He returned to the sofa to resume his place next to Alice. 'Except that—' After a moment's hesitation, he went on to explain Mona's visit to his office and what she had said. 'We had some slight acquaintance, and she'd come to tell me she was leaving, and to say goodbye. It was only incidentally that she made the remark about Mr Latimer needing to be careful. It puzzled me slightly, but to tell the truth I didn't give it much thought at first.' He kept his eyes on Alice as he said, 'It was only Mrs Latimer's concern that her husband was worried over something that made me begin to wonder what she had meant by it. But, as you must appreciate, there's always a certain amount of interaction between us and the Nationalist office and I simply concluded she was warning him to be a little more diplomatic in what he said. Mr Latimer was known for his sometimes rather acerbic opinions. Perhaps someone was taking exception. They're a touchy lot, the Nationalists, but it's a quid pro quo situation: we support them over Home Rule, they support us by voting with us in domestic matters. That's common knowledge – a necessary evil since we Liberals have such a small majority.'

'Hmm. So you would think it unlikely that Mr Latimer was being threatened in some way, over this Home Rule business, say?'

'Threatened? Indeed, no, but in the unlikely event that he was, it wouldn't have made much difference. Emotions are running high at the moment, but he was not a man easily swayed. In any case, we are on the same side, are we not?'

'But something must have happened to make him think of resigning his career.'

A silence fell.

David waited. He had expected more reaction after his relation of what and who he'd seen at Prosser Street, yet the name of Erskine Childers in this context had seemed neither to surprise nor alarm either policeman. But now, he saw them exchanging glances, after which Gaines appeared to come to some decision and said easily, 'Well now, that's all speculation, which isn't going to take us very far just now, is it? Let's get back to Tooley. The thing is, Mr Moresby, we urgently need to speak to a man called Daniel O'Rourke and we have reason to believe he may have taken refuge in Paddy Tooley's house, or been helped by him to find somewhere else.'

'He's not there now,' Inskip said. They had gone to some trouble, even calling in the resources of the Special Branch to make certain of it. This was the section of the Criminal Investigation Department at Scotland Yard whose knowledge of troublesome immigrants, Irish or otherwise, was extensive, but even they, with their extensive intelligence network, hadn't come up with any information about Daniel O'Rourke. Tooley's house had been searched but if ever O'Rourke had been there, he wasn't now.

'Why exactly do you need to speak to this man?' Alice asked.

'He's wanted in connection with the murder of your cousin, Dudley Nichol, Mrs Latimer.' She stiffened. 'I'm sorry to bring that up just now. Your family's had a very trying time recently. First little Lucy being kidnapped, then your cousin being killed, but—'

'I can understand you're anxious to catch Nichol's killer, of course, but may I ask what it has to do with Mr Latimer?' Moresby interrupted.

'Most likely nothing at all.' Gaines looked at them both, summing them up, making his mind up as to whether he should trust them further. Alice Latimer he had few doubts about. His previous encounters with her had given him reason to respect her level-headed approach and her ability to keep her own counsel. He had trusted her from the first, but politicians were a tricky breed, and he was automatically wary of them. At the same time, he instinctively liked the cut of Moresby's jib. He was cautious, but seemed sincere. Alice Latimer had hung on his words and clearly looked up to him, while he was obviously protective of her. It didn't need a clairvoyant to spot that his feelings for her went well beyond those of friendship or respect for a colleague's wife.

At last he said, 'It looks very much as though your cousin may have got himself mixed up in some murky dealings to do with Irish politics, Mrs Latimer. And since your husband was directly concerned with Irish affairs that could well be why he got in touch with you after so many years. And why he disappeared so mysteriously.'

It took Alice a moment to get her breath. 'You are suggesting he was *spying* on Edmund? But Dudley was—' What exactly he was seemed to escape her and she began again. 'They never spoke politics. To be honest, they spoke very little together. Edmund – well, to be honest, he didn't suffer fools gladly and he never had much patience with the sort of people who fritter their lives away. I'm afraid he thought Dudley was a hopeless case. The little they had to do with one another wasn't about anything important anyway, certainly not about Irish politics.'

She didn't trouble to hide her scepticism over the idea that there could have been any communication between her husband and her cousin, and Moresby was evidently not prepared to give the idea much credence, either. 'There is always a good deal of lobbying going on,' he said shortly. 'There are dozens of ways anyone in politics can be pressurized in some way, we all know that, but if you're inferring that Edmund could be influenced at all you are very wrong. It's ludicrous even to think it. You'd need

more political weight than Latimer had in any case to change
what has already been agreed.'

Gaines' prediction that their attempts to see Violet Martens would
come to nothing proved to be correct, as they found when they
went through to the Martens' apartments. She wasn't well enough,
her husband repeated, and Gaines didn't insist. Ferdie himself was
willing enough to talk but, although he was clearly shocked at
the turn of events, he could offer no insights into the reasons for
his brother-in-law to have shot himself. Gaines suspected that he
and Latimer had had little in common. They were poles apart,
Ferdie who was content to take life on the surface, who asked
little beyond an agreeable social life and the occasional excitements of the racetrack, and the serious, ambitious man who had
been deeply involved in matters concerning the government of
the country.

The Another visit to the study before they left was indicated. While
they had been otherwise occupied, Latimer's body had been removed
and the knowledgeable team who were called in to deal with the
aftermath of death had been and done everything that was necessary
in the way of taking photographs, clearing up, taking away everything
they thought might be useful in the way of evidence. The room
was more or less restored to normality, although there was now a
pale rectangle on the wall where the black-and-white etching had
hung, and behind it the hole in the wall, surrounded by cracked
plaster and torn wallpaper, from which the bullet had been extracted.
But the blood splashes were still there on the wallpaper, a gruesome
reminder of what had occurred.

The study was a room at the back of the house and commanded
a view of the garden, which was not large but attractively laid out.
Latimer had chosen to set his desk facing into the room, maybe as
a stern reminder not to waste time gazing out of the window at the
garden, just now a pink froth of cherry blossom that the sun of the
last few days had brought out. A swathe of daffodils stretched out
towards the bottom, which might be past their best on closer inspection. To one side the baby's wicker pram stood under another cherry
tree. Its silk canopy had been raised against the sun and today Lucy
slept peacefully under it. Even as Gaines looked, Emma Pavel came
out of the house, peeped into the pram and tucked the blanket more

carefully around her before tiptoeing away. It would be some time before anyone was easy leaving Lucy without someone watching over her.

Now that the experts had done their work and departed, and if you ignored the damage to the wall, Latimer's study could be seen as conventional and rather characterless, dominated by his large mahogany desk. Standing on it was the green-shaded lamp which had been undamaged in its tumble to the floor, and because of that had miraculously escaped contamination and now stood in what was presumably its original place on the green leather top beside the inkstand which had remained in place throughout. A bookcase was set against one wall, its shelves mostly filled with a series of dull-looking volumes, carefully arranged according to subject. Among them were several copies of the books Erskine Childers had written.

'Have you read this, sir?'

'No, don't get much time for that sort of thing,' Gaines said, following Inskip's pointing finger towards the best-selling spy novel which had brought Childers such fame. It sat, faintly incongruous, between his more serious non-fiction works about his experiences as a volunteer artillery driver in the Boer War and those on cavalry warfare, criticising the outmoded arms presently being used and recommending the employment of modern machine weaponry, and his latest publication, in which he had set out what he called a framework for Home Rule of Ireland. This was bringing him almost as much publicity as his famous work of fiction.

'You should try it, it's a cracking read.'

Gaines slid *The Riddle of the Sands* from its shelf. That Inskip, not noted for reading, had actually picked up the book at all, never mind read it, must have something to recommend it. It looked new, and appeared to be unread, a complimentary copy signed by the author. A folded sheet of letter paper had been tucked inside the flap. 'Well, well. Read this, Sergeant,' he said to Inskip when he had done so himself.

It was a short note to Latimer from Childers, the purpose of which was to thank him very sincerely for his recent, very generous, donations to the Cause. '*I have come to value our growing friendship greatly,*' it went on, '*and know only too well the hardships of the path you are treading. Having trodden the same way myself I know the difficulties you face, and the struggle between conscience and loyalty. I have, thank God, emerged from the dark and I am confident that now you have made your decision and your doubts have been resolved, you will feel the same sense of freedom.'* It was simply signed, Childers.

So that was it, Latimer's reason for suicide. He had thrown in his lot with the extremists, but contrary to what Childers had evidently thought, he had still been plagued by doubts, struggling between conscience and remorse, in which neither had won. Yet he wouldn't have been the first to switch allegiance from one party to another over a principle, and survive. It hadn't harmed Winston Churchill when he had crossed the floor from the Conservative benches to join the Liberal party, nor impeded his almost meteoric rise to Home Secretary. Yet . . . were Latimer's doubts enough for him to have taken that fatal step?

At least, it went some way to explaining that odd message the woman Mona Reagan had asked David Moresby to pass on to Latimer. It now seemed more than possible that as a person working in the Nationalist party offices, she had overheard some gossip about Latimer's possible defection to the other side. But what connection could they have had, that she felt it necessary to warn him, possibly at risk to herself? It was an interesting question, but it hardly mattered now.

There was little else left in the room to interest them, but Gaines found himself staring at a large group of family photographs ranged on the top of a chest of drawers that seemed, in view of its extent, and given what was known of him, to reveal a somewhat surprising aspect of Latimer's character: a stiffly seated Victorian couple, presumably his parents, Latimer as a boy, as a young man in tennis whites with a group of friends, a wedding photograph of himself and Alice. Latimer holding the hand of his little sister, Violet, and smiling down at her. More of Violet alone, a pretty little girl who seemed to have enjoyed from an early age having her picture taken, being dressed up for the occasion in flouncy clothes, jewellery and, as a tiny girl in one picture, wearing a white party frock, pretty slippers and – extraordinarily – white gloves.

He thought that Edmund Latimer must have been something of an enigma. The personal revelation of family feeling was unexpected, and sadly seemed to emphasize the sense of emptiness in the room, over which, despite the apparent normality, the taint of death remained, a stain in the air. The very silence seemed to underline the horror of what had happened here, those few moments when a man had taken the ultimate step of deciding to pull a trigger and blow out his brains.

He stood in the centre of the room, gauging something and trying to work out what it was as he gazed round. Dust motes danced in a beam of sunlight. He deliberately brought back to mind his initial impressions of the room, and the large desk as he had first seen it. An unusually tidy desk, he recalled – apart from Latimer's body sprawled across it. Otherwise, only a stack of blank paper on one side, waiting to be used, a blotter, both previously unmarked before the shooting had made such a mess of them. They'd been taken away for examination, as had the fountain pen, uncapped, which had rolled to the floor.

'Noisy things, guns,' he remarked at last. 'Yet not one person in the house hears one going off.'

'It was only a small gun, and it's a big house,' Inskip said, but he spoke doubtfully because he understood what Gaines was getting at, unlikely as it seemed. 'His study's here on the ground floor, and everyone was asleep upstairs.'

There was a French window and when Gaines tried it, he found it was unlocked. 'Careless. Anyone could have got in that way.' He looked even more thoughtful.

Inskip said, 'You're not suggesting . . . sir?'

Gaines didn't reply.

'Because when the gun's fingerprinted it will show—'

He stopped, and Gaines supplied, 'It'll show his own finger-prints, of course . . . which could have been left when the gun was wiped and put back in his hand.' He saw Inskip's expression and sighed. 'All right, I know. I'm being fanciful.' Fanciful in his book was something that wasn't permitted. 'I'm pushing it because I can't see a way through all this yet. What's been happening to these people?' Inskip shrugged non-committally. 'Oh, come on, Sergeant, don't tell me you haven't been thinking the same thing. This is somehow all part of what's already happened. The baby's kidnap, Dudley Nichol, your Danny boy, and now – now this little lot.'

About which, he gloomily predicted, there were going to be repercussions. It was likely to go well beyond Edmund Latimer's so far inexplicable suicide.

'You're right, sir,' Inskip said. 'If you don't mind my saying, it is a bit fanciful.'

'I know. I was just trying it out.' But against Gaines' instincts, the notion that the MP hadn't died by his own hand was one he had to admit he'd been toying with ever since he'd first seen the body. He doubted very much if it would stand up to scrutiny, and in any case he'd now ceased to believe it himself, but it had been worth considering, if only to be ruled out. All the same, he led the way out via the French window, just to show how easy it might have been, and locked it behind them.

When they reached the front of the house, they came face to face with David Moresby, who was also just leaving, setting off to hire a taxi as soon as he saw one, he said.

'Lucky to have caught you then,' Gaines said, 'if you could spare a minute or two, sir, we'd be grateful.'

'Well.' He frowned and pulled his watch from his top pocket. 'Is there something else? I was under the impression you had finished with me.'

'I think you've been keeping something from us, Mr Moresby.'

'What?' His politely correct manner seemed to be in danger of deserting him. 'Look here, I've told you everything I know that might be of use in clearing up this sad business. If you still think Latimer was being forced to act in a way he felt was dishonourable, that he was in some way mixed up in some dirty business, you could not be more mistaken. What I said about Mona Reagan—'

'It's nothing to do with Mona Reagan, Mr Moresby. Unless she was involved with him in a personal way, if you get my meaning.'

'Personal? Mona?' He laughed shortly. 'You're on the wrong track there, Inspector.' He was trying to brush it off, but he wasn't entirely succeeding. Blustering didn't come naturally to him, Gaines thought.

'I said "unless" Mr Moresby.' The other man went silent. 'We shall find out if that was the case, sooner or later, if there is anything in it,' Gaines reminded him gently, 'you know that. But I said it had nothing to do with her.'

Still Moresby hesitated. 'Wouldn't it be better to have the truth of the matter from you? I realize you probably didn't want to say anything about it in front of Mrs Latimer, which is why I didn't ask you earlier, but I can promise discretion, in so far as I am able.'

Suddenly, Moresby's common sense took over and he gave in. 'Is there somewhere we can talk?'

'We can go back into the study, we won't be disturbed there. It's locked, but we have the keys.'

'The study?' He looked slightly appalled at the prospect of entering the room where the tragedy had taken place.

Inskip said, 'It's been cleared by now.' He led the way round to the back where he unlocked the French window and they once more entered.

Moresby's eyes went immediately to the damaged wall and the arc of blood splashes still defacing the wallpaper and he hesitated for a moment, but in the end he stepped into the room. Inskip, displaying unusual tact, indicated a seat that had its back to the bloody reminder, well out of range of the desk. Not everyone was accustomed to looking at sights like that, he admitted. Averting his eyes, Moresby took the seat.

'You assumed correctly that I was reluctant to speak in front of Mrs Latimer,' he began immediately the other two had found chairs for themselves. 'When you hear what I have to say, you'll realize why.' Gaines, who had already guessed something of what was coming, didn't reply. 'But that wasn't the only reason I didn't say anything. I wasn't supposed to know about it, for one thing, and for another, I suppose it could turn out he was being blackmailed for it, which I suppose is what you're getting at. I doubt it, though, and in any case, I don't believe Latimer would have reacted in the way he has. Whatever else, he wasn't a coward, he would have faced it, ridden out the scandal. And he would certainly have appreciated that it was not the way to cover up. Nothing stays hidden when someone has taken his life, does it?'

He looked down at the toes of his polished shoes for a while and then met their combined regard squarely. He seemed to realize he hadn't been making a great deal of sense. 'I feel pretty bad about me being the one to tell you this. I'm certain Alice – Mrs Latimer – has no idea, though I don't suppose it will be long before some kind person informs her. I'm amazed it's been kept from her so far. You can stop looking for political motives for what he has done. Latimer and I have worked together for a good while and I owe him a great deal,' he said honestly. 'The least I can do is to prevent it going on record that he took his life because of any chicanery in that direction. He was not dishonest.'

Whatever else, he had said. Gaines knew then he had been right in his earlier assumption that there had been little love lost between the two men. 'I assume you are saying he was having an affair?'

'That's what it amounts to, I suppose, though an affair implies a temporary thing, a fling that's soon over. And as far as I know – I'm certain, in fact – this was more serious than that. You – you will want details, her name . . .'

'Yes, though I doubt very much that it isn't known already. As a politician yourself, Mr Moresby, in the public eye, you must be aware that it's in the interest of national security to keep tabs on anyone of importance in the Government.'

'The Special Branch, I suppose,' Moresby said with resignation.

'Yes, they've already been notified about Mr Latimer's death and we will be working together,' Gaines said neutrally, giving no indication this was not something he precisely welcomed, either, although he had often worked closely with them. The Branch saw themselves as an elite corps and were inclined to want to take over the whole operation. But since they were chiefly concerned with all matters pertaining to national security, part of the Branch's area of responsibility was to keep themselves up-to-date with politicians and all their activities, extramarital or otherwise. It was inevitable, having been a minister at the Home Office, that Latimer's background would be known to them.

'Are you sure Mrs Latimer knows nothing?' In Gaines' experience, wives who were presumed to be innocent of such matters were often quite well aware of what was going on, even if, for various reasons, they chose to keep the knowledge to themselves.

'Yes, I'm certain she doesn't. But she will have to know, it seems. I think I must go to her now and warn her,' he said, though he looked wretched at the prospect. 'Before she hears it in the wrong way. I should have thought about it before. It's better she's told straight off, rather than hear of it in a roundabout way, which she's certain to do, one way and another.'

He half rose from his chair before recollecting that he hadn't yet said all he needed to. 'You want to know about Connie Fiore,' he said.

Fifteen

Daniel O'Rourke lay inadequately propped against the cast-iron bed frame by a thin pillow, gasping on a cigarette. It was the last thing he needed with this cough, though it helped to disguise the fusty smell of the pillow, had he been in any condition to notice or care about such things – about the pillow, or its stained black-striped ticking, the lumps in the mattress, or the coarse grey blanket. Living as a hunted man, you got used to discomfort, and this was luxury compared to some of the places he'd slept in. A room to himself. Food sometimes, though he couldn't force much down at present – but what was food, as long as he had his cigarettes? The craving for a drink was a different matter. He was desperate for a drop so he could think better, but she wouldn't bring him any, only water.

He'd got drunk that night with Dudley Nichol, or Lennie Croxton as he'd called himself when he came back to England. It was a pity about what had happened later, but never in this world had he imagined Dudley getting cold feet, becoming dangerous and therefore dispensable. Inoffensive as he'd outwardly appeared, he'd had passions he shared with every true patriot – stronger passions than his own, Daniel owned, in moments of the honesty which admittedly didn't come to him very often. Like most converts, Dudley had been more fervent in the cause and less tolerant of those who opposed its aims than many of those who were born into it. He had a fire in his belly although, back in Ireland, he hadn't shown himself capable of the cold, calculated violence which many of their brotherhood, including Daniel himself, were deeming necessary.

The rats were starting their nightly scuttering behind the skirting board. They were worse at night. He had killed one the night before last when it had ventured into the room. He'd reached down from the bed for one of his heavy, nailed boots and made a lucky throw. The rat lay dead on the floor. He couldn't stomach the thought of it lying there, beginning to smell maybe, but when, weak as he was, he'd managed to get himself out of bed and pick it up by its tail it squirmed and came alive again, only stunned by the boot. He'd twisted its neck and thrown it out of the window and into the other rubbish in the yard below, wedged his boot into the hole it had come from, then crawled back to bed. By morning, the leather had been gnawed through by more rats and he'd had to ask her to get him another pair.

'You'll not be needing boots for a while,' she said, holding the water glass to his lips to help him drink.

God, but he could do with a drink now. Not water, though, a drop of the hard stuff was what he needed. The pain in his chest was like a red-hot knife and he was beginning to sweat again. He knew he had a fever, what with the burning, then the shaking cold coming after, with only moments of clarity among the confusion in his mind. He'd got soaking wet on too many of those bloody vigils outside Manessa House and then again in the pouring rain that night. It had been a queer old to-do all round, that night, ending up with him drenched to the skin and exhausted. He'd dropped on to the bed and fallen asleep as he was, there in his wet clothes, shutting out the remembrance of a man being killed. Not the first death he'd encountered, by any means, but he hadn't imagined it would be like that, that the enemy being shot in an ambush was a different matter from the knifing to death of one of your own.

The agonizing cough rattled again in his chest, doubling him over. When it was finished, he leaned back and let his eyes close and when he opened them again a feeble light was trying to penetrate the murk on the soot-streaked skylight. He thought he felt a bit better for the sleep, and reached for the water on the orange box beside his bed. The pain sliced through his chest again.

Coughing his damned lungs up was no damned good. He had to get shot of this lot, and soon. He couldn't stay here indefinitely, imprisoned in this attic. He'd already been here too long – how long, he couldn't work out and didn't dare to try. He only knew he should have been away long since, shaken the dust of London from his feet, but he still had several more guns promised, and if he wanted the good opinion of Leary, the cold man who led his cell in Ireland, then he had to stay here until he'd finished the job . . . even though it seemed to have taken a wrong turning somewhere along the way.

Gone wrong in the same way as the plan Lennie had hatched,

which might have brought them all to disaster, and only by luck that it hadn't.

No use thinking of that now. Instead, he tried to focus on the news that Tooley had brought him – was it one, or two nights ago? Only his mind wasn't functioning as it should. He kept floating off. Did he remember rightly what Tooley had said, yesterday, the day before . . . or when? That the matter was being taken out of their hands by a great plan to smuggle weapons to Ireland that would make his own efforts look like nothing. Or was he hallucinating again? Tooley wasn't what you'd call reliable. A greedy bastard, and stupid with it. But what he'd said was the truth, it would account for the murderous thoughts Daniel kept having. He broke out in a thick sweat. God, he should try and pull himself together. He couldn't afford weakness like this now.

It was too much effort even to light another cigarette. The house was only a one-up-and-one-down, plus this attic, and he could hear the sounds from below, Maureen's husband's cough nearly as bad as his own, herself in the kitchen, clattering pans about in her slapdash way as she cooked, every now and then flinging the door open and yelling to the kids playing outside to go and make their bloody noise somewhere else, the kids cheeking her back. Other street noises floated up through the cracked pane in the skylight, a horse and cart rumbling on the street cobbles, the striking of a church clock. Our Lady's, that would be, not Father Finucane's . . .

Daniel O'Rourke had been born here, in the East End. He hadn't had much schooling and had never had a trade, but had worked wherever he could find a job, lining up for work as a docker when there was any to be had, as a porter at Smithfield, navvying, anything he could get. The jobs had come and gone, but he'd mostly been lucky, usually one of the first to be taken on because he was a big strong fella, standing out in the crowd of hopefuls who turned up to be hired. East Enders were poor specimens on the whole, underfed and puny; poverty and living conditions here were not calculated to produce a race of he-men. Daniel had been lucky in that his parents, first-generation immigrants from Ireland, had been a thrifty pair, determined against odds to sustain a decent living for themselves and their only child. His father had worked all his life for the same company as a brewer's drayman, and his mother, who was a skilled needlewoman, had even managed to save the odd shilling now and then from what she earned working for the Jews in the garment trade. Remembering only too well what they'd left behind in Ireland, they'd made something of a life for themselves here, settled and dug themselves in with no intention of ever leaving. Daniel himself had never set foot out of London until the day, six or seven years ago, when he'd been forced to flee to Dublin after the business of Cathleen Hennessy. He had broken his mother's heart with that, they said. She died a year later and Daniel had not come home for the funeral. His father still worked for the brewery but he hadn't been to see him either since he came back.

Cathleen had been an indiscretion Daniel had regretted, though he still didn't see it as being all his fault. It took two to make a bargain. He could have married her, she was a fine girl, but the truth was, the thought of being trapped into family life, children, and all that entailed, had terrified him, though he told himself he would eventually have done right by her, if she hadn't gone and killed herself. He hadn't been keen to stay after that, and when he heard her brothers were after his blood he'd cleared off, taken the ferry from Holyhead to Dublin. There he'd got himself in with the boyos who were ripe for a fight, the rebels who said they were doing it because they loved their country, though not everyone supported them, by any means, nothing but a gang of oul' Fenians they were, never mind they called themselves soldiers. Their unswerving dedication to the cause was something Daniel didn't fully understand or even care much about. He'd joined them anyway, more because he enjoyed a good scrap for its own sake than for any political conviction.

Until he'd arrived in Ireland he'd never thought too much about the struggle going on there, although no one who'd grown up in the environment he'd been brought up in could have avoided knowing about it, not with the endless talk that went on among those who'd left the shores of their native land for whatever reason . . . starvation, eviction by the landlords, religious struggles. In Ireland it was different. There, the talk was being translated into action by those who were proud to work for a day when Ireland would be free to rule herself. The need for violence was unfortunate, they said, but there was no denying how many of them liked what they were doing, got a taste for it.

Since he'd grown up with incendiary sentiments, Daniel took it for granted that it was how his new friends would feel, but he was at sea when it came to understanding somebody like Dudley Nichol, who didn't have to fight for Ireland but had wanted to, was burning to do so, nourished by his mother on stories of Ireland's heroes and the fight against oppression. And yet in the end, when it came down to it, Dudley hadn't been a fighter. He was a dreamer, full of high ideals but short on reality.

Take that business with the Martens' baby. It had been the craziest idea in the world, Daniel knew that right from the first and he hadn't wanted to go along with it. For one thing, he didn't see how it could succeed and for another, he had his own reasons for not wanting to bring any attention to himself: these things had a way of getting out and he didn't want to be around if any hint that he was here in London reached the Hennessys, Cathleen's brothers. All he had to do was to keep his mind on the job he'd risked coming back to London for, and in any case, he hadn't seen the point of going to all that trouble, not to mention danger, of kidnapping a baby for the surprisingly paltry sum Dudley had suggested – surprising because Dudley never had tuppence to rub together, and even more since it was to be shared. Even when that was pointed out to him, he'd refused to increase it. He was like that, away with the faeries most of the time. But once fired up, he wasn't going to give up the idea. It was only afterwards that he had begun to lose his nerve about the whole idea, but by then the baby had been taken.

It was the wrong thing to do, he'd said, too late. 'We must give her back.'

'Are you mad, Croxton?' Tooley said. 'Do you realize what that would mean?'

No, he wasn't mad. He was in deadly earnest. And Daniel had learned that when Lennie Croxton, aka Dudley Nichol, got an idea into his head, it took a sledgehammer to drive it out. Daniel hadn't liked the idea of them getting rid of him but they couldn't think of any other way to silence him.

And yet the problem hadn't ended there. It had run through all Daniel's fevered nights since then. What were they to do about the baby now that Dudley was dead? he kept asking them all. 'Sure, we can get a better price for it, now he's out of the way,' was all Tooley would say.

Somehow, it had got to be night again. The door opened and Maureen came in with a cup of soup she'd made and began to urge him to try to take a drop. She was a big, blowsy, untidy woman and her house was no better, but as well as knowing how to pull a pint at the Nag with just the right head on it, she was a good cook, and had a heart as generous as herself – if you got on the right side of her. He took a spoonful of soup from her but that was as much as he could manage.

'Ah, come on, that's not going to do you any good. You can't live on water.'

He turned his head away. She stood the soup cup on the orange box and put a hand on his forehead. She looked worried. 'We'll have to get you a doctor, you know.'

'No.' The effort that went into even that made him cough again.

She'd brought a bowl of water and a cloth as well as the soup. 'Let me send for one, Danny,' she pleaded, wringing the cloth out and wiping his face. It felt good, like he was a child and it was his mother wiping round his sticky mouth; he hadn't known she had that much gentleness in her.

'Don't need one.'

Maureen shook her head, attempted to straighten the roil of his sheets and then, with another look at his face, left him.

No, it isn't a doctor you're needing, Daniel O'Rourke, it's a priest. Yet, however ill he was, belated fright consumed her at the thought of letting anyone know he was here. She was a good-natured woman and willing to oblige, but not if her liberty depended on it.

Sixteen

Murder took officers of the law into strange and various places. Nor was it any respecter of race, religion or class. The house, tall and white-stuccoed, was in an elegant Georgian terrace in wealthy Belgravia, the agreeable face of London, with its tree-lined roads, its fine architecture, parks and gardens. The knocker was brass and shone against the gleaming, black-painted door, which was presently opened by a pleasant-faced maid in a starched white apron and cap. Inskip announced who they were. 'Mrs Fiore is expecting us.'

'Ah, yes. Please come in. I'll let her know you're here.' She led them into a room at the front of the house that overlooked the street and invited them to take a seat while they waited.

Sunlight poured into a grey-walled room which was gently fragrant with beeswax and pot-pourri. The window was open and champagne net curtains moved gently in the breeze. Daffodils in the widow boxes outside showed their waving heads. The room was furnished with no-expense-spared good taste: oriental rugs on polished floors and deep, comfortable chairs, a pair of elegant mirrors and one or two pieces of fine porcelain. Every hard surface gleamed, the deep blue velvet draperies and cushions complemented everything else. A clock ticked discreetly. It was another world.

'Blimey!' said Inskip under his breath. He was not at his best in situations like this. He felt awkward and that made him act bolshie. He looked around, not knowing where to sit lest his clodhopping police presence might dirty something. Eventually he settled, as Gaines had done, for one of the straight chairs variously placed around the room. It mollified him to notice Gaines looked as uncomfortable as he himself felt.

Mrs Fiore did not keep them waiting. Like the room itself, she looked discreetly expensive, her brown hair dressed wide as was the fashion, with pearl drops depending from her ear-lobes and a pearl choker round her neck. Holding her figure very upright, she gave the impression of being taller than she actually was. Impressive, thought Gaines, noting that although she smiled pleasantly, she was very pale and her eyes were shadowed. She shook hands and bade them resume their seats in a voice that held only the trace of an American accent. Almost immediately, the maid who had opened the door to them entered with a tray.

She had a natural manner that put them at their ease in this alien environment, serving them cups of excellent coffee. When they were settled, and Inskip was attempting to deal with the crumbs from one of the delicately thin almond biscuits that had come with the coffee, she began calmly, 'Let's not waste any time, mine or yours. We all know why you're here, so without any rudeness on my part, I would be grateful if we could get it over with as soon as possible. I'll do my best to answer as many questions as I can. But tell me first: is it usual for a detective inspector and his sergeant to go so far into a matter of . . . suicide?'

'Only in so far as it impinges on the main focus of our investigations, ma'am,' Gaines replied, not showing that he was taken aback.

'In that case . . .' She wasn't restrained by British politeness, and there had been only the slight hesitation before the word suicide. She was being honest and Gaines liked her for it, but her directness had him a bit flummoxed. He was struggling to find an opening to what he had to ask when she said, quietly, 'Very well. It's hard to know what is the right thing to say, but let me start by saying that I'm aware you must already know that Mr Latimer and I had – a long association, so you can dispense with the preliminaries.'

'It's been a shock for you. I am sorry, Mrs Fiore.' And Gaines found he was, deeply sorry. You didn't have to be a strict churchgoer to deplore the sin of cheating on one's wife – and that was what he thought it was, a sin – but at the same time, he couldn't look at this woman's face and not be aware that she was suffering as much as Alice Latimer was, perhaps even more.

'That's kind of you. It won't be most people's response,' she said, and rather bitterly added, 'In my position, I shall not be allowed to grieve, but I daresay I shall deal with that in my own way. I can only say now how stunned I was by the news and—'

She stopped abruptly, evidently not as much in command of herself as she believed. Bending her head, hiding her face, she reached out towards a box that stood on a nearby table, its black lacquer reflected in the polished rosewood surface. After extracting a cigarette and a book of safety matches, she asked, 'Do you mind if I smoke?'

Though Inskip didn't mind one way or another, Gaines didn't smoke himself and hadn't yet accustomed himself to seeing women smoking, either, but he didn't object, and after they both declined to join her, she detached a match from the book, inserted the cigarette into a mother-of-pearl holder, lit it and breathed deeply. Her hand was not quite steady.

In spite of her declared willingness to be frank, Gaines was beginning to wonder if he should not be wary of this woman's responses and he wanted to watch her reactions. He took the opportunity to catch Inskip's eye and nodded to him to take up the questioning.

Inskip, uncomfortable in an unfamiliar situation, obviously didn't want to, but had no option. 'Had Mr Latimer ever given you any indication that he was worried, or upset about anything?'

'If you are in politics, Sergeant, you can't escape that. He was a conscientious man and he was always concerned about something or other regarding his work, especially over what's been happening lately. He was always anxious to do the right thing, but like all politicians, he'd learned not to allow anything to prey on his mind. You don't have to take my word for it: no one who knew him would ever have anticipated this.'

It was no more than could have been expected, no more information than had been given to them by Latimer's wife, thought Inskip. The next part was going to be more tricky. He was going to have to tread on eggshells and he had never really understood the meaning of tact. He ran a finger under his collar and inwardly cursed Gaines for letting him in for this.

'I understand what you say. But that was his professional life. What about his private concerns? His friends, for instance?'

He licked his pencil, ready to take down the names, but at that moment deliverance came. Gaines had noticed a copy of *The Riddle of the Sands* on an adjacent table and his interest had immediately sharpened. 'You admire Mr Childers' work, Mrs Fiore?' he asked, indicating the book.

She shrugged. 'It's not quite my cup of tea, but he's a personal friend, through his wife, Molly. She's American, too, and we expatriates tend to stick together.'

'I suppose that meant Mr Latimer was a friend of theirs, too?'

'He did not know Molly, though I believe he had some

acquaintance with her husband.' Her transatlantic accent had become more pronounced. She was treading warily, Gaines thought.

'I expect they found much to discuss – on the future of Ireland, for instance. Mr Childers holds strong views about that.'

'I doubt they knew each other well enough to have *discussions,* about Ireland or anything else. If they did, Edmund never told me of any. The little time he and I could spend together was time for him to relax and he rarely discussed his work with me.' Again, these were almost exactly the words Alice Latimer had used. Edmund Latimer's reputation as a bit of an enigma obviously extended to his private life.

'I won't pretend the situation we found ourselves in was easy,' she went on sadly. 'It won't be of any importance to you, but you can believe me when I say that what Edmund and I had was more than a passing flirtation. We had been together more than ten years – we couldn't marry, because my husband was still alive then. Edmund's own marriage was . . . an expediency. I'm sure you understand that it's advisable for any man in his position to have a wife – a single man, unless he's an obvious womanizer, is always suspect, I'm afraid. It would have been a pity to let unjustified gossip jeopardize his career. We were always discreet, and I know Edmund didn't believe his wife ever knew about us, or even suspected. He respected Alice, he would never have done anything to hurt her.'

Gaines was constantly amazed that men in positions such as Latimer had held could risk everything they had worked for all their lives, all that they held dear, families, wives and children, all for the sake of another woman. That Latimer had allowed it to go on for so long, and had in fact got away with it, was still more incredible. He must always have been aware that he faced inevitable discovery and retribution, one day. Not that he was alone in that direction. Rumours circulated about others in public life, about Lloyd George to name but one notorious philanderer for instance, although, being the man he was, the Chancellor had somehow always managed to circumvent them. Nevertheless, it never did to underestimate the power of gossip and rumour and what it could do to a reputation, however good society was at turning a blind eye when necessary, and no one would understand this more than politicians.

'Do you know Mrs Latimer?'

'We have met, once or twice, briefly. She was, I believe, a good wife to Edmund.' She had finished her cigarette and put it out. The disagreeable smell rising from the ashtray almost overwhelmed the delicate scent of the pot-pourri, but it didn't seem to bother her.

They were not getting very far and he decided there was nothing for it but to copy her own directness. 'Mrs Fiore, it's a terrible thing when someone's life has reached a point when it's no longer worth anything to him. You were, I believe, important enough in Mr Latimer's life to know that he must have been under some considerable strain.'

Her eyes flickered. 'Strain? In what way?'

'That's what we're trying to find out. It seems more than possible he was being blackmailed. Forgive me, but you must have realized his position laid him open to that sort of thing. Can you throw any light on that?'

Her hand strayed towards the cigarette box again but she withdrew it and sat with her hands clasped on her lap. At length, she said, 'We were treading a tightrope, I guess. Yes, of course, it was always there, the possibility that someone would try to use the situation for their own purposes. My own position in society is not so important to me, but Edmund's career was another matter.' She fell silent again. Several minutes passed.

'Are you saying you have something to tell us?' he prompted.

She merely looked at him. The smart clip of approaching horses' hooves sounded from the road outside and a hansom cab bowled in front of the window, throwing a passing darkness across the window and shadowing her face for a moment. 'Mrs Fiore, I believe you do know he was being blackmailed, and you also know the source of it.' When she still didn't reply, he said, 'Surely you don't wish to leave the cause of his death unexplained?'

He thought she was going to remain stubbornly silent on that one, too, but in the end she said, 'It's not worth pursuing.'

Not worth pursuing the source of her lover's suicide? He let the silence continue while the nebulous thought which had come to him in Edmund Latimer's study began to take on more shape and form. He stood up. 'Very well. I understand your reluctance to name names, Mrs Fiore, but it doesn't matter in the long run. Thank you for your time, and your honesty.'

* * *

Yesterday, he'd been sitting in a scented, sunlit, luxurious room in Belgravia, sipping coffee and eating almond biscuits. Him, Joseph Inskip. What would Emma think of that when he told her? Could anything be more of a contrast to that than this dark hell-hole where he was now? he wondered, as the two of them, he and DC Watts, plunged into the Stygian darkness of the dark, narrow passageway and emerged into the hemmed-in square of tottering tenements. Jubilee Court, it was called. Possibly named in an excess of patriotism to celebrate the old Queen's sixty years' reign. No, that was only fifteen years past, and these ancient crowded hovels had surely existed before then, before the Stone Age conceivably. Enough rot and filth had accumulated here to believe that possible, except that Stone Age dwellings would have been cleaner. Even so, he thought he would rather be here than in Gaines' shoes at this moment, facing the task he was about to undertake.

He pounded on the door of number three, whose grimy windows looked a little cleaner than some of the others, if not by much, and waited.

'We've got company,' said Watts. When they had come through the passage, there had been no one about, not even the usual gang of rowdy children. It was understandable. Even the unchoosy urchins who inhabited these tenements wouldn't want to hang around on this patch, a yard, enclosed on four sides. If it had ever had the benefit of cobbles, which was doubtful, decades of stamped down rubbish had buried them. It was now just a filthy black scum of trodden earth. Thank God it wasn't raining. Then, it must be nothing more than a sea of mud that stuck to the boot soles and got trampled into the houses. Not that such concerns would bother most of the occupants, not a few of whom had miraculously appeared and were now hanging around, women in doorways with their arms folded and men standing about in various exaggeratedly non-menacing attitudes, all of them eyeing them covertly. Having been despatched here while Gaines attended to business elsewhere, Inskip was glad he'd picked Watts to accompany him. A strapping lad like him would make catsmeat of any of them stupid enough to try anything on. He thumped the door again, louder. And this time it was answered.

'Maureen.'

'Well? What do *you* want?' The blowsy barmaid from the Nag

wasn't pleased to see him, but he hadn't expected she would be. 'Can we have a word?'

'It's not convenient.' She made a half-hearted attempt to push the door shut, but he had his foot there.

'Where is he, Maureen?' She looked past his shoulder and saw the square full of onlookers, and as Inskip showed no sign of moving, after a moment she decided to step aside, but not before she'd screeched out to the audience, 'Seen enough, have you, so?' Watts followed the two of them inside. She banged the door shut and faced Inskip, arms akimbo.

'Where is he?' he asked again.

'If you mean my husband, he's still in his bed, where he's been for the last six weeks, and I'd ask you to have the decency not to disturb him, poor soul.'

'I'm not talking about your husband, I'm talking about O'Rourke.'

'And which O'Rourke would that be? I know at least half a dozen that go by the name, and none of them are here, so you can sling your hooks, both of you.'

'I'm talking about Danny O'Rourke, Maureen. Him that used to go with Cathleen Hennessy, remember?'

'And what makes you think he's here? You've got no cause to go disturbing innocent folks, looking for the likes of that one.' She was full of righteous indignation, which didn't fool either of them.

'Come on, Maureen. We're not going until we've had a look round.'

'Go on, then, look. If nothing else will satisfy you, look around all you want. You won't find him. But don't you go bothering Michael.' For the first time she looked anxious.

'We'll have to take a look in his room, but we won't disturb him.'

There were few places to hide in that barely furnished house – and nor did they find anything, after searching from attic to cellar, even in the sick Michael Maguire's bedroom, after a hasty apology to its occupant. Nothing except, in the attic, an old iron bedstead, an orange crate and a vile, acrid smell that made Inskip gag, which Watts cheerfully ascribed to rats. Maureen said yes, they did occasionally take in a lodger but she had enough to do now, looking after Michael, without that.

So Mona Reagan had given him false information – or been mistaken, which Inskip preferred to believe. He'd had a message from Corrigan at the Nag that she had something to tell him and to meet her in the same place as before. He had done as she asked, and when they met, found she'd had a change of heart after all. She had at last admitted she might have an idea where he might find O'Rourke. 'But you must promise me you won't get the people there into trouble,' she'd insisted before she would say a word.

'I can't promise that, if they've been hiding him.'

Then she wasn't going to tell. But in the end, she did.

'Maureen Maguire's my sister – the woman who works at the Nag, you know? She's not a widow but she soon will be – her husband's dying of the consumption in the front room and nothing to be done about it. Nothing coming in, either, so she was glad of it when Michael Corrigan gave her that job. She's hopeless, to tell the truth, but she does her best. Her house isn't big enough to swing a cat, but she has to take in the occasional lodger in the attic to make ends meet.' She gave him a steady look. 'If you understand me.'

'O'Rourke's the lodger now?'

She didn't say yes, but she didn't say no, either. 'I hope I'm not going to live to regret this, but anything that'll help you to get that swine.' Again, he wondered what had caused her to hate O'Rourke so much she was prepared to sacrifice her sister. 'As long as you don't tell Maureen it was me who told you, sure she'd murder me. She's doing it for the money, that's all, so I can't blame her. But you just promise she won't get into trouble – I won't be here to help her, I'm leaving, going back home. I've had enough.'

'I'll do my best, that's all I can say.' Enough of what? he wondered. 'Though I don't suppose much more than a warning will happen to her, if she swears she didn't know he was wanted.' He hoped that wasn't wishful thinking on his part.

'To tell the truth, I'm not sure she does know what it is he's done, though anybody else but Mo might have a good idea, the daft spalpeen.'

'Why didn't you tell me this before?'

He didn't expect an answer to that one, but she said, 'Well, I've told you now. You never know, it might drive some sense into her thick noddle.' She laughed shortly. 'Just listen to me, the pot calling the kettle black!'

'I have to thank you, Mona, for this. But before you go, tell me . . . what do you know about Lennie Croxton?'

'Oh, him!' she said, curling her lip. Then, 'I'm sorry, I shouldn't speak ill of the dead.'

'But he and O'Rourke – they were in something together?'

He had tried her too far, he saw. She looked scared. 'I'm sorry he's dead – Lennie. But he is now and nothing to be done about it. He was up to his neck in it over in Ireland, you know, and doing things he'd no right to do over here, and . . . no, I can't say anything else.'

After that, he hadn't pushed her further. After all, she'd been brave to go as far as she had, even though they hadn't found O'Rourke.

Mona had hoped they would, and that searching her sister's house would make Maureen Maguire see sense, but he doubted much would do that. Unlike her sister, Maureen was not, as Mona had intimated, very bright. More than that, she was a slattern. If O'Rourke had been holing up here, he must have been glad to depart. On the other hand, she was devotedly doing her best to look after a husband who patently wouldn't see out another winter.

He was disappointed not to have found O'Rourke in Jubilee Court, but he would have been more surprised if they had. Too much to expect. Too easy. Maybe he had been here when Mona had spoken to him, but these people operated their own network and O'Rourke was most likely moving from house to house, not staying long in any one of them. If he was still hanging around London, there must be a compelling reason, but he couldn't hope to escape detection for ever. With the resources of the Special Branch behind them, they would find him, sooner or later.

While Inskip was holding his nose at the odours of Jubilee Court, Gaines was interviewing Violet Martens in her lavender-scented sitting room.

'Rather you than me, sir,' Inskip had said, rolling his eyes after they had discussed the hypothesis Gaines had put forward and Gaines had announced his intention of seeing Mrs Martens. 'And the best of luck,' he added with a grin.

So now the inspector was left alone with her after the reluctant departure of the sour-faced Newcombe, who had been with her when he was shown in. He sat facing her, his solid frame on an upright chair, his feet planted squarely on the ground. That she didn't welcome his presence or the prospect of conversation with him was more than obvious, but at least she was being coolly polite.

She was looking better than when he had last seen her. Recent events in this household must have taken their toll, but it didn't show. She was wearing black, because of her brother, of course, from head to toe, but in no way did it resemble the deep mourning it was meant to be. Her dress was fashionably cut to show off her slim figure and no other colour but black could have enhanced her dazzling complexion to such an extent. She was wearing no jewellery, except for a shiny jet mourning brooch at the throat of her high-collared dress, and more jet in her ears.

'I'm sorry we haven't had the opportunity to speak since your brother died, Mrs Martens,' he began.

She raised delicately drawn eyebrows. 'I would hardly have thought that was necessary. I'm afraid I can't be of any help to you there.'

'May I offer my condolences?'

'Thank you.' She inclined her head in acknowledgement and smiled the closed, tucked-in smile that never seemed to be really amused. 'It's all been very unfortunate.'

'Indeed. I'm afraid your family's had a series of unfortunate happenings lately.' If she noticed the irony, she didn't show it.

'That's true, Inspector. But at least my baby's been returned.'

'She's shown no after effects, I hope?'

'None, according to Nanny.'

Her impatience was beginning to show. She only just avoided looking pointedly at the clock, but she picked up some sewing that was nearby and began to stitch, her slender fingers moving quickly, a plain enough indication that she thought he was wasting her time. He decided she was quite capable of continuing indefinitely with her monosyllabic responses to his questions, but he didn't intend to let it stop him. What he had come here to say would be difficult for him, a man who normally didn't use words more than he had to. But before he could begin, she spoke lightly. 'It was all very mysterious, was it not, the kidnapping?'

She had unwittingly given him his opening, 'That's true, but perhaps not so mysterious as you might wish us to believe, Mrs Martens.'

'What?' She stared at him, her colour rising. 'Would you mind telling me just what you mean by that?'

'I'll try to explain myself more clearly. But before we go any further, I must ask you if you would like your husband to be present as well.'

'He's not at home, he's at the bank.' Her breathing was coming more quickly, but she asked coldly, 'Why should I want that?'

'Because there are questions I need to ask, to which he's entitled to know the answer. Unless, of course, you don't want him to hear.'

She put the sewing aside very deliberately and stood up. 'I believe you are exceeding your welcome, Inspector. How dare you? I must ask you to leave.'

'I'm prepared to do that, but not before you have heard what I have to say.'

For answer, she simply turned her back and pressed the bell by the fireplace whereupon the maid, Newcombe, entered, so quickly it was easy to see she had been outside the door listening, or attempting to listen, to what was going on inside. How much did she know? he wondered, not for the first time. He said, 'I don't intend to go just yet, not until we have talked. Are you sure you want your maid to hear?'

Newcombe looked daggers at him from under drawn brows. If Violet Martens ever needed a formidable watchdog, she had one in this woman. It wouldn't have amazed him to see her showing her teeth, ready to bite. He was pretty certain that what Emma Pavel had told Inskip was likely to be true enough, that she would do anything for her mistress. Assuming a headache at the time of the so-called kidnapping would have been nothing to her.

'Is everything in order, Mrs Martens?' she asked.

For a split second, Violet hesitated, then she shook her head, 'You may go, Newcombe. I'm sorry, I rang the bell by mistake.'

The woman scowled her disbelief, but as Violet fluttered her hand in dismissal she had no option but to obey. Sitting down again, Violet looked at her feet. He waited several minutes but she kept her head down, silently tracing the carpet's pattern with the toe of her shoe.

'All right, then let's start with this, Mrs Martens, shall we?'

At last she raised her head. 'What – what is that you're holding?'

He stretched out his palm so that she could see the little silver bracelet more clearly, but her expression didn't change as she stared wordlessly at it. 'The bracelet your daughter was wearing when she

was returned, of course. You recognize it? You should; I think I'm
right in believing it once belonged to you.'

'To *me*?'

'When you were a child. You must remember it, you were wearing
it in several of the photographs your brother was so proud of, all
those he kept in his study.'

He could feel the frost from where he sat. 'That's a totally
unjustified supposition. A cheap little mass produced thing like
that, there must be hundreds about.'

Her insistence on the bracelet's tawdriness wouldn't hold up. It
was a pretty, delicate little thing, craftsman made, and though not
an expensive object, it was not something to be despised. He said
nothing for several moments, but her stare didn't waver. Her eyes
were beautifully shaped, with thick lashes, the same shade of forget-
me-not blue as her little daughter's, though there the similarity
ended. He'd never thought of it before, but it struck him now that
hers were the unnerving eyes of a china doll, diamond hard and just
as lifeless. She kept them fixed on him and he saw she wasn't going
to own up to the bracelet. 'All right' he said at last. 'We'll leave that
for now. Let's talk about Dudley Nichol.' Her immaculate brows rose
again. 'Mrs Latimer's cousin, the young man who was murdered.'

'I know who you mean. What about him?'

'There's quite a lot I need to ask you about him, but I'm not
here for the duration,' he said, dispensing with politeness. 'So I'm
going to leave the questions for the moment and tell you that we
now have a fairly clear picture of what has been happening in this
house lately. I believe it started, for you, when Dudley Nichol
arrived, though for him it began when he discovered his cousin,
Alice, was married to your brother, a senior politician. He brought
himself to stay with them for a particular reason. Did you never
wonder what he was doing here?'

'He was a guest of my sister-in-law. It was not up to me to pry
into his personal life.'

'You became quite friendly with him, though . . . were you aware
he had been living in the East End under an assumed name?'

'Certainly not – and if he was, the reasons for it were his own
business.'

'Even if he was working with Irish troublemakers?'

'I'm afraid I don't understand what you're talking about.'

'Don't you read the papers, Mrs Martens? Don't you know anything of what's happening in Ireland, in Parliament, over this Home Rule business? Then let me tell you, it's more than a difference of opinion that's going on over there. It's going to be more than a scrap . . . there are some who think it goes so deep it might even lead to civil war. And there's no shortage of people who are getting ready for it, who are desperate to raise money to buy arms. Why do you think Nichol wanted money?'

Her eyes flickered, but she shrugged at such a needless question. 'Why does anyone want money? If he did.'

So she hadn't known the truth about Nichol, at least not then. But he sensed a dawning comprehension, and perhaps anxiety for what was coming.

'Dudley Nichol was playing a risky game, perhaps more so than he knew, associating with dangerous people. He made a serious error of judgement – and he wasn't the only one, as I think you now know, Mrs Martens. No, no! Listen, and hear what I have to say.' He settled his bulk more comfortably and went on, 'When your brother and his wife were out of the house, Nichol fell into the habit of visiting you. And together you made a plan for the apparent kidnapping of Lucy.'

She gave a smothered exclamation and tried to speak, but he held up his hand. 'You can have your say when I'm finished. You planned to ask for money for her return, five thousand pounds to be exact, which you were going to share, half for you and half for Nichol. And for that,' he said deliberately, 'you were prepared to put your child in danger.'

He had at last succeeded in touching a nerve and she could contain herself no longer. 'Please stop this nonsense. You're getting it all wrong! Lucy was never in the slightest danger.' She stopped. Her colour came and went rapidly as she realized what she had admitted in her agitation.

'No, I don't believe she was. Because she never was kidnapped, was she? She was taken away with your consent.'

'If she was, there was no question at any time that she wouldn't be looked after properly.' She was visibly trembling now, too agitated to refute the accusation.

'How did you know that? Did you visit her to make sure she was being looked after?'

'Lucinda was— Well, she was with my old nanny, the one I had as a child, if you must know. She was in no danger *at all,* and she was happy. She knows Nanny Ryan because she's been taken to visit her regularly, and Nanny adores her. She was delighted to look after her.'

'She was the one who fastened the bracelet around Lucy's wrist, wasn't she?'

She snatched up the discarded sewing again, but her hands were shaking. She threw it down and finally said, 'Very well then, yes. Yes, I'm afraid it was. She is a darling, but she's old now, and . . . old-fashioned. She loves Lucinda and for some reason the idea of her having something that belonged to me as a child pleases her.' She toyed nervously with the brooch at her neck, her fingers restless against the black silk of her dress as he began to press her further.

Yes, she was forced to admit after a while, the bracelet had been given to her at her christening by her godmother. She had worn it often as a child, until it grew too small. Nanny Ryan had been scandalized when she'd later been going to dispose of it along with other childish things, dolls and so on, and took charge of it herself. 'It really wasn't worth keeping. You may not have noticed, Inspector, but I am fussy about my jewellery.'

Gaines didn't recall that she'd ever worn very much of it, but he was trained to notice these things and had remarked on the quality of what she did wear: a ring with diamonds of the first water, a string of gleaming pearls probably worth more than he could ever hope to earn. The jet brooch and earrings she was wearing now were set in a fine tracery of gold.

It was the bracelet that had given her away and roused his suspicions when Lucy had been returned wearing it on her wrist. Despite her denials, it had been patently obvious that the trinket was familiar to her. It was when he saw it, and realized what it might mean, that Gaines had first begun to regret having so summarily dismissed Inskip's original suggestion that the parents might have been involved with the baby's kidnapping. He should have realized it could not have been accomplished without the connivance of the mother: the opportune absence of staff; Newcombe's obliging indisposition, which he was certain now had also been conveniently arranged between her and her mistress;

Violet taking her daughter herself to the park . . . And then, there had been Violet's rage at the sum demanded in the ransom note when it arrived, which had clinched it for him, and in part went to explain how Dudley Nichol had become involved in the affair. She had been hoping to share the ransom with Nichol, but even she had seen the whole scheme was losing credibility by the impossible sum demanded. The more he thought about it, the more possible it had seemed, but it wasn't until he had seen those photographs of her as child, wearing that bracelet, that he had finally become convinced.

'Agreeing for someone like Nichol to take your baby, that took some courage, Mrs Martens, I'll grant you that.'

'How many times do I have to tell you? She was absolutely safe with Nanny Ryan.'

'All the same, you must have been desperate for money to have run such a risk. Knowing your husband's father as you do, it was by no means certain that he would eventually pay out the money, was it?'

'No? Then let me tell you something about Emil Martens. You might find it hard to believe, but it's very necessary indeed to him that he should be seen in a good light, that people should have a good opinion of him . . . why else do you think he makes sure his donations to charity are made so public? He needs everyone to feel Martens Bank is founded on trust and respect. He would have paid, eventually, no doubt about it. But not five thousand pounds, that was simply ridiculous! I never agreed to that at all.'

'How did it come to be asked for, then?'

'I've told you. I don't know. And I've nothing more to say.'

'In your own interests, Mrs Martens, I would strongly advise that you tell me everything you know.' She shook her head, stubbornly mute, but he wasn't going to let her get away with that. He'd come up against silent tactics before now. It took something of a struggle, akin to drawing teeth, but at last she seemed to see that ultimately she could not win, and eventually, bit by bit, he began to get the rest of the sorry story from her.

She had asked Nanny Ryan to look after Lucy for a few days, giving her the reason that she was between nannies. She seemed to take it for granted that he would understand how desperate that situation would make her seem. 'She knew Struthers had left, but

I told her the new one hadn't yet arrived and there was no one to look after Lucinda, and she was more than delighted to do as I asked. She lives alone now she's retired, but she misses the children she used to look after.'

The plan, she went on, had been that Dudley should arrange for a woman to meet her in the park, where the baby would be handed over. The woman would simply wheel Lucy to where Nichol was waiting with a motor car in which baby and perambulator could be stowed. After which Dudley would then drive with her to Nanny Ryan's house in Hampstead, where she would be looked after for a few days.

'Longer than you had agreed, though, before the ransom was demanded?'

'Much longer. That was when I knew something had gone wrong. Everything went quiet, we heard nothing, until . . . It was quite dreadful, I knew Nanny would be wondering why I wasn't taking Lucy home, although I was also certain she would be quite content to keep her as long as necessary. But I didn't know what to do. Dudley had left here the day before Lucinda was . . . taken . . . and I had no idea where he was. He had told me he would get in touch, afterwards.'

'And then the ransom note arrived.'

'Five thousand pounds, yes! Asking for a sum like that made the whole thing look ridiculous – and Dudley wasn't stupid. But then, Lucinda was brought back and it was all over, wasn't it?'

All over. The very words she had used then. But he also recalled her agitation – or had it simply been bewilderment?

'You saw the bracelet and you thought it was your Nanny Ryan who had brought her back?'

'Good gracious, no! Not at all. She's too old to have walked with the pram all the way from Hampstead. I thought it must have been Dudley, of course. But I didn't really *care* who'd brought her back. I was just too thankful she was with us again.'

'But when you heard Dudley Nichol had been killed, you must have wondered who else had been involved. And about so many other things as well – not least, questions about that ransom note.'

'There was no point in worrying about something I could do nothing about.'

And, he thought, as far as she was concerned that really was the end of it. A regrettable incident that had occurred but could now be forgotten. She was not to blame, her child had been taken into the care of someone whom she trusted, with her permission. She felt fully justified and free of guilt, notwithstanding she had wasted police time and resources, about which she seemed ignorant that she might yet be charged.

'Who was the woman you met in the park?' he asked.

She shrugged. 'Just someone Dudley knew.'

'And how much of all this did your husband know?' he asked suddenly.

'Ferdie? He knew nothing!' Sudden panic caused her voice to rise. 'And he mustn't know, ever! It's over, with no harm done.'

It wasn't the first time Gaines had noticed the relationship between Martens and his wife was not perhaps what it seemed on the surface. Other instances sprang to mind of when he had shown that there was probably more of his father in Ferdinand Martens than anyone suspected.

'Why do you think your brother killed himself, Mrs Martens?' he asked suddenly.

'Edmund?' The abrupt switch startled her. 'Who could possibly know that?'

'Did you know about his affair with Mrs Fiore?'

'Well, yes, of course I did. I've known about it for years. My God, *everyone* knew about his affair with that woman. What has that to do with anything?' she asked sharply. Then her eyes widened. 'You don't seriously believe that had anything to do with his death?'

'If you knew about her, you must have realized that it might have everything to do with it.'

By now he had come to think there wasn't anything much he wouldn't be prepared to believe of Violet Martens. He could now see through the play-acting he'd witnessed that first day, when Lucy was supposedly taken from her in the park. He had been sorry for her then, but now . . . He believed there were evil men – and women – who had committed far worse acts than she had ever done, as well as those of limited intelligence who were not responsible for their actions. Violet Martens did not have either excuse. She was an intelligent woman and far from evil. But he had rarely encountered anyone so monumentally self-centred. And he thought she was also astute enough to know exactly what he was implying, however much she was pretending.

'Oh, come now, Inspector. This really is too much. If you are thinking anyone would blackmail him over that, your imagination really is running away with you.' She laughed.

Dudley Nichol's original idea about the kidnapping had been inherently stupid and in the end ineffectual, but he was pretty sure he was right in thinking she might not have been willing to abandon the basic principle and had attempted to use the idea of blackmail on her brother. To an honourable man who publicly acclaimed integrity above all things, his sense of self-worth already lowered by doubts regarding the future of his hitherto unblemished political career, might not the threat to expose what had been going on in his private life have been the last straw? It would not have been, of course. Men had emerged intact through much worse. It probably wouldn't have mattered, ultimately, to anyone in a similar position to Latimer's. The point was, however, that Latimer had in all probability believed that it would.

She hadn't answered his question, but now she said, almost defiantly, 'Well, we shall never know why my brother did what he did, shall we, Inspector?'

Sadly he had to admit she was right. He was pretty certain his theory was correct, that the crisis over his political beliefs wasn't the only cause, but he couldn't see how he could ever find any proof of that.

Seventeen

Alice had been determined not to let the tragedy of Edmund's death keep her from her duties at the Dorcas, for the clinic felt to be the one stable point in her life at the moment. Once there, she could put aside the desolate thoughts that threatened to swamp her, and begin to face the questions hanging over her future.

Charles Markham, Edmund's solicitor and close friend from schooldays, had spent time with her, discussing the terms of Edmund's will. 'I'm afraid he's left Manessa House, in its entirety, to his sister,' he'd said in some slight embarrassment. 'Do you have any problems with that?'

'None at all, since he's inserted the proviso that I may live here, in our part of the house, as long as I wish. Which won't be for long – but it will give me time to find somewhere of my own. After all, I shall hardly be destitute with what he has left me.' There had not been as much as had been expected: large withdrawals over the last few months had been left unaccounted for. But by her standards she would do well enough, with money to buy a more modest property of her own, and to help keep her in moderate comfort for the rest of her life. 'I'm happy that Violet should have the house.'

As a consequence of this, Violet was being especially agreeable to her, though she herself was obviously looking and feeling very much under the weather, an understandable reaction, Alice decided, to what she had been through, the awfulness of Lucy's kidnapping, and then the loss of her brother. Alice well understood this. She herself was still dealing with the guilt she knew a suicide death always left behind, questioning how much of it had been her fault. If she had been more understanding and sympathetic, if she had encouraged Edmund to be more open and talk about his inner feelings, might this not have happened?

After they had finished discussing the terms of Edmund's will, Charles Markham had said, 'He wanted you to have this.' He handed her a letter. 'And his diaries,' he added, taking a sizeable parcel from a drawer. The diaries all politicians kept if they ever intended to write their memoirs, Edmund had told her at the beginning of their marriage. He called them his daybooks, there was nothing personal in them, they were simply a record of events, meetings and conversations with other MPs. Chilled by the thought that he had after all left her some communication, she had felt quite unable to read them immediately, especially the letter, which had been left to be opened by her, tellingly, 'in the event of my death'. It was as she had thought: he had been ambivalent about taking his life, right up to the last moment. Its contents might give her a clue as to why, but just now, she did not feel strong enough to bear the burden of the torment that must have faced him.

Resolutely she had forced herself not to dwell on these dark thoughts – they would get her nowhere. Far wiser to concentrate on her work at the Dorcas, where she insisted on going every day to work. She was being thought odd in doing this, people were rather shocked, for some reason, but that only made her feel rebellious. She was in mourning, but that didn't mean she should remain in purdah.

Today, the influx of needy patients having dispersed, she pressed on with bringing her records up to date, and when she had finished that and tidied her desk, she picked up the notes she'd made for her meeting with Sam in a few minutes. On the way out, catching sight of herself in the small mirror in the corner, she paused to smooth her hair, then turned away and left the room, refusing to acknowledge how pale she was looking.

Sam was by the open front door, talking to a dirty-faced boy in patched fustian trousers cut short at the knee, bare-legged and wearing ill-fitting boots, who had just delivered what appeared to be an urgent summons. 'I'm sorry, Alice, we can't have that talk just now,' he said. 'I'm needed elsewhere. Tomorrow?'

'Of course. It's not important.' He raised his eyebrows and she suspected he knew very well that the private conversation she'd requested was very important to her. He had guessed she was going to ask him to reconsider her position here at the clinic. She hoped she wasn't being unduly optimistic about his likely reaction to her proposal. She didn't really think he would be averse to her going into partnership with him, and thought he would welcome the sharing of the work and the expenses of running the clinic, but she was also sure he would urge her not to be too hasty about making such a decision. He had already told her she should take more time off to get her bearings, as he put it, but that was the very last thing she wanted to do, to have the empty hours stretching before her with nothing else to do but relive the traumatic events of the last few days. Did nobody understand that the work here was her salvation, as it always had been?

She took another look at him now, his stocky frame leaning against the doorpost, almost as though he needed its support. He looked very tired indeed. Sam, with his seemingly inexhaustible energy, who was normally able to put in an amount of work that would have killed a lesser man! She knew he'd been called out twice the previous night. Added to that, Hannah was nearing her time and caring for a pair of boisterous twins in her condition, and in their cramped quarters, was no easy ride. It was taking its toll on her. Emma Pavel had supplied them with the name of a girl to help out but the situation still laid heavy demands on Sam, too.

The boy on the doorstep was shuffling from one booted foot to the other, waiting for an answer, no doubt anxious about the fate of the coppers he'd earn by running the errand – but only after he'd delivered the message and received a reply. 'He said you was to come right away, Doctor. She's asking for you.'

'All right, sonny,' Sam said with a sigh. He patted the lad's shoulder. 'Tell him I'm on my way.'

The boy shot off and Alice asked, 'Who is it? Who's asking for you so urgently?'

'Old Mrs Tooley, Prosser Street. Sorry about this, I promise we'll talk tomorrow, Alice,' he said, turning to fetch his bag.

'I'll go.'

'What?'

'She's your patient, but I'm sure I can cope with whatever's needed.'

He looked sorely tempted, but then he shook his head. 'She has me on a bit of a string, old Roisin, to tell the truth, and I doubt if she's at death's door, but you never know with her, and she is nearly ninety.'

'There isn't anything you can do that I can't.'

He really did look exhausted, but he shook his head. Then he laughed suddenly. 'Well, I suppose if the old biddy's asking for me and not the priest, she can't be that bad. You're a brick, Alice, but don't forget to tell Paddy Tooley it was me sent you to look after his mother.'

He gave her Mrs Tooley's notes and they spoke briefly about the heart condition she suffered from. She was, he said, very much inclined to play on this, sending for him whenever she felt like it, enjoying the drama of it and not least the opportunity to show the world she had the means to pay for a doctor's visits. But since there was always the chance she could go at any time, for that reason alone Sam couldn't afford to ignore any summons. 'And why not, if the Tooleys are prepared to pay?' he asked, affecting a cynicism Alice knew he didn't feel. 'Don't let her intimidate you . . . she can be an old tyrant and she will do that if she sees she can, but she's all right if you stick up to her and don't object to being called Doctor Alice.'

A lot of people used the familiarity and Alice never minded. It was their way of lessening the distance between themselves and someone they all too often imagined could perform miracles. If Sam, with his jocular bedside manner, was Doctor Sam to Mrs Tooley, it meant he was as much a favourite with the old lady as he was with most of his regular patients, she guessed.

'All the same, go easy on her, she's not the old witch you might think.' He laughed again, as if recalling something she'd said or done that amused him.

She went to fetch her bicycle out of the backyard and wheeled it along the narrow passage which ran from front to back of the house. She had a general idea of the direction of Prosser Street, but Sam had given her more precise directions and as she made her wobbly way over the cobbles, she began to wonder where her impulse was going to lead her, what she'd let herself in for. She felt a stab of uncertainty, but the name of Tooley at that address had been too much to ignore.

The door was opened by a big, heavily built man with gingerish hair and small brownish eyes. He looked at her suspiciously, and even when she informed him she had come in place of Doctor Weston and with his recommendation, he didn't alter his stance, not bothering to hide the prejudice she had by now become accustomed to against women doctors.

'Very well,' she said eventually. 'If you're not going to let me in,

Mr Tooley, it seems as though your mother will have to wait until Doctor Weston can come himself.' She turned to go down the steps, but he hurriedly called her back. Her first impression hadn't been wrong. He was the sort of man who was all bluster, and not very intelligent either, she suspected.

'There's no need to be so hasty, now. And I'd bring that machine inside, if I was you. If you don't want to have to walk home, that is.'

He watched her manoeuvring the bicycle up the steps, not offering to help, but once inside, he relented and pushed it further along towards the back of the hallway until he found a spot where he could rest it against the dado. He was a rough-looking customer but he had the soft, musical lilt of his native Ireland in his speech, even though he was not making any attempt to be pleasant. Either it was deliberately assumed, or he couldn't have lived over here for long, she thought. 'Mrs Tooley's up the stairs,' he said. 'I don't like to think of what she'll say when she sees it's not Doctor Weston who's come.'

There wasn't much she could reply to that and she followed him up two flights without speaking. Although the stairs were uncarpeted, they were fairly clean. Recalling what David and the police had said, she knew that the Tooleys did not occupy the house alone. If they, Paddy or old Roisin herself, owned the house, renting rooms must be how they made their money. It had once been large and handsome, and even run down as it now was, it was enough to provide the cramped sort of accommodation which sufficed in these parts for several families, and the rents would mount up to a profitable operation. They passed several scruffy doors with peeling paint, from behind which various domestic noises emanated, although she heard no piping voices of children, or babies crying. On the third floor, they reached a door which had attempted a touch of class, due to a rather tatty shamrock wreath nailed to it, left over from St Patrick's Day last month. It made her catch her breath, reminded of Lucy's bracelet.

Sam had told her the old woman, Tooley's mother, was not bedridden, but today she had taken to her bed. She was barely a bump under the bedclothes. She lay with skeletal hands outside the covers, her rosary twisted between her fingers, and showed no sign of movement when Alice entered with her son, but a pair of small, shrewd eyes followed her progress, which sharpened when she heard the explanation for her being there. 'Get you away now, Paddy.

Leave the women to it.' And though her voice was barely above an exhausted whisper, and had the same soft accent as that of her son, it held a command which he didn't hesitate to obey.

The room was dark and stifling, and Alice's first impulse was to throw open the one tiny window that offered all the illumination there was, had she not guessed it would be jammed shut. The small, cast-iron bedroom grate was empty, so the heat wasn't generated by a piled up fire, as it often was in an invalid's room. The smothering effect was due more to the room being crammed with overstuffed furniture, heavy draperies, and the numerous rugs that overlapped each other on the floor. A musty smell arose from the furnishings, and from the bed itself, where the old woman lay under heaped-up quilts. The pattern of the wallpaper could scarcely be seen, so many holy pictures were hanging there. In addition, a large crucifix hung over the bedhead, beneath it a picture of the Virgin Mary. Alice averted her eyes from another, Jesus with an all too realistically bleeding heart, as she approached the bed where Roisin lay. Her skin resembled the crazing on old china and her lips were cyanosed. She was nearly bald, but what was left of her hair showed it had once been red. A wig of that colour hung from the bedpost.

'Hello, Mrs Tooley. I'm Doctor Alice,' she introduced herself, mindful of Sam's advice.

There was little doubt that Roisin Tooley was a chronically sick woman. She was, however, clearly not in need of urgent medical attention, and Alice couldn't prevent herself from thinking of all those who truly needed medical help and couldn't even afford simple medicines. All she would say was that she'd had a pain, but she'd had worse, she'd taken her capsule and it was gone now and she wasn't done for yet, evidently expecting the sort of joshing reply to this Sam would no doubt have given.

Alice didn't bother, and yet as she started to examine the old woman her annoyance at having made this pointless journey dissolved. She curbed her intolerance, knowing that patients often needed reassurance as much, if not more, than treatment and medicines, even someone like Roisin Tooley. Sometimes they were lonely and only wanted to talk. Old Roisin was nearly ninety and frail as the dried shamrock leaves that had fallen from Dudley's prayer book. She looked liable to fall into dust, as they had, at a touch. Whatever medical attention she was given could be merely palliative, to ease her last weeks through this world – or even, Alice was afraid, her last days. But those sharp eyes still held a distinctly indomitable gleam.

As if divining her thoughts, the old woman's lips parted in a broken-toothed smile and she repeated, 'I'm not for the next world yet, you may be sure of that.' But even as she spoke, a claw-like hand emerged from under the bedclothes to make the sign of the cross. And for a second or two, dread showed in her face. Despite what she said, Roisin Tooley had not yet accepted the inevitable.

'You go on believing that, Mrs Tooley, it'll do you good,' Alice smiled, reaching for what felt like nothing more than a loose bundle of bones to take her pulse, knowing Sam's prognosis had been correct, and that it was doubtful she could survive much longer. Her heart condition was serious, even if she did choose to use it to exploit the situation. Clearly, she liked to have a doctor dancing attendance on her, but both Alice and the old lady knew there was nothing to be done except to ensure she was left as comfortable as possible, with a supply of her medicine handy. Alice was in fact getting ready to leave, when Roisin said suddenly, and quite strongly, 'You look like the sort of young woman who can keep her tongue between her teeth. I'm right, aren't I?'

Alice paused in the act of stowing her stethoscope into her bag. 'I hope I can keep quiet when necessary, yes,' she answered, wondering what was coming.

'It's a great gift.'

She said nothing more for a moment or two, then her hand dived back under the bedclothes, this time bringing out a small cloth bag. 'Take it,' she said, 'and give it to Doctor Sam for his new babby. It was my dear mother's, God rest her soul, and it was herself put it round my neck when I was no more than six weeks old and where it's been ever since. You can take a look at it, if you like.'

In the bag was a tiny mother of pearl crucifix on a silver chain. 'There's no one else for it. I'd be after giving it to a grandchild if I had one, but Paddy's never given me any. Or not that I know of.' She gave a dry cackle. 'I can tell you that one's going to be a girl, and I want her to have it. Promise me you won't forget to hand it over.'

'I won't.'

'You haven't been blessed with children yourself.' The sharp old eyes rested on her.

Alice felt her colour rising. 'No.'

'It's a queer old life we're given sometimes, but don't you fret.' She nodded her balding head. 'You've been through the darkness but the night doesn't last forever. You'll get what you wish for, one day.'

It was unsettling, to be read so easily. The old woman clearly believed she really had got the second sight and maybe she had. There was something distinctly sibylline about her and her predictions.

'Thank you for coming, Doctor. I took me pill and told Paddy there was no need, but he insisted, for all he's used to seeing me like that. He's a good son to his old mother.'

'I'm sure he is.' It was true that there had been no need, and Paddy Tooley was used to his mother and maybe ought to have known that. But such attacks could be alarmingly frightening things for relatives to witness, and the old lady herself, as Sam had said, seemed more than capable of using emotional blackmail in order to hand over the little cross, which could be the real reason for requesting the visit. Roisin had been expecting Sam, so it probably was. It seemed to Alice that the intuition that had prompted her to volunteer for this visit had failed her. What had she expected to find, after all? The woman, Mona Reagan?

Roisin lay back on her pillows under the smothering quilts, passing her rosary beads through her fingers again, her eyes never leaving Alice. 'I'm sorry if you think you've been brought here on false pretences, Doctor Alice.' Reading her again.

'I'm a doctor, Mrs Tooley. I hope nobody's ever afraid of calling me out.'

'Well, don't forget to leave your bill. Not that you will, or if you do, you'll be the first doctor I've known that has,' she added wickedly. 'Paddy will pay you if you give him a shout.'

Alice laughed and thought she saw why Sam had a soft spot for old Roisin.

There was no need to call for Paddy. He was waiting for her outside the door. He had decided to put his previous obstructiveness to one side and had assumed a smile she found even more irritating and certainly unconvincing. 'If you could kindly see it in your way to spare a moment or two longer, Doctor, I'd appreciate it. There's someone else in need of the benefit of your expertise.'

She didn't for a moment think it was a request. She felt her flesh crawl as he put out a beefy hand and for a nasty moment she thought he was actually going to detain her physically, although she had shown no intention of refusing to do what he was asking. Her heart began to thump, with a premonition of what was coming. She hadn't been mistaken, after all. This was why Roisin had pretended to need a doctor. She wasn't the one who needed medical attention.

She told herself there was nothing to be afraid of. No one knew who Doctor Alice was, or that she herself had any reason to have heard of anyone who lived here. But still she felt a qualm. Perhaps she ought not to have stepped in, and let Sam come here, after all. Sam would not have allowed himself to be coerced like this, even without the 'persuasion' of a little mother of pearl cross for his new baby. All the same, she followed Tooley into another room. And what would Sam have done faced with the man on the bed – whom Tooley said was called Frank Doyle, but whom she had not the slightest doubt was the Daniel O'Rourke who was suspected of murdering her cousin, and whom the police were seeking so urgently?

The telephone was by no means Alice's preferred means of communication. It was quick and convenient, a modern-day invention that was improving all the time, but it wasn't yet always entirely reliable. Lines invariably crackled and not infrequently went dead. In no way did it equal talking face to face, or even communicating by a letter or postcard which would get there the same day. But there was no time for any of that. The telephone it would have to be.

The staff at the Dorcas had gone home, Sam was upstairs with his family and she had the hallway and the telephone to herself. She asked for Inspector Gaines when she got through to Scotland Yard, on a line that for once didn't break up, but he wasn't there. She was put through to the dapper Sergeant Inskip, he who seemed to have taken a fancy to Lucy's nanny, Emma. He listened attentively, only interrupting with a few sharp questions, as she told him how her visit to Prosser Street had come about.

'Blow me,' he said when she'd finished, and added, 'We might have guessed, I suppose; it's an old trick, moving around, going back to a place we've already searched. Twice, in this case.' He thanked her, sounding jubilant. 'But don't do anything more, Mrs Latimer. We'll be in touch and let you know what's happened.'

David was less pleased when she rang him with the story. 'You did *what?* What possessed you, Alice? No, don't say anything more. I'm coming over to see you immediately – no, dammit, I've got a meeting in ten minutes. But stay where you are and I'll be over as soon—' The line went dead.

It was in fact less than an hour before he arrived and she admitted him into her surgery.

'There's no need to fuss – I wasn't exactly in danger, you know. They didn't know who I was for a start, I never gave my name. To them I was just any old doctor.'

'Don't joke about it. I just wish you hadn't gone there. What made you do it?'

Alice didn't say she had wondered the same herself, when she'd been manoeuvred into that room, though she soon saw that all they wanted of her was her professional advice.

She had tried the only way she could see to manipulate the situation. 'This man should be in hospital,' she had said after examining him, wanting to get him away from this house, but by no means certain that there was any chance of him being admitted into overcrowded wards, even at her urgent request, when there was nothing more they could do for him than what she could do here. She need not have worried. The suggestion was met with a flat refusal from the man lying in the bed, immediately endorsed by Tooley.

The man, O'Rourke, was obviously a gaunt shadow of his former self, but when he'd had a shave and got dressed, he would no doubt look very different. His looks were not distinguished, the sort of fellow you passed every day in the street without remembering them, a narrow, dark face and deep-set eyes. Fit and well, she thought he would have the sort of looks that seemed to appeal to some women, simply because they couldn't read them. 'I'll be able to travel soon?' he'd asked with some urgency. 'I have to get back to Ireland as soon as possible.'

The police hadn't mentioned his background. She had imagined, from his name and those he had associated with, that he must be

Irish but his accent, unlike Tooley's, owed nothing to Ireland. He sounded like a Londoner, born and bred.

'They told me his name was Frank Doyle,' she told David, 'but I'm sure it was O'Rourke I saw. I suspected at first, the way they'd wanted a doctor in to see to him, that he must have been shot and they needed a bullet removing, but it wasn't that. He's had a virulent fever which has left him very weak, and he still looked pretty bad, but actually he's on the mend, apart from his cough. He's feeling pretty sorry for himself, but they needn't have bothered with a doctor. He was well able to talk to me and he seemed clear-headed, though he swore he'd no idea what caused him to be ill.'

'What do you think it was?'

'Could be anything. Not taking care of himself when he had a cold . . . influenza . . . I left him with something that should help his cough and when I told him to be sure to eat well, he said there should be no problem with that, he'd been able to eat nothing for days and was feeling ravenous by now. So I suppose he'll be up and about within a few days. By which time the police will have got him. Sergeant Inskip promised to let me know when they have him in custody.'

But two days passed without hearing anything from the police.

Gaines hadn't the least idea what the delay was about, why Special Branch hadn't gone in immediately, as he would have done, but he kept his opinion to himself. He needed their cooperation more than he needed conflict with them. In any case, he knew they would only say they had their reasons. And they *had* put a strict watch on the house in Prosser Street for the last two days, so that there was no possibility O'Rourke could have slipped away without their knowing.

But now there was to be a full-scale search, led by the Branch's Inspector Ted Williams, still smarting a little from the previous failed searches at Prosser Street. Gaines was satisfied with what was to be done. When he was apprehended, he wanted O'Rourke pulled in for questioning in connection with the murder of Dudley Nichol. Williams had additional reasons. There was enough suspicion hanging over him that he might be connected with smuggling contraband firearms and ammunition to have pulled out all the stops.

Williams was a tall man, with a physique that was not threatening, so thin his jacket seemed to hang across his shoulders, rather than fit, but anyone who knew him had learned not to underestimate him. He was obviously keyed up but he made light of the proposed search. 'The sort of people we're dealing with here aren't major players. Forget the Childers of this world, we know who they are. They're dangerous, they have the money and the means to raise funds to buy guns and they'll do it sooner or later, but they'll get their comeuppance, we'll see to that. That doesn't mean, of course, that they're not prepared to stir up feelings . . . easy enough to do, God knows, with these Irish, you don't need me to tell you that. How many fights have you seen after closing time on a Friday night when they're roaring drunk?'

Gaines had lost count. As a young copper he had once narrowly missed losing his eye when he'd come into contact with a bottle hurled across the street in one of the late night brawls the fighting Irish were notorious for. After a drink or two, it was mayhem in the Irish quarters.

'Are you saying O'Rourke's not dangerous?'

'I'm saying he's *bloody* dangerous. Amateurs always are. The fact that they don't know what they're doing half the time is enough to put the wind up anyone.'

He was right in that, of course. The people he was talking about were so-called patriots, but often no more than a rag, tag and bobtail lot with only the instinct to be part of a fight. If any of them other than O'Rourke had been involved in the murder of Dudley Nichol, or Lucy's kidnap, it would only have been incidental to the main cause.

Williams was expecting violence and since the British police were not permitted to use guns, he could only pray these Irishmen wouldn't have any either, or at any rate not find themselves in a position to use them. He agreed that Gaines might go along with him, and Inskip, who would have been mortified at being kept away. Two of his own men were with him and five uniformed constables were stationed outside, together with a horse-drawn police van.

The sun was shining when they arrived at the Tooley house in Prosser Street, and every curtain was drawn – though not, apparently, against the sun. They were taken aback to find also that the door knocker was wrapped in black cloth to muffle its sounds. This was disconcerting, but after a moment, Williams gave the signal to proceed. He didn't much like entering what appeared to be a house of mourning, but even that couldn't be allowed to deter them. He thought it was quite possible, anyway, that in this case it might be nothing more than a specially set up façade.

Tooley himself greeted them, however, his tough bulk tightly encased in a black suit, and with a long face informed them that his mother, God rest her soul, had died the day before and they were making arrangements for her coffin to be sent back to Ireland for burial there among her kin. He scowled at Inskip, doubtless remembering their last meeting, but he made only token objections to them entering when he saw how many more were waiting outside.

Although all the curtains were closed, the clocks had been stopped and the mirrors turned to the wall, the house was by no means hushed and silent. Neighbours and friends seemed to be coming and going all the time to pay their last respects, and family mourners had gathered there for Roisin Tooley's wake. Williams had them all shunted into the front parlour where the coffin lay and a constable was stationed at the front door while the rest of the house was searched.

The inspector's face lengthened as no sign whatever of Daniel O'Rourke manifested itself in their search through rooms showing that most of the occupants weren't particular about sharing their living space. There were more beds jammed into small spaces than anyone would have thought possible and the kitchen seemed to have been a communal affair. But at least they encountered none of the sort of violence they had been led to expect, which was just as well, unarmed as they were. Room after room, as well as the cellar and the two attics, was thoroughly searched, but without success. Gloom was beginning to descend on the searchers as they finished at last and stood outside the room of the old woman, Roisin Tooley, realizing they were facing another failure and wondering what next to do. Williams hesitated, then belatedly remembering that this room's late occupant now lay downstairs in her coffin, finally gave the nod for them to enter.

And that was where they found him. As the bedroom door swung open, they saw a foot protruding from under the bed that Roisin no longer had any need of.

It was an ignominious capture. He was dragged out, half dressed, and emerged coughing, sneezing and covered in fluff. He and the man who had yanked him out faced each other. 'And not before time,' Inskip said, grasping his arm. Gaines' hand reached out and locked on Inskip's other arm like steel, but the sergeant made no move to hit O'Rourke. He just threw him a look of contempt, released him then stood back. Gaines relaxed his grip and gave him a satisfied nod.

After O'Rourke had been taken away, they went to find Tooley. Technically, he hadn't committed any crime by harbouring O'Rourke, but Gaines for one needed to speak to him. He was in the front parlour with those of the mourners still left.

Watch over the body was being kept in the darkened room, where the coffin lay on a table draped with a cloth, lighted candles at either end, a statue of the Blessed Virgin at its head, but there were no gloomy faces. The wake was a cheerful affair and the relations and most of the mourners who had been ushered into the room while the search went on were allowed out and had dispersed themselves about the house, showing no disposition to leave. They had gathered there to pay their last respects to old Mrs Tooley, to talk and reminisce about the old lady and what a character she'd been, but they weren't about to be deprived of this new source of gossip. There was a lot of laughter and joking, possibly not unconnected with the fact that every new arrival had a glass immediately thrust into their hands. Tooley had remained in the parlour and Gaines and Williams went in to speak to him.

Of course he hadn't known O'Rourke was hiding from the police, he protested indignantly. Wasn't he just a friend who was ill and needed somewhere to get better? No, why should he ever have heard of a man by the name of Dudley Nichol? No, he knew nothing . . .

'All right, never mind that just now. But we're going to need a statement from you later,' Gaines said, and looked to Williams to see whether he had any questions. He seemed to have his mind on something else.

Williams wasn't a Catholic, so he couldn't have said for certain, but wasn't the coffin usually left open while the mourners came in and paid their last respects? He couldn't answer his own question, but what he did know was that the last time he and his team had been here looking for O'Rourke, Mrs Tooley hadn't yet taken to her bed. A very little lady, he recalled, not reaching up to his shoulder, not weighing much more than a wet dishcloth. And very angry she'd been at having her house's privacy violated. His ears still burned from her colourful Irish invective. Size didn't enter into it when it came to outrage.

'That's a very big coffin for a very small lady, Mr Tooley,' he remarked.

'Sure, but isn't she going back to be laid to rest in the oul' country among her kin, and wouldn't she be wanting all her precious treasures with her?' Paddy replied, at his most Irish.

'Like the Egyptians,' Williams said.

'What? What's that, then?'

'Grave goods, to see them through the afterlife,' Williams explained, aware that offence could be taken, but not inclined to pander to the susceptibilities of somebody like Tooley, even in a situation like this. 'We'll just take a look at these treasures, eh?'

Tooley paled visibly. 'You can't do that,' he said, aghast. 'That's a dead woman in there!'

One of the women crossed herself. Everyone else went silent.

'I don't mean any disrespect, ma'am,' Williams said to the lady. 'But we've just apprehended a wanted man and—'

'And I suppose it's another you're hoping to find in the coffin?' She laughed scornfully.

'All the same.' He walked towards the table and the coffin with its closed lid, and looked around for the means to open it.

'Jayz,' said Tooley to no one in particular. 'The fat's in the fire now.'

Eighteen

Roisin Tooley had been laid to rest in her coffin with the accompaniment of half a dozen rifles, an ancient flint-lock pistol, a Browning revolver, two sophisticated long-range Mausers and sundry other weapons of assorted sizes, ages and capabilities, with as many rounds of ammunition as could be packed into the space that was left. An array of lethal weaponry, a veritable cache that left Williams jubilant, in spite of the caustic comments he made about most of them. They'd forgotten the bows and arrows, he said.

Removing them was a delicate business, requiring some tact. The mourners who still remained in the house had to be ushered out of the way while it was done, and while O'Rourke and Tooley were taken away, followed by Gaines and Inskip.

O'Rourke looked dreadful, gaunt and hollow-eyed, still weak from his fever, but he was a normally fit and healthy man, Gaines judged, tall and broad-shouldered, and was quite up to facing any amount of questioning. He did the interviewing himself. Inskip, to his chagrin, was being kept away for now, but Gaines decided he had enough to deal with, without the prospect of having to keep an eye on his sergeant if things got sticky. When he had pulled O'Rourke from under the bed, he'd done well and kept the promise he'd made not to let his loathing of O'Rourke get in the way of his duty, but Gaines didn't want to push his luck too far.

After the sortie at Prosser Street, the weather had turned. It was a dreadful day, the weather mirroring the night of the murder, and rain beat incessantly against the windows, adding to the sense of gloom as Gaines faced O'Rourke across the table in an interviewing room, with DC Watts, elated at being allowed the honour of taking notes, sitting beside him.

He very soon found out that O'Rourke was not so debilitated that he wasn't also quite capable of deftly deflecting any questions addressed to him. He denied knowledge of anyone called Dudley Nichol, but admitted to meeting Lennie Croxton. Yes, he had called at Mrs Maclusky's house with messages from her relatives in Ireland

and been introduced to him. They had gone out for a drink together, parted about eleven o'clock, and that was the first and last he'd ever seen or heard of him.

'Did you not hear he was dead?'

He hadn't heard that. 'What was it that took him? He didn't weigh no more than a ha'p'orth of humbugs, but he looked chipper enough to me. Very happy, too, when we parted. He could down a pint with the best.'

Gaines didn't bother to answer the question. 'Where did you go for your drink? The Nag?'

'Nah. Well, it might've been, but to tell truth, I don't rightly remember. I'd had a few meself.'

Daniel O'Rourke didn't actually look as though he ever lost control so far as to allow himself to get drunk. He had watchful, deep-set eyes and an expression that was hard to fathom. Since it had been a fair cop regarding the armaments, both he and Tooley knew they were in for it. The illegal possession of firearms and the purposes for which they were intended was a serious matter indeed, regardless of other crimes the pair of them had committed to get money for the guns they'd acquired . . . thieving, extortion and God knew what else. They still had to face Williams after Gaines had finished with them, but as far as the murder of the man he had known as Lennie Croxton went, O'Rourke was keeping his mouth shut. He was sticking to the story that he had met Croxton for the first time that night, that he'd never heard of him being murdered.

Tooley had not been so reticent. When Inskip questioned him, he admitted to knowing Croxton, who'd only gone to lodge with Orla Maclusky because there had been no room at Prosser Street at the time he had arrived in London from Ireland. He'd been living over there for a couple of years, but Tooley hadn't the least idea what he'd been doing there. He'd heard he'd been murdered and he'd been sorry to hear it. Yes, Lennie had been hot on the subject of Irish independence, and why not? It was true he was always full of big talk about raising money to buy guns, but no, Tooley didn't know anything about the kidnapping of any baby, he swore, looking shifty.

'All right, O'Rourke, where were you headed for when you hailed that cab?' Gaines asked now.

'Cab? What cab?'

'The one you got in with Lennie Croxton. The one where you knifed him.'

O'Rourke stuck his hands in his pockets. 'Can I have a cigarette? I talk better when I can smoke.'

'No.'

He sighed exaggeratedly. He was nervous, as well he might be in view of the serious charges he was facing, but he was not showing it. 'I never went in no cab,' he repeated. 'I left him outside the boozer, as I said. It was tipping down, like now, I was soaked to the skin and I wanted to get home.'

Gaines didn't believe a word. He had never been more sure that O'Rourke had been the man in the cab with Nichol. He had used the knife on him, and he had laughed as he got out and left him there.

He eyed him with disfavour and carried on with the questions, the rain beat against the windows and the clock ticked away the time, but they still weren't really getting anywhere. Gaines was tenacious, but so was the man on the opposite side of the table. He terminated the interview for the time being and went to find Inskip.

'Get Sheldyke in,' he told him. He hoped the cabbie's claim that he would recognize the killer again would hold up.

An identification parade was hurriedly assembled, including Tooley as well as O'Rourke. Sheldyke arrived, cheerful and cocky, looking better than he had when they had last seen him, though he insisted it was more than a cold he'd had. It had been a right old dose of flu or something like it, and he still wasn't feeling very clever. 'I didn't rightly oughter be out in this weather, but I know my duty,' he said virtuously, wiping raindrops from his moustache. Perhaps it was he who had passed on his flu or whatever it had been to O'Rourke.

Asked to pick out the man who had ridden in his cab with Nichol, Sheldyke took his time, but in the end he made a decision. 'Seen that one before,' he said, pointing to O'Rourke. Inskip let his face slip into a happy grin. 'But he ain't the one that was in me cab. That's him we left standing there by the gas lamp.'

Nobody said anything until at last Gaines found his voice. 'There was someone else with them?'

'I just said, didn't I?'

The parade was dismissed and they sat down with Sheldyke again.

'You never told us there were three men when you stopped to pick up your fare, Mr Sheldyke.'

'Why should I? Far as I knew, you was only interested in the poor sod what copped it and the one what did it.'

'You're sure they were together, the three men?'

'Well, they was talking to each other, and they said goodnight when we pulled away so I should think so.'

'Would you recognize the other man, the one who got in?'

'I would. I've a good memory for faces. It pays in my line of business. Anyhow, I couldn't hardly fail, could I? Seeing him plain as day under the gas lamp, and with a face like that?'

Latimer.

The man Sheldyke described could have been no one else but Edmund Latimer. He fitted the description like a glove. Big man, well dressed, with a posh accent. The cabbie had been certain his fare had spoken like a toff, and unless O'Rourke was a bloomin' good actor – which he might well be, of course, given the performance he was putting on now – it certainly ruled him out. But above all, there was the only too recognizable birthmark, the port wine stain which Sheldyke swore he had seen very clearly.

It was little use berating the cabbie for neglecting to mention earlier either that or the fact that there had been three men together when he had picked up his fares: the unprecedented happening had prevented the man from getting home to a hot toddy for his cold and a warm bed. He had clearly been feeling groggy, and in no position to think of every detail. In any case, it was highly unlikely that Sheldyke, unless he followed political gossip avidly, would have recognized his fare as Edmund Latimer, unlikely that he had ever seen him before, except maybe in a grainy newspaper photograph which would not have shown up his birthmark clearly.

But – *Latimer?*

There were links with Dudley Nichol, of course. Nichol had stayed under his roof for several weeks and it was not wholly inconceivable that some trouble might have arisen while he was there. But what the devil was he doing out at Bishopsgate, that time of night? And whatever had been between them, could it possibly have been enough to constitute a motivation for murder?

Even supposing Latimer had somehow got wind of Nichol being involved in his niece Lucy's kidnapping, it was scarcely enough for him to seek out and kill Nichol for it. And then to have shot himself, in remorse? Gaines didn't think so, but could the truth of his suicide lie with something other than his political problems or the threat of blackmail over his affair with Mrs Fiore?

'Are you absolutely sure he was the one who got into your cab with the man who was killed, Mr Sheldyke?'

'We-ell.' The cabbie was sounding less confident now. 'I know he was one of them under the lamp, but whether he was the one as actually got into the cab – as to that, I wouldn't swear on the 'oly Bible. It was raining cats and dogs, remember. But that's what I thought.'

He wouldn't be moved from that. Gaines went back to O'Rourke and this time he decided to take Inskip with him.

When faced with what the cabbie had said, O'Rourke eventually admitted that the three men had met and had a drink together. 'I wasn't told his name,' he said. 'Lennie only said he was his cousin's husband. But I could see they was a bit edgy with one another. Turned out the two of them had had a row that morning. Some bust-up about the other bloke's wife.'

'Whose wife? Not Latimer's?' Inskip asked.

'If that was his name,' O'Rourke answered cagily. 'Well, all right then, this Latimer had told Lennie to leave his house – seems he'd been living with them lately.'

'Latimer had told him to leave? Then why did he go to meet him again?'

'Search me. Said he wanted to apologize, didn't he? We had a few drinks together and he got a bit soppy over it, you know? Ready to burst into tears any minute. Said he'd thought there was something going on between Lennie and his wife, but he was sorry for thinking such a thing afterwards, so he'd come looking for him to shake his hand.'

'How did he find Croxton? Latimer's wife said he had left no address.'

'I dunno. I think he'd just been looking around for him.' O'Rourke looked vague.

Alice Latimer had admitted to a slight fondness for her cousin, but the idea of anything more going on between them was patently absurd. But if O'Rourke was to be believed, that was not perhaps how Latimer had seen it. He was a middle-aged man with a much younger and attractive wife. And jealousy was a corrosive emotion Gaines had seen men hanged for. Humiliation that their wives or sweethearts had preferred someone else, rage that anyone had something which they regarded as belonging to *them*. Loss of control and power over what they regarded as their possession. Latimer was a man who was accustomed to both. But surely no one could seriously associate that sort of emotion with a level-headed, rational and shrewd politician such as he had been? And what about the double standards there? What had he to be jealous about, anyway, considering his ten-year relationship with Connie Fiore?

It was far more probable that the row between the two men had nothing to do with that, especially given what they now suspected of Nichol and his involvement in the Irish troubles – and not forgetting the part he'd played in the kidnap. Obtaining money to buy guns for use in Ireland was what had ultimately been behind that, and Latimer had secretly been making heavy contributions to the fund. Supposing Nichol had threatened to make this public, and that was what the row had been about? And so Latimer had later gone to meet Nichol, armed with a knife? Forgetting the one thing which had so distinguished him from other men, his 'trademark', as it were, that made him so memorable? Drinking with Nichol and his crony and making up some cock and bull story about his wife and Nichol?

None of that made any sense at all.

Neither could Gaines see Latimer cutting Dudley Nichol's throat. He remained as convinced as Inskip that O'Rourke had been the one to have done it, but unless new evidence ever came to light, he didn't see how the murder as it stood could ever be pinned on him. Sheldyke had wavered about positively identifying the passenger who had entered his cab on that fateful night as either Latimer or O'Rourke and wouldn't now commit himself to anything further than saying it might have been. He knew he had seen the three men standing together under the gas lamp, had noticed one of them had a striking birthmark on his face, and he had *thought* O'Rourke was the one he had left standing there, but he couldn't be absolutely certain. He would certainly never swear to it in a court of law. All of which was, of course, academic. How could there ever be a trial, when both victim and suspected murderer were dead?

'He's guilty as sin,' Inskip said, 'and he's going to get away with it.'

'Not quite.'

O'Rourke wouldn't go scot free. He had coughed up more about the guns and the means of obtaining and disseminating them than was good for him. His friends across the Irish Channel were not known for their forgiving natures and he wouldn't be allowed to get away with it. 'It's justice, of a sort, Joseph,' he said. 'Rough justice.'

'Not my sort, though.'

It was the least satisfactory way for an investigation to have ended that Gaines could think of, but it was the best they were going to get. Dudley Nichol's murder would just go down in the books as an unsolved crime. Latimer's untimely end would be regretted. He would be remembered for what he had achieved as a public servant, there would be sadness for what he might have become, but ultimately his name would pass into history. The Martens family were reunited. Events in Ireland would take their course, whether towards a bloody civil war or a peaceful end was in the lap of the gods.

Epilogue

Outside the Dorcas, the gusty autumn wind was adding to the detritus that was part of the scenery of life around there, blowing dead leaves to drift in hidden corners, to clog the gutters and blow inside whenever doors were opened, but there weren't really enough of them to make much difference to the general scruffiness. Spitalfields didn't go in for trees much.

Gaines had timed his visit for late afternoon, when he thought the main business at the clinic would be drawing to a close, when most patients had departed. He congratulated himself when he found his calculations had been right on the nail and that Doctor Latimer was free to see him. She held out her hand with obvious pleasure when he was shown into her surgery. He had always felt they liked and respected each other, and he was glad she hadn't wanted to avoid him. But he would have understood if she had.

'Come in, Inspector, and take a seat.'

'You are looking well, Doctor Latimer.' He felt free to address her as such now, after noticing her name on the new brass name-plate outside the door. He hoped it was an indication that she was coming to terms with her husband's suicide and accepting what must be her drastically changed circumstances, and thought she most probably was. He had spoken the truth: she was looking well. A little older, perhaps, and a trifle thinner, but she'd gained a healthy summer tan and he fancied she had lost the shadowed look from her eyes.

She smiled and a faint colour touched her cheeks. 'I've just had a holiday in Derbyshire. Have you ever been there, Inspector?'

No, he had never visited the area, he admitted, recalling that was where David Moresby's constituency lay, though he didn't think it necessary to mention that.

'Oh, but you should, it's lovely. Rather grim in places, awe-inspiring, really, but otherwise so beautiful. Walking there is something to be recommended.'

'A good holiday does wonders, so I'm told. Never gone much

on them myself. Maybe I should try it some day.' He wasn't one for walking, either, or not for pleasure. In his opinion he got enough of it in his daily job.

She offered tea and when she'd made it, they took refuge in small talk for a while, skirting round the reason why he was here. She had moved house, she told him; she had learned to drive and bought herself a little motor car, a small Austin that made getting around so much easier. 'I'm thinking of getting one myself,' he said, 'if I can persuade my wife it's a good investment and not a waste of money.'

She smiled and refilled his cup.

'I've tried to get in touch with you before, Doctor, but they told me you were away. I had the idea you might like to know what's been happening, but if you'd rather not—'

He had in fact debated whether to come and see her at all. He had no wish to open up old wounds, which talking over the situation would inevitably do, but he felt she had the right to know what had happened, if she so wished. It was, after all, due to her that they had apprehended O'Rourke sooner, rather than later. But he was aware of the need to tread carefully, because he didn't know how much she knew, or was willing to admit.

He doubted very much if he would have told her everything that had been found out, even without the directions from on high which had not so much filtered down as landed on him with a thump. They had been explicit. No hint should ever leak out that a senior minister of His Majesty's Government might have been suspected of committing murder, or even been in any way involved in it. There was no proof to connect Edmund Latimer with Dudley Nichol's death, nothing which could connect him with anything else that might be suspect, either, and for those reasons the investigation must be considered closed. Apart from unavoidable gossip about a minor peccadillo in the shape of an extramarital affair, his reputation, and therefore that of his Party, must remain unblemished. The verdict on his death had been suicide while the balance of his mind was disturbed, and that was how it had been fed to the press and the public. The matter was classed as sensitive and no hint of Latimer's political doubts and waverings must ever be disclosed.

But he had to wonder how much of all this Alice Latimer, who was neither naive nor a fool, could go along with if ever she was made aware of it. After her husband's suicide, Moresby had wisely prepared her for the gossip that would be bound to circulate about her husband and Mrs Fiore, and however hard this had been for her to take, she had apparently accepted it as the reason for Latimer's uncharacteristic behaviour before his death. She also knew why Lucy had been kidnapped, and by whom, though not of Violet's part in it. But, like the iceberg which had sunk the *Titanic*, there was so much more down below all this than appeared on the surface, and she must have known that.

'I came to tell you that Daniel O'Rourke is dead.'

For a moment she didn't understand, and looked at him blankly. 'But—' Of course she knew that O'Rourke hadn't hanged, as he would have done if it could ever have been proved he had killed Dudley Nichol. If the case had ever come to trial. Yet it had almost seemed for a moment as though she had thought he had. 'How?' she asked at last.

'He . . . died, in prison. I don't rightly know how,' he lied, in no way prepared to go into specific detail. That wasn't for her ears. In any case, he knew little more than that O'Rourke had opened his mouth too wide, about those guns and more, given information that put others in danger. There were ways of getting at such men, in or out of prison. He wouldn't give much for Paddy Tooley's chances, either.

She struggled with that for a bit. 'I think you mean he was killed,' she said eventually. 'How appalling. How sad and pointless this whole business has been.' She sat silently contemplating her cold tea. 'He *did* kill my cousin, of course,' she said eventually.

'Oh, yes.' Gaines had no need of proof to believe that.

'My husband saw him that night, you know. O'Rourke and Dudley.'

'What?'

'He – Edmund – left me a letter.' He waited, listening to the wind rattling the window in its frame and a door banging somewhere while she braced herself to go on.

She had read that letter eventually, though she'd been curiously reluctant to do so. Finally, she had steeled herself to do it – to read the letter and Edmund's 'daybooks' too, or at least the most recent of them. As diaries, they were merely a dry and detailed daily record of events, current affairs, meetings in his own North

London constituency, sub-committees, conversations with colleagues and so on. But there were notes with them that served to reinforce those barely comprehensible lines he had left behind when he shot himself. Latterly, he had come to regret deeply his decision to support the supplying of arms to those dedicated to bringing about Home Rule, those for whom a fight to the death would not be going too far. He recorded a conversation he had had with the Prime Minister, and Asquith's belief that such provisions could only add to the certainty of tumult, riot and bloodshed, which had echoed the doubts already set up in his mind. But it was the letter, not the diaries, which had revealed exactly how much he had been disturbed, not only by the commitment he had made and whether he had enough courage enough to see it through, but also his concerns with his personal life.

The letter had been full of regrets for the situation as it concerned Alice and himself. She was sad that he should have blamed himself for marrying her at all, for what he termed a marriage of convenience, as if she had been a starry-eyed young girl just emerging from the schoolroom that he had deliberately taken advantage of. Whereas she had been twenty-five years old, brought up by a practical, sensible and experienced father who had taught her not to view the world through rose-coloured spectacles, but to evaluate situations and people for what they were, and she had gone into her marriage with her eyes wide open, not expecting a fairy-tale romance. And she had not been actively unhappy. Edmund had always been a kind, generous and considerate husband and he had, moreover, taken pains to ensure she didn't learn of his affair with Mrs Fiore. Nevertheless, she couldn't deny that it had been a shock, learning how she had been deceived, and it had hurt badly. The fact that it had apparently been going on even before their marriage did not lessen the hurt.

Clearly, whatever he had chosen to do hadn't been without cost to him, and yet she had never suspected just how tormented he had become. '*I sleep hardly at all, and when I do, I have nightmares,*' he had written. '*I believe I am on the verge of a nervous breakdown. Literally going mad, doubting my own judgements and unable to make decisions, which leads to mistakes and makes me no longer fitted for the position I hold. I even have doubts about my ability to carry out my intention to end it all, though I can see no other solution. It is a sad irony that if you are reading this, my dear Alice, I shall, after all, have managed to accomplish that at least.'*

How little we know other people, even those nearest to us, Alice had thought through her tears. To think how little it was, really, to have brought him to the point where he felt the only solution was to end his life. Who would ever have suspected that beneath that confident and competent exterior self-recrimination and doubt over so many things was building up to that final, fatal step?

'*But that is not the worst of it,'* he had continued, evidently feeling the necessity to unburden himself of everything. '*I believe I was contributory to your cousin's death. I lied to you when I told you I had not seen him the morning he left Manessa House. I did as you and I had agreed and went to tell him he must leave, and we ended by having high words. I will not encumber you with the sordid details, enough to say that I told him to pack his bags immediately. Later, I was sorry for what I had said. I knew there was no basis for the accusations I had thrown at him. I was simply jealous of the easy friendship he had with you. I went back home, not expecting him to be there and he was not, but I found the note he had left for you. He had given no address, simply stating that he was going back to Spitalfields.*

'*I did not dine with Hugh Palfreyman, as I told you, that night. After leaving the Essendines', I went instead to Spitalfields, without any clear idea of where I might find Dudley, if at all, and simply wandered aimlessly around. I did not expect to encounter him in a public house but I was by then in need of a drink and when I went into one which looked reasonably respectable, there he was, with a companion. Perhaps it was fate, giving me the chance to apologize for my behaviour, which I did. He accepted with good grace, that I will say. The last I saw of him was when he and his friend hailed a taxi and drove away.'*

Gaines coughed and Alice brought her thoughts back to the present, to find him looking at her expectantly. 'Your husband left you a letter?' he prompted.

'Yes.' She hesitated, then explained briefly what he had written about meeting Dudley the night he was murdered. 'I would have come forward and told you that if necessary, of course I would, as I believe Edmund would have done, but as it was . . . O'Rourke was already in prison for his other offences and . . .' To have shown that letter, so essentially private, to the police, would have been a betrayal of Edmund's deepest feelings, especially after it became evident that the case would never reach the point where O'Rourke would face trial for the murder. 'Do you think I was wrong, not to let you know, Inspector?'

'Yes, Doctor Latimer, I do. He might then have hanged for his crime.'

She flushed. 'But he has paid the price.'

He said nothing to that. A gulf of misunderstanding stretched between them.

At last she broke the silence. 'You should see Lucy, how she's grown. She's walking now – or staggering, I should say. I'm afraid she's going to have to have a new nanny, though, now that Emma is leaving.'

'And I may be looking for a new sergeant. He's anxious for promotion now that he'll have a wife.'

'I'm so glad for her. But it's a pity she's going. Lucy loves her and it will be difficult to find someone as good – in Ferdie's eyes. He's besotted with that child.' She let moments go by, then she said cautiously, 'They were both so happy, he and Violet, to have her home again, they never questioned why she was brought home like that.'

'Indeed.' The Martens had been surprisingly content to leave the outcome of the kidnapping as it was, so long as Lucy was safely home with them once more, but he had never seen Alice as being happy with such a solution, any more than he had been himself. He was therefore not surprised at what she said next.

'But I'm afraid I just didn't believe she was brought home simply because the kidnappers had got cold feet after Dudley was killed, as everyone seemed to think.'

'It was one possibility.'

'But not the correct one, was it?' She hung back, undecided for a moment, then, apropos of nothing, she said, 'Emil Martens has decided to take a back seat at the bank – or what he calls a back seat. At least he's allowing Ferdie more say in running the business, though I'm not sure how Ferdie feels about the responsibility. I think maybe he'll jump to it, though. It's very easy to underestimate him.'

'I had noticed.'

'I thought you might have.'

It had occurred to him more than once to wonder why the obvious solution to Lucy's return hadn't presented itself to him at the time. Ferdie, distraught by the thoughts of his daughter out there somewhere. Unable to sleep, walking the streets, trawling in his motor car looking for her, incapable of fixing his mind on anything other than that. And then, Lucy being miraculously, if mysteriously, retuned.

It was his turn to speak, Alice was waiting for him to take her up on what she'd begun, but he couldn't help her out. At last she sighed and said, 'It seemed like a miracle, you know, just to find her there, back home.' She paused, then rushed on. 'We'd all grown so used to Ferdie going out looking for her and coming and going at all hours. If he'd been out that morning, no one would have remarked on it – but that's just what happened, isn't it? It was Ferdie who brought her home and left her out there in her pram.'

It was even more of a miracle that he had known where to find her. Violet certainly hadn't told him. She had been as startled as any of them when Lucy had been returned. Yet who else but Ferdie would have thought of Violet's former, beloved nanny? And who else would Nanny Ryan have surrendered the child to but her own father? At some point, he must have eventually suspected Violet's part in the kidnapping of their own child. It wouldn't have been difficult, even for him, to put two and two together. In actual fact, that should have been no surprise at all. Ferdie, perhaps more than most, had the measure of his wife.

'So you knew, Inspector.'

'Maybe I suspected.'

'There won't be any – repercussions?'

'The case is closed, Doctor Latimer,' he said, and saw her visibly relax. That was what she wanted to hear, why she'd mentioned it at all, having guessed that he must have worked it out. To his mind, what Violet Martens had done was a monstrous thing for any woman to have agreed to, but the business was now nothing to do with him, for which he was duly thankful. He could leave the family to sort out with one another what it had done to their relationships.

It had begun to grow darker while he was inside the clinic and the street outside was for the moment a strange oasis of quiet in the noisy clamour of the warrens of streets, alleys and courts surrounding it. The street lamps had come on but they looked pale and anaemic in the fading afternoon light. It was the dark of the moon tonight and the sky would soon be inky black, but when night came the lamps would shine brightly by contrast and the darkness beyond would recede. For a moment, he thought of three men, standing in a circle of lamplight, but he didn't allow the thought to linger. One thing he'd learned as a policeman was when to refuse to let doubts hang around any longer.

He stepped outside the Dorcas, turned his coat collar up against the wind that was blowing leaves and grit and old bits of newspaper, and turned his steps away from the squalid streets towards home.